ACE OF SPADES

ALSO BY SANDRA OWENS

Aces & Eights

Jack of Hearts
King of Clubs

K2 Team Series

Crazy for Her
Someone Like Her
Falling for Her
Lost in Her
Only Her

Regencies

The Duke's Obsession
The Training of a Marquess
The Letter

ACE OF SPADES

Aces & Eights – Book Three

SANDRA OWENS

Montlake Romance

This is a work of fiction. Names, characters, organizations, places, events, and incidents are either products of the author's imagination or are used fictitiously.

Published by Montlake Romance, Seattle

www.apub.com

ISBN-13: 9781503948990
ISBN-10: 1503948994

Cover design by Letitia Hasser

Printed in the United States of America

This book is dedicated to the best cheerleaders in the world, the Sandra's Book Salon gang. Ladies, your friendship and support, along with the fun we have in our group, means the world to me. You haven't been at all patient in waiting for Nate's book, and I love that you've been dying to see Nate get his happily ever after. So here you go, my friends.
Enjoy!

PROLOGUE

"Take us with you, Mama," Nate Gentry said. She couldn't just walk away and leave them with the old man. He would blame them when he found her gone, and that meant a beating.

She put her hand—rough from hard work—on his cheek. "This is the hardest day of my life. If I take you, he will find us and kill us all. This he has sworn to do if I dared such a thing. There is a reason I must go, but you are strong boys, and you will grow up to be men I can be proud of."

She kissed each of them as tears streamed down her face. "Nathan, you will see that you and your brothers study hard and get good grades. Court, you will help your older brother protect Alex." She knelt. "My baby. This will be the hardest for you, but be brave and strong for your brothers. Can you do that, Alex?"

Seven-year-old Alex burst into tears. Nate fisted his hands, hating that their mother was making his baby brother cry. Even Court's lips were trembling, but for some reason he refused to look at her. There was something in his middle brother's eyes, almost like hate, that Nate didn't understand.

"Please, Mama. Don't leave us with him." Nate hated begging, but he had to make her take them, too. She stood, the tears still coursing down her face, and he was sure that meant she would agree.

"I'm sorry, son. If I did, he wouldn't stop until he found us." Suddenly, she pulled him to her, hugging him hard. "Always know that I love you, Nathan." She let go of him and glanced down the dirt road. "I must go before he returns."

She picked up the garbage bag holding her meager belongings, gave the boys one last sad smile, and then walked away, her shoulders slumped. A few steps down the road, she stopped and turned, and openly sobbing now, blew them a kiss before continuing on. Nate squeezed his eyes shut. He was eleven years old. He was too old to cry.

"Go do your chores before he comes home," Nate told his brothers. They shuffled away, Alex's sobs fading as the boys rounded the corner of the two-bedroom house, badly in need of a coat of paint and a new roof. As soon as they were out of sight, Nate slipped into the trees lining the dirt road and followed his mother. In his young mind, he thought if he knew where she was moving to, he could gather up his brothers and just show up one day. She was their mother. She wouldn't turn them away.

His parents had had a fight earlier, and the old man had knocked her around. Nate didn't know what it was about this time. Most days, his father didn't need a reason, especially when he was drunk. They'd all been on the receiving end of those fists far too often, especially their mother. He didn't blame her for leaving, but she should have taken them with her.

At the end of the dirt road, he stopped behind a tree, and watched in disbelief as Harmon Baker opened the passenger door of his old pickup truck. After Nate's mother got in, Harmon glanced up and down the two-lane country road, then ran around the front of the truck, jumped in, and took off. Harmon occasionally did odd jobs for their old man. Sometimes Nate had wished that he were their father because he was nice to them, but now he hated the man for taking their mother away. He hated his mother even more for choosing Harmon over her sons, and for that he would never forgive her.

Nate heard his father's truck—which had needed a new muffler for as long as he could remember—coming down the road. He ran as fast as he could back to the house. By the time the old man walked out to the pigsty, Nate was busy mucking it out.

"Where's your ma, boy?"

"In the house, I reckon." He kept his back to his father, afraid he'd see the lie on his face.

"No she ain't."

"Then I don't know." He narrowed his eyes at his brothers, signaling them to keep their mouths shut. When the old man stomped off, Nate said, "We don't know nothing, okay?" Alex nodded, his eyes filling with tears again, but Court's gaze shifted away.

"What's wrong with you?" Nate asked Court. He knew his brothers, and there was something going on with Court beyond their mother leaving.

"Leave me alone." Court threw his shovel across the pen, almost hitting the pig, then took off, running for the woods.

Nate watched him for a minute, then picked up Alex. "Hey, little man, what say we go for a swim in the pond?"

"Okay," Alex said around the thumb he sucked on. Until now, it had been five years since his baby brother had last sucked his thumb.

They were going to get a beating when the old man finally realized their mother was gone, and whether or not they finished their chores wouldn't matter. They might as well do something to deserve the coming punishment.

The next day when his teacher asked about his black eye, he said that he'd fallen when he'd gotten up in the middle of the night to go to the bathroom. She never asked why he was wearing a long-sleeved shirt on a hot Florida day.

The beating from the old man had been the worst yet—and there had been many over the years—since he was the only one in the house during his father's drunken rage. Nate had hidden his brothers in the woods that night so their father couldn't get his hands on them. Nate never told them their mother had run away with another man.

CHAPTER ONE

Nate Gentry sat in his car, studying the small house on the other side of the street. Harmon Baker had left Ocala, disappearing the same time Nate's mother had. Back then, it had only reinforced Nate's belief they'd run away together. Now he questioned his young self's conclusion, and the time had come to find out the truth.

He'd tracked Harmon to this run-down house in Dunnellon, a mere thirty-minute drive from Ocala, where Nate had grown up. When he'd run a search for Harmon Baker, he'd been surprised to learn the man had never married. Was his mother in there? Ever since his middle brother had shared the secret he'd kept since the day their mother had walked away from them, Nate didn't know what to think anymore.

According to Court, their mother had been pregnant and had run away because their bastard of a father had tried to beat the baby out of her. The revelation had shaken Nate to his core. He opened the car door, getting out. Had he been wrong about her all these years? If he had been, shame on him. Guess he was about to find out.

He probably should have at least stayed for Court's wedding reception, but after hearing his brother's confession, as soon as the ceremony was over, he'd left. Not cool, but too many bad memories had broken out of the mind boxes he'd locked them into when he'd been a boy. It was either leave as soon as he could or ruin the rest of Court's wedding reception because of his rotten mood. He loved his brother too much to do that.

So he'd pulled his boss aside as soon as the ceremony was over, asked for and had been granted two days off. Now he was digging into the past, something he'd tried hard to never think about. Did he want to do this? Open old wounds?

Nate paused a few feet from the door. Alex and Court were determined to find their mother, Nate's opinion on the matter be damned. Before he'd allow them to be hurt all over again, he'd get answers. He'd been their protector from the day each was born, and he didn't know how to stop now. If their mother had left them for something other than another man, he wanted to know.

As he took a step toward the house, his phone rang with the tone Nate had set for his boss, special agent in charge of the Miami office of the FBI. As usual, Rothmire's timing sucked. Bringing the phone to his ear, Nate headed back to his car. If the boss was calling at eight in the morning—after giving Nate two days off—it wasn't to chat about what they each planned for breakfast.

"What's up?" Nate asked.

"Another woman at the same dumping ground as the first two. The local police got an anonymous tip on where to find the body."

Damn. Three meant they had a serial killer on their hands. When the second body had been found, the evidence pointing to the same killer, the bureau had been put on alert. With this third one, the FBI would be taking over the investigation.

Nate headed back to his car. "The first two were found in the Everglades, right?"

"Yep. Since they were prostitutes, it's likely we'll find out this one was, too, once she's identified. I want you on the scene."

Nate glanced at his watch. "I'm in Dunnellon." Which Rothmire already knew, since his agents went nowhere without the boss being aware of their locations at all times. "It'll take me four or five hours to get there."

"No it won't. There's a helicopter on the way to the Dunnellon airport to pick you up. Rand's riding along with the copter. He'll drive your car back. One of the local cops will be waiting for you to take you to the scene."

"Why am I going there?" He worked undercover.

"You're the lead on this one. Taylor should get there about the time you do." Rothmire hung up without waiting for an answer, which was typical.

Nate stared at his phone in confusion. This wasn't an undercover operation. Taking the lead would make him visible. What was Rothmire up to? Until the boss was ready to clue him in, he would remain in the dark.

Shrugging, he slid behind the wheel of his car. Harmon Baker and his secrets would have to wait. As he pulled away, he glanced at the house that looked like a heavy wind could knock it over. A dingy curtain in the front window fluttered closed. Someone had been watching him. As tempted as he was to stop the car and knock on the door now that he was here, he didn't have the time to spare. Whatever answers that house held would have to wait.

♠♠♠

When Nate arrived at the scene, Taylor Collins, his fellow agent, was already there. At the sight of her, Nate's heart did a little bounce. "Stop that," he muttered, warning his stupid heart to quit wanting what it couldn't have. She was special, not for the likes of him. Besides, she was his best friend, and he wasn't about to screw that up by having an affair when he had nothing to offer her or any other woman.

As he walked toward her, his gaze roamed over her—as it always did, whether he wanted it to or not. Sleek blonde hair an inch longer than her ears, blue eyes that reminded him of his beloved ocean, and legs that went on forever. In the darkest hours of the night, when he was alone in his bed, he would imagine them wrapped around him.

She glanced over and, at seeing him, a smile curved her lips that seemed like they were made for kissing. He didn't smile back, nor did she expect him to. But he craved hers, and when she did gift him with that smile—unlike any she gave others—it seemed as if the sun had suddenly appeared on a cloudy day. So far, he'd managed to hide his reaction to her, but that was getting harder to do.

"Morning, boss," she said, saluting him. "I was surprised when Rothmire said you're heading up this investigation. Are you putting your undercover days behind you?"

"Beats me," he said, coming to a stop next to her. "You know Rothmire. I'll learn the answer to that when he's ready for me to." He subtly inhaled her citrusy fragrance. Her tart, fresh smell had been a surprise the first time he'd been close enough to catch her scent. He'd expected something flowery. On meeting her for the first time, men—him included—often made the mistake of thinking she was a fragile female in need of their protection.

He inwardly snorted. She was so far from fragile that it was a rare man who could best her. She was an expert markswoman, held a Krav Maga black belt, could hit a bull's-eye with a knife without trying, and had twice his brainpower. In other words, she was the hottest woman he'd ever met. And one he could never have. So even though she'd given off signals that she was interested, he'd pretended not to notice. That was getting harder to do, too.

She bumped his shoulder with hers. "Did you complete your mission?"

"No. Rothmire called right as I was walking up to the door." Although their boss knew where Nate had gone, Taylor was the only one who knew why. As for his brothers, he hadn't shared his plans and wouldn't until he got answers. He wouldn't get their hopes up that their mother was still alive or would want to see them.

"Bummer," she said. "Well, let's catch this bastard so you can finish what you started."

She was right. Now that their perp had moved into serial-killer status, their time would be devoted to the case 24/7 until they caught him or her.

"Let's go piss off some cops, then." Nate had great respect for all members of law enforcement, but the ones he could hear trampling around inside the tree line were from a small town and didn't have a fraction of the training he and Taylor had on how to look for and preserve evidence. They weren't going to appreciate the FBI taking over, but whatever. It wasn't his job to soothe their hurt feelings.

♠♠♠

"That went well," Taylor said, after they'd sent four grumbling cops and their captain to handle traffic control. Drivers were slowing their cars at seeing the police cruisers, their blue lights flashing, parked along the side of Tamiami Trail, better known to the locals as Alligator Alley.

Nate snorted. "You have a talent for understatement, my friend."

"My talents are many, Nate." She winked at him as she snapped on a pair of rubber gloves.

Stop saying things like that, Taylor. He watched her walk away, taking a moment to restart his brain before he followed her into the swamp. Why'd their killer have to use this place as his dumping ground? He slapped his arm, smashing a mosquito. What was wrong with a dumpster in the city or an alley in town where there weren't things that wanted to bite you?

"Christ, something ate her leg off," Nate said as he came in full view of the body.

"An alligator, I imagine."

Nate scanned around him. If there was a gator nearby, he wanted to know. "I guess we're lucky he didn't drag her to his lair." He frowned. "Do they have lairs?"

"Beats me. I'm a city girl. Look at this." She bent over the body, eyeing the victim's left hand. "Rothmire thinks that she'll be a prostitute like the other two, but she's wearing a wedding ring. Most prostitutes aren't married. And her dress . . . White isn't a color a street hooker tends to buy. Too hard to keep clean."

Taylor would know. Her Russian-born mother had turned to prostitution after her American boyfriend had abandoned her and their young daughter, leaving them homeless and hungry.

"Do we know what the first two were wearing?" When Taylor shook her head, he took out his phone. "I'll call Rothmire. See what we have on them." He studied the dead woman while he waited for the boss to answer. She appeared to be in her early thirties and had all the signs of a drug user—hollow cheeks from malnutrition, and, because her mouth was open, he could see she was missing two bottom teeth.

"It's me," he said when Rothmire answered. "We're at the scene. It's not pretty, let me tell you. When will the crime scene people be here?"

"Ten minutes, give or take. Can you tell how she was killed?"

Nate eyed the body. "From the bruises on her neck, she appears to have been strangled." Of course, they wouldn't know for sure until they got the results of the autopsy, but Taylor was right. Something didn't add up.

"I have the reports from the first two victims," Rothmire said. "They both were strangled."

"Were either wearing a wedding ring?" He heard the rustling of pages as Rothmire searched for an answer to his question. "Also, what kinds of clothes were they wearing?"

"Now, that's interesting you asked. Yes, both had a gold band on their left ring finger. Both have been identified, and neither were married. As to what they were wearing, also interesting. Each had on a white dress."

Nate watched Taylor as she took pictures with her phone. "Well, we've just confirmed all three were killed by the same person, then."

"You can ride back with Taylor. Head here as soon as the crime scene techs get there. We need to get on this. Three in two months means we'll have another one soon if we don't stop him."

"Will do." After hanging up, Nate filled Taylor in on the dresses and rings.

As was her habit when upset or thinking, she chewed on her bottom lip. "I'm going to catch this bastard, Nate. No woman deserves to end up in a swamp with body parts missing." She pushed his hand away when Nate, understanding she was thinking of her mother, touched her arm. "He married them, or made them think he did."

He let her pretend that she wasn't hurting, even though he knew she was. "Maybe offered them a way to get off the streets?" Movement to her left drew his eyes. "Shit. Snake!" The slithery thing was headed straight for them, its tongue flickering as it tasted the air.

Before Nate could get to his gun, Taylor had hers out, her shot exploding the snake's head. He eyed her in admiration. Damn, she was hot. "Nice shooting, tiger."

She grinned. "I'll let you take out the next one."

"No way. You're my hero. You see a snake anywhere near me, you go for it." He gave an exaggerated shudder. "Hate the things."

Taylor patted Nate's arm, amused that he was afraid of a snake twenty feet away from them. "I'll save you from all the slithery creatures." She reluctantly stopped touching him. She'd been in love with Nate Gentry for almost a year, and sometimes she was sure she saw heat in his eyes when he looked at her. Sadly, he'd put himself off-limits. She wasn't sure why, but she was working on figuring it out, and when she did, all bets were off.

The local police captain came running toward them, his gun drawn. "What's happening? I heard gunfire."

Nate stepped in front of Taylor as if to protect her from the excitable cop. Standing behind his back, she rolled her eyes. But she'd just killed a snake for him, so she let him play protector for her.

"Easy, man. Put your gun away," Nate said, holding up a hand. "She shot a snake is all."

"Oh, okay." He slipped his weapon back into his holster, then bent over, bracing his hands on his knees as he sucked air into his lungs.

Taylor stepped to Nate's side, exchanging an amused glance with him. She and Nate trained together three or four times a week, and their regimen would likely give the man his first heart attack. There was also a lot of sexual tension between them when they fought on the mat that carried over at odd moments. Like now. Nate didn't smile, he rarely did, but if he didn't want her panting over him, he should stop looking at her like that.

"I sent all but one of my boys back to the station. How long you people gonna be out here?"

"We're about done," she said. "Our team will be here any minute to take over." It was hot, they were both sweaty from the humid Everglades air, mosquitoes were buzzing around them, and she was past ready to get out of here.

"Why don't you leave your man behind to keep the traffic moving? No reason for you to stay." Nate swatted at a mosquito about to land on his nose. "Unless you feel like sticking around and donating blood to the insect population."

"Nope. I prefer to keep my blood. You people keep me informed, you hear?"

"We will," Nate said. "Not," he muttered after the police captain was gone.

No, they wouldn't. The FBI didn't play well with others. Taylor eyed the body. Although she wanted to shed tears for the woman, she would wait to do that in private. Even Nate, her best friend, the one person who knew her story, wouldn't understand the sadness she felt at seeing how this woman's life had ended.

Nate touched her arm. "You okay?"

Maybe he did understand a little. "Yeah." She forced a smile she didn't feel, but it turned real at the sight of the people walking toward them. "Our forensic team arrives. Oh, good, the M.E.'s with them. I vote for getting out of here." The medical examiner was one of the best in his field, and would have his preliminary report to them by tonight or tomorrow, along with more photos.

"I'm riding back with you," Nate said as they headed for her car after briefing the new arrivals. "Rothmire wants us to go straight to the office. He's got the files on the first two already."

When he slid into the passenger seat, he adjusted it as far back as it would go to accommodate his legs. Normally, Taylor would enjoy a long ride with him, but she wished today that she could be alone with her thoughts. It wasn't often that her past reared up, but the dead prostitute had her remembering things she did her best to keep locked away.

"Want to talk about it?"

She glanced at him. "We need to check the national database. See if any murders in other cities—"

"That's not what I'm asking."

No, it wasn't, but she didn't want to talk about her mother. Not today. "I'm fine. I want to catch this bastard before he kills again."

Nate put his hand on her arm. "Don't let this become personal, Taylor."

It already was. "When are you going back to Dunnellon?" she asked, hoping to divert his attention. They both had issues they hadn't dealt with concerning their mothers, which she supposed was one reason they understood each other so well.

"Depends on this case, I guess."

"You could slip away tomorrow before things heat up."

He shrugged. "They always say be careful what you ask for. Maybe I should just leave it alone."

"Court and Alex are determined to find your mother, or at least find out what happened to her, so you should go back soon. Get the answers so you'll know how to handle it with them."

"You're sneaky, you know? We're supposed to be talking about you and what's going through your mind. Since you don't want to do that, I'm going to take a little nap." He popped a wintergreen-flavored Tic Tac candy—his one addiction—into his mouth, reclined his seat, and closed his eyes.

Pot to kettle, my friend. A nap was his way to avoid talking about his mother, too. She wished she could fall asleep that fast. While he slept, she studied him, something she liked to do when he wasn't paying attention.

There were very few men Taylor liked long hair on, but Nate was one. The ponytail he always wore suited him, as did the one ruby stud earring. Even though she rarely saw him in anything other than black, red was his color. Since he worked undercover at his biker bar, Aces & Eights, he typically dressed like a biker: black T-shirts, jeans or leather pants, chains hanging from his pockets, motorcycle boots, and her favorite thing, the black leather bands he wore on his wrists. It all added up to one very hot man.

One of her favorite fantasies was of him, his body covering hers, and while he devoured her with those fathomless black eyes, she would pull the leather band from his ponytail. His black hair would fall around his shoulders like some long-ago warrior, and she would comb her hands through it, then trail them down to the shoulders bunching with muscles before—

"Stop staring at me."

Busted! Heat crept up her neck as she choked out a laugh. "You're cute when you drool."

He swiped his hand over his mouth. "Don't drool."

"Besides, you were asleep, so you don't know if I was looking at you or not."

"I felt your eyes on me." He brought his seat back upright. "Sorry for conking out."

Was he really so attuned to her that he could sense her watching him even though his eyes were closed? If so, that was very interesting.

CHAPTER TWO

The man changing a tire that hadn't needed changing ducked his head when the car with the female FBI agent inside drove by. He'd parked on the side of the road, far enough away from the crime scene so as not to draw attention. With binoculars, he'd been able to see *her* up close and personal. She was beautiful, with her sun-kissed blonde hair and pale skin. It had been hard to see the color of her eyes, but he already knew they were blue.

His first two angels had been found almost immediately. One by a man needing to make a pit stop and the other by a photographer who'd set out to get pictures of the Everglades and its slithery inhabitants. The man chuckled at thinking how surprised the photographer must have been.

When his latest angel's body hadn't been found after two days, he'd called in a tip from a burner phone. He'd done his research and knew the FBI would take over with this one. He wasn't afraid of the FBI. After all, he was smarter than they were. Everything he'd done and planned to do was for her.

After calling in the tip, he'd driven to this spot to wait. He hadn't been sure she would be assigned to the case, but when she'd appeared, he knew it was a sign that his mission was blessed.

A little later, she walked into view again, heading back to her car. He brought the binoculars back to his eyes, frowning when the man who'd arrived after her got into the car with her. He'd never seen her with a man before and took that as another sign. She was waiting for him.

When her car passed again, heading back to Miami, he assumed, he'd only allowed himself a brief glance at her. Then he kept his head down, concentrating on putting the last of the lug nuts on, even though he'd longed to look up again. To look in her eyes. To let her see him. But it was too soon for that.

Who was the man who had been in the car with her? The question burned in his mind long after she was gone from sight. He sure hadn't looked like an FBI agent. Did she have a boyfriend? The thought sent anger coursing through his bloodstream. He slammed the lug wrench against the bumper, leaving a dent.

She was his, and no one was going to keep him from claiming her.

CHAPTER THREE

"No rumblings from any of the biker gangs about this?" Rothmire asked, after they'd taken seats in the conference room.

Nate shook his head. "Not even a hint, and I don't recall her ever making an appearance at Aces and Eights with Ramirez." Aces & Eights was the biker bar he and his brothers owned. It was also a cover for their covert operations. No one suspected that the owners of a biker bar were FBI agents. Although that might change with Rothmire's decision to make him the lead on this case.

"Well, if she was his"—Taylor made air quotes as her lips curled in distaste—"'old lady,' why didn't he report her missing?"

"I'll see what I can tease out of him next time he comes in," Nate said. "In the meantime, you and Rand need to pay him a visit. Find out what he has to say about her."

According to the report from the detective on the case, the first prostitute, twenty-seven-year-old Alana Gilmore, had been an on-and-off girlfriend of Hector Ramirez, a.k.a. Stud. A member of the Cubanos Motorcycle Club, Hector had the looks to go with his handle. Unlike many club members, he'd never once brought a woman with him to Aces & Eights.

The second victim, Stacy Wimberley, age twenty-two, had been reported missing by her roommate, another prostitute. The last anyone saw of her, she was getting in a car that might have been dark blue, dark green, or black.

"I'll go with Taylor to interview him," Rothmire said.

Huh? Nate glanced at the boss. "Why not Rand?"

"I'm having him lie low for a while." At Nate's raised eyebrow, Rothmire shrugged. "I have my reasons. He'll still work on the case, but from behind the scenes."

He looked at his watch. "Gotta go. My daughter's a fairy princess in her school play. If I don't make an appearance, you'll be investigating my murder instead of this one. My wife and daughter aren't women I want to cross." He grinned as if two murderous women were the most awesome things in the world.

"And rightfully so," Taylor said.

His grin grew wider. "Considering Gwen's the first black princess in her school's history, they wouldn't have to kill me. I'd shoot myself if I missed such a momentous event. Figure out how to catch this bastard. Keep me informed." He stood, then turned his attention on Nate. "When this case is closed, we need to talk."

"Yes, sir." Talk about what? Why was he the lead on a case that would likely expose him? And why was Rand being kept on the down low? But until Rothmire was ready to share, all he could do was nod.

Rothmire was Nate's second bureau chief since he'd joined the FBI. All his first boss had cared about was advancing up the ladder, taking the credit for his agents' successes while blaming them for any failures on his part. Fortunately, that man was now sitting at a desk in the basement at headquarters, analyzing meaningless emails, after one of his agents had been killed because of his ineptitude. Good riddance as far as Nate was concerned.

Rothmire was the best thing to ever happen to the Miami bureau. He was sharp, didn't put up with anyone's bullshit, and always had his agents' backs. Nate loved him, but he was leery of his boss's devious mind.

"What does he want to talk to you about, and what's the deal with Rand?" Taylor asked after they were alone.

"Beats me, but I'm quaking in my boots. He always has something up his sleeve. Just wish it wasn't anything to do with me or mine." "Mine" meaning his brothers. They loved what they did and were good at it. Nate didn't like the thought of his boat being rocked, which Rothmire excelled at doing.

Nate studied the photos of the three victims, pictures of the latest one sent over by the M.E. only minutes ago. Hopefully, she had an arrest record and her fingerprints were in the database. In the meantime, Taylor and Josh Sheridan, their newest agent, would be hitting the streets tonight, showing her photo, hoping to find someone who knew her.

He wished he could team up with them, but with his new assignment, he was already exposing himself more than he should. Like being sent to this morning's crime scene where anyone paying attention could have seen him.

The boss was cagy, cunning, and devious, and Nate's Spidey senses screamed that something was up. But until the boss deemed it time for him to know what he had going on in his mind, Nate knew he might as well wish to touch the moon for all the good it would do him.

The plan they settled on was to release the photo of their latest victim to the news stations. As soon as her death became public, he'd be able to talk about it at the bar, see what he could turn up.

He tapped a finger on one of the photos. "He's targeting blondes with blue eyes."

"We're sure our bad guy's a he?" Taylor asked.

Nate looked at the blonde-haired, blue-eyed woman sitting across from him, not liking the shiver that snaked down his spine. The someone-just-walked-over-his-grave kind of shiver. He gave himself a mental shake. Just because Taylor shared the same hair and eye color with the dead women didn't mean anything.

"Aren't you?" he said.

Her gaze fell to the photos, and he knew the sadness in her eyes was for her mother. "I'm sure, but we still need to keep open the possibility that it's a she."

"Agreed, but our killer's almost certainly a male. This is about something from his childhood, something that messed with his head."

Taylor nodded. "Something he's trying to make right. In his mind, anyway."

"You left out sick. In his sick mind."

"Isn't that how it always is with these people?" She stood. "I need a shower and a change of clothes before I meet Josh."

Nate squashed the urge to tell her to be careful. She was more than capable of taking care of herself. And he somehow managed not to say, "You're not hitting the streets without me there to protect you," instead saying, "Call me when you get home."

She smiled, too much understanding in her eyes. "Because you won't sleep until I do?"

"I don't have a problem sleeping." True, except when he knew she was out on the mean streets of Miami. "I'll just want to know if you turned anything up."

"Ah, Nate." She trailed her fingers over his shoulder. "You truly amuse me."

He sat at the table after she left, alone with his thoughts, his shoulder still tingling where she'd touched him.

How many times was he going to have to tell himself she was off-limits before his brain got the message? It would help if she stopped flirting with him, stopped touching him. He snorted. Who was he kidding? Neither of those things would make a difference. He gathered up what little they had on all three victims, then flicked off the lights as he left the room.

♠♠♠

Nate sighed. “Spider, if Fish doesn’t kill you, I will.” The little man grinned back at him as if Nate had just told him he’d get free beers for the rest of the night. He grabbed the back of Spider’s vest, hauling him out of the line of fire.

Fish was a probate, hoping to be accepted by the Dominos Motorcycle Club, and had decided to toy with Spider to impress the gang members. Once Fish was voted into the Dominos, he’d get patched.

And Spider? The idiot thought Fish liked him. The problem with Spider was that he loved Aces & Eights and its customers. Because he did, he failed to comprehend that everyone didn’t love him back. Most did, but jerks like Fish got off on toying with Spider, amusing themselves at the trusting man’s expense.

Except for Saturdays, Nate and his brothers had assigned certain nights each club could spend at Aces & Eights. Otherwise, they’d have gang fights every night of the week if they let them mix. Saturday was open to all bikers. Usually that wasn’t a problem, since on that night, the gangs were at their own clubs, so there wasn’t much mixing going on at Aces & Eights.

Spider, being gangless and something of the bar’s mascot, was there every day of the week except Sundays, and that was only because the bar was closed. Most of the clubs liked him, even rubbing his bald head for good luck before they headed out to ride.

Monday nights belonged to the Dominos, and although they weren’t the baddest of the bad, they could raise hell as good as the next club when it suited them. Nate pushed Spider onto a barstool next to Alex. "Keep this fool here until Fish and friends forget he exists," he said to his baby brother.

"Spider, my man, how's life?" Alex said, slapping Spider on his back.

For some strange reason, Alex liked Spider. Said the man amused him. Spider didn't amuse Nate, but then few things did. As he walked away, he tried to remember the last time he'd been happy. Maybe truly never. Sure, he loved his job, loved his brothers, loved keeping the world safe from bad guys. He was satisfied with his life. Honest-to-God happiness wasn't something he thought to wish for. Wouldn't know it if it slapped him in the face.

He went to the opposite side of the bar and grabbed the remote to the large-screen TV. "Game's gonna be on in a few minutes," he said to the three bikers next to him. "A round on me if Florida State wins."

"Hell yeah," Dirty Dan, Nate's least favorite customer, said.

"At least you won't have to steal one." He'd lost count of how many times he'd caught Dirty Dan stealing beers.

Dirty Dan smirked. "Takes all the fun out of it."

Ass. Nate picked up the remote, turning up the volume. Minutes before the game, a news alert was scheduled to air, asking if anyone recognized their latest victim.

The station flashed a news-alert banner across the screen. "What's going on now?" Nate said to get the three men to pay attention.

"The cops probably shot someone again," one of the guys said.

Nate nodded. "Wouldn't be surprised." He hated dissing the cops, but it came with the territory.

The female anchor appeared on the screen. "The body of a murdered woman was found this morning near Tamiami Trail. The police are asking if anyone recognizes this woman to please call the number on the bottom of the screen."

At seeing the artist rendering of their last victim, Nate said, "She looks familiar. Has she been in here before?" He watched the three men's reactions.

"I know her."

Nate swiveled on the barstool, his gaze landing on Spider. "Dude, really?"

"That's Peaches. Don't know her real name, but she's a regular over on Seventh Avenue and Seventy-Eighth Street."

"In Liberty City?"

Spider nodded, his gaze on the TV. "Yeah. Always at that corner. She was a nice girl."

"And you don't know her real name?" he asked.

"Nope. She's just Peaches."

Although that didn't help much, it gave them a little something to go on.

"Sometimes I'd give her a few dollars because she always looked hungry."

More like she was strung out. "You know anything else about her? Where she lived? Who she was friends with?"

"Nope. She's just Peaches."

"Yeah, you already said that."

Spider narrowed his eyes. "Why all the questions, Ace?"

Nate decided that Spider wasn't as stupid as he pretended to be. "No reason. Just bothered me to think I might have seen her around." He headed to the office to call Taylor.

♠♠♠

"She's not a regular around here," Taylor said.

Josh nodded. "Yeah, someone would've recognized her by now if she was."

"Where to next?" They'd started near downtown Miami, showing their murder victim's artist rendering to everyone they came across. Taylor's phone rang, and her heart skipped a beat at seeing Nate's name on the screen.

"Hey," she said.

"Any luck on an identification?"

"Well, hello to you, too." He was always all business, and she couldn't resist needling him at every opportunity. She smiled when she heard his sigh.

"Hello, Taylor."

"See, that wasn't so hard." When Josh mouthed *Nate?* she nodded. "To answer your question, no luck on an identity yet."

"I've got something for you. One of my customers recognized her from the news bulletin. Said she went by Peaches, and that she worked around Seventh Avenue and Seventy-Eighth Street in Liberty City."

"That's a start. We'll head over there now."

"Just be careful, okay?"

She chuckled. "It's sweet that you're worried about me."

"I'm not sweet. Call me when you get home."

"Will do." No, he wasn't sweet, but he was protective of those he cared for, which seemed to include her.

Nate was an intensely private man. She had no idea why he was so open with her, telling her things she wasn't sure he shared with his brothers. What she did know was that the man had fascinated her since the day she'd met him.

For a good six or seven months after first reporting to the Miami field office, she'd been too afraid to even try to talk to him. But she'd find herself watching him, and as time had passed, she'd learned that underneath his daunting exterior was a man who cared deeply about justice, his brothers, and his team members.

First, she'd grown to respect him, and then over time, they'd become friends. After she'd been assigned to work with him behind the scenes on his undercover investigations, and they'd spent more time together, they'd somehow become best friends. That had surprised her, because he wasn't the kind of man who—with the exception of his brothers—let anyone get too close. Why he'd let her in, she didn't know.

She hadn't meant for it to happen, but one day she'd looked at him and out of the clear blue, her heart had said, *I love him*. She might as well have fallen for Prince Harry for all the good it would do her. Nate might consider her his best friend, but he'd erected an impenetrable wall that she could only bang her head against. On one side, a close friendship was allowed, and on the other side was no man's land—or, more accurately, no Taylor's land.

Yet more than once, she'd caught him looking at her as if she were the proverbial glass of water to a man emerging from a barren desert. That heat directed at her in his eyes when he thought she wasn't paying attention fed the hope that someday she could do the impossible and obliterate that wall.

There wasn't any rule against dating a fellow agent, and there had been married agents at one time or another. Not that Nate would ever ask her out on a date, so Taylor wasn't sure why she was thinking of the possibility that would ever happen.

"Where to?" Josh asked after they were in the car.

"Oh, um, Liberty City. Nate said one of his customers recognized her when they showed our artist rendering on TV. Her working name was Peaches."

"Shouldn't take us long to ID her, then."

She hoped not. She was ready for a hot bath, a glass of wine, and a good book that would take her mind off their victims. They were women who'd had no one to care about them, but Taylor did. Her empathy came from having a mother who'd been a prostitute, from having grown up with other prostitutes babysitting her when her mom was working, and watching women she'd loved die because of the needle they'd stuck in their veins one too many times.

The only person who knew the depths of her sorrow was Nate. He understood why she was determined to catch the murderer. It was a miracle that she hadn't ended up on the streets herself, and she probably would have if not for Rosie.

Rosita Manuela had taken in that frightened six-year-old girl after her mother had died. Overlooked by social services—fortunately, in Taylor's opinion—Rosie had carted Taylor home with her after finding her crying over her mother's body.

At least, that was what Rosie had told her. Taylor didn't remember a thing from that night. But Rosie had always been evasive about exactly what had happened, still was, and it wasn't until Taylor had joined the FBI and had searched for and found a police report that she'd learned her mother had been killed by one of her johns.

"Let's see if we can get a name and get back to the car while it still has wheels," Josh said, pulling to a stop at the corner their victim had worked.

Her trip down memory lane interrupted, Taylor glanced around, seeing the hostile stares of young men and women who didn't have a chance for a better life. She wished each one of them could have a Rosie in their life. Of course, she and Josh were made as cops right away, so hopefully that would lend a little protection to the car.

"Keep an eye on the man in the red T-shirt, leaning against the wall. He's carrying."

Josh's gaze scanned the group. "Probably not the only one."

When they exited the car, Red T-shirt took off, followed by several of his friends. One girl and a few others held their ground; the girl's eyes daring them to mess with her. Taylor stepped up to her, showing her badge.

"We're not after anyone here, okay? Just want to show you a picture, see if you can give us a name."

The girl smirked. "We ain't helping no pigs."

"And I don't expect you to, but this woman is from around here." She held out the artist rendering. "She went by Peaches." Taylor saw recognition in the girl's eyes.

"What she done?" a boy standing behind the girl said.

"She was killed. We'd like to let her family know, that's all. Do you know her name?"

He exchanged a glance with the girl, as if asking permission to tell them. At her nod, he said, "Linda Harding. Showed up around here 'bout two months ago." He pointed to an abandoned building across the street. "Slept there most nights." With that said, the boy turned and walked away, the remaining kids trailing after him.

Taylor stood on the sidewalk next to Josh, both of them eyeing the building. "I so don't want to go in there," she said. Especially at night. She hated rats, a leftover phobia from her childhood, and she just bet that place was crawling with them.

"If she's been missing for two days, whatever possessions she had are long gone by now." Josh gave an exaggerated shudder. "God knows what vermin call that place home."

All true, but they still had to check out the building. She'd lived in such places as a child, knew that the people who called abandoned buildings home were desperate, sometimes dangerous.

"We need backup." Taylor called Nate. While they waited, she and Josh returned to the car, put on Kevlar vests, jackets with "FBI" emblazoned on the backs, headsets, and ball caps that would hopefully keep the spiders out of their hair. She wished she had a hazmat suit, to be honest.

After stuffing some small bills into her jacket pocket—a few dollars in the hands of people desperate to know where their next meal or fix would come from might get questions answered—she turned and faced her nightmare. The building seemed like a big black hole out of a Stephen King novel, ready to suck her back into a past she'd tried her best to forget.

CHAPTER FOUR

After Nate arrived with his brother, he walked over to Taylor. She was standing ramrod straight, and when she glanced at him, he didn't like the apprehensive look in her eyes. Her gaze skittered away from him, focusing on the building across the street.

Stopping next to her, he put a hand on her shoulder. "That building?" He didn't miss that as she leaned into his touch, the tense muscles under his palm relaxed a little.

"Yeah. Peaches was the working name for Linda Harding, and that was what she called home." She shuddered. "I hate rats. I can remember hearing them scurrying around on the floor at night and being afraid they'd climb in my bed."

So her trepidation was because of childhood memories. Had she lived in places like that?

"Hope the thing doesn't fall down on our heads," Alex muttered as he and Josh joined them.

The place did look like it might fall in on itself at any moment. Why hadn't the city condemned it and torn it down? At some point in the past, there had been a fire on the top floor, resulting in a corner of the roof missing.

"Well, at least it's only three stories we have to search," Nate said. "Alex, you and Josh start at the top. Taylor and I will work our way up." He exchanged a look with his brother, Alex immediately understanding that something was going on with Taylor.

"Anyone else shaking in their boots at the thought of going in there, or am I the only wuss?" Alex said.

Nate gave him a slight dip of his chin in approval. Alex had a way of making fun of himself that eased tensions.

"Can't say I'm excited about it." Josh flipped the switch on his headset. "Let's get this over with."

"You guys are wimps," Taylor said, resolutely marching toward the building.

"Is she going to be okay?" Alex quietly asked after both Josh and Taylor were out of earshot.

"I'll make sure of it." Nate slapped his brother on the back, then jogged to Taylor. Alex didn't know of Taylor's childhood, but his baby brother was observant enough to pick up on her tension and would probably have questions later. It was her story to tell, when and if she wanted anyone else to know.

They both activated their headsets and turned on their flashlights. As they stepped inside the building, Nate stayed next to Taylor, letting his arm brush hers, a reminder that he was with her. It took a good twenty minutes to clear the bottom floor. As they headed up the stairs, something small and furry raced ahead of them.

"Damn rats," Taylor said, again shuddering.

Nate put his hand on her lower back, following her up. Normally, he wouldn't touch her during a search, but he sensed she needed reassurance that he was there. Taylor Collins was one of the best agents he'd ever worked with. She was highly trained, kept herself in excellent shape, and had a brain she knew how to use.

Her anxiety had nothing to do with being incapable of doing her job. It was the memories assaulting her mind that had her so on edge. He wished he could take them away, erase all the bad in her past. Since he couldn't do that, he'd do the one thing he could. Be here for her, while not making her feel incompetent.

"There's someone sleeping in that corner." She aimed her flashlight on a filthy mattress.

Nate followed her, and when they were close enough, he saw two girls huddled together as they slept. He guessed one to be in her early teens and the other to be a year or two younger, sisters from the looks of them. Too young to be alone and unprotected. Next to the bed were a half-full jar of peanut butter and an almost-empty package of saltine crackers.

Although his mother had left them, and his father was a son of a bitch who'd beaten them for the least offense, he and his brothers had grown up with a roof over their heads, and sometimes the old man had actually brought food home.

Taylor knelt beside the mattress, and when she gently brushed the hair away from the face of one of the girls, Nate swallowed past the lump in his throat. Had this been Taylor's life until Rosie had taken her away?

"Sweetheart, wake up," she said to the older of the two, lightly shaking her arm.

The girl shot up, rapidly blinking as she focused on them. Her eyes widened, she scooted in front of her sister—shielding her from view—and pulled a knife from under the one pillow they both shared. She jabbed her weapon at them.

"Easy, sweetie," Taylor said in a soft voice. "We're not going to hurt you."

The girl darted her gaze to Nate. "You try to touch us, I'll stab you."

Following Taylor's example, he knelt, staying at the end of the mattress. "I'm not going to touch you or your sister. We're here to help you."

The girl glared at him. "Yeah, like I haven't heard that one before."

Taylor opened her jacket, letting the girl see her gun. "If he tries to touch you, I'll shoot him. What's your name?"

"You the cops?"

"My name's Taylor, and we're with the FBI." When the girl's eyes skittered over to him, Taylor said, "That's Nate. I promise that he won't hurt you."

Taylor glanced at him, and he got her message loud and clear. She wasn't about to leave these two girls behind. Not surprised, he nodded. There was no way they could let these girls stay here, but they needed to know if their mother or father was around. You couldn't just go and take someone's kids.

"What's your name?" Taylor asked again.

"Mellie."

The younger girl sat up, and at seeing Nate at the end of her bed, she frowned. "Is he here for Mama?"

So their mother was a prostitute. If this was where Linda Harding called home, their mother would probably know her.

"Mellie, where is your mother?" Taylor said.

The girl pressed her lips together, refusing to answer. Their mother was probably in some rent-by-the-hour motel room with a john. Nate had to respect the girl's loyalty.

Taylor edged onto the mattress. "Okay, you don't have to tell me. I'm going to show you a picture. Do you know this woman?" She handed the oldest girl the artist rendering.

"Why do you have a picture of our mama?" the youngest said, peering over her sister's shoulder.

"Shut up, Becky!" Mellie said.

Well, shit. Linda Harding had children.

"Third floor's clear," Alex said in his ear.

"I'll give you a minute with them," Nate told Taylor, then walked to the opposite wall. "Come down to the second floor. Taylor and I found

Linda Harding's daughters. We're in the southeast corner, but I think there're some others sleeping in some of these rooms. You two check them out, make sure no one bothers us."

"Roger."

Next, he called Child Protective Services, arranging for a social worker to meet them in an hour at the police station. Taylor walked to him as he finished the call.

"They haven't seen their mother in three days. Mellie said she sometimes disappears for days at a time but that she always comes back." She glanced over at the girls. "I haven't told them she's dead."

He hated the tremble in her voice. "Let's get them out of here before you tell them."

"I wish . . ."

"You can't take them home with you, Taylor."

"I was thinking just for one night before they get lost in the system."

He stroked his thumb over her cheek, brushing away her tears. "You know you can't."

"Yeah, I know." She swiped at her other cheek with her fist, then inhaled a deep breath. "They're not going to want to leave. They think she's coming back any time now."

"What would someone have had to say to you to get you to go with them?"

"I don't know. Rosie didn't give me a choice. She just dragged me home with her."

"Then I guess we don't give them a choice." He nodded at Alex and Josh as they walked up. "All good?"

"Yeah. An old man threatened to gut us if we didn't leave him alone," Alex said. "In another room, a couple getting it on asked if we wanted to stay and watch." He gave an exaggerated shudder. "I'm traumatized for life."

Josh grinned. "Yeah, I need a cigarette and a beer now," he said, getting a laugh from Taylor. He lifted his chin toward the girls huddling on the mattress. "What's the plan?"

"Someone from Child Protective Services is meeting us at the police station. Taylor wants to wait until we get them away from here to tell them their mother's never coming back."

Nate was glad to see Taylor laughing. Josh and Alex could always bring a grin to her face or make her laugh; him, not so much. Yet another reason he refused to give in to his desire for her. She needed a man who could make her happy, not one who had never once made her laugh. He walked back to the girls.

Taylor passed him, kneeling on the mattress. "Mellie, we're going to find a safe place for you and Becky to stay."

The girl shook her head. "No, we have to wait here for Mama."

"Your mother would want both of you to trust Taylor," Alex said, squatting next to Taylor. "What if I wrote a note telling her where to find you?" He glanced at the jar of peanut butter. "While you're waiting for her, we'll have some dinner. How does a cheeseburger and chocolate milkshake sound?"

"I want a cheeseburger and milkshake," Becky said. She drummed her hands on her sister's back. "Cheeseburger. Cheeseburger. Cheeseburger," she chanted.

Mellie reached behind her, grabbing Becky's fingers. "Stop it. Mama said we're not supposed to leave."

Not wanting to intimidate the girls, Nate stood back with Josh. Between them, Alex and Taylor finally convinced the girls to willingly come with them. Alex left a note on the mattress that Linda Harding would never read.

♠♠♠

"You're letting this case get to you. You can't save all the lost children, Taylor."

"You think I don't know that?" But she could damn well try. Taylor handed Nate a beer. He'd insisted on bringing her home after they'd seen the girls safely into the hands of the social worker. It had shredded her heart to watch them holding each other after learning their mother would never return, their sobs still echoing in her ears long after the car carrying them away had disappeared.

The few times Nate had been in Taylor's small apartment, the place had seemed to shrink in size. It wasn't only because he was a big man, but his persona was sometimes bigger than life. Not one to care much about fancy belongings, her furniture was secondhand. Her extra money was better spent on more important things, like Rosie. And her girls. *Nothing* was more important than her girls.

Although she did have a weakness for pretty clothes and shoes, things she'd never had growing up. Since she didn't go out much, she didn't need many outfits, so she kept a firm rein on her clothing budget. For work, her chosen wardrobe was black pants; a tailored jacket; red, blue, or white blouses; and shoes she could run in when necessary.

After Nate's first visit, when she'd been afraid the chair he sat in might break, Taylor had gone out and bought her first brand-new piece, a sturdy blue leather recliner. He hadn't hesitated to claim it as his own whenever he was here, and at the moment, he was sprawled on it, looking perfectly at home.

She liked him here most times, but she didn't need a lecture tonight. All she really wanted to do was kick him out and then crawl into bed, where she'd probably cry the night away. He knew that, which was why he seemed prepared to greet the morning from *his* chair. Sometimes she wished he didn't know her so well.

"We'll need to talk to them again soon," she said, sitting on her plaid couch and tucking her legs under her. "But let's give them a day or two." Once the girls had been told their mother wasn't coming back, they hadn't been in any condition to be questioned. At least the social worker who'd come to collect them had seemed like a compassionate, nice woman. Some were so burned out that they had no empathy for the children in their care.

"They probably don't know much, but yeah, we'll have to talk to them . . . Or you will. I think I scare them."

"You're a scary man." To someone who didn't know him, he was definitely intimidating, but as much as he tried to hide it, he was a softie inside. The man was prepared to spend the night in a chair because he didn't think she should be alone right now. Probably the only people who understood his heart was one giant marshmallow were her, his brothers, and their wives.

Taylor smiled. "Stop scowling. It's true. And besides, you like everyone thinking you're the big, bad wolf."

There was the slightest twitch of his lips. "Keeps them from messing with me."

Someday, she was going to make him actually laugh. It was her number-one goal in life. She shifted her gaze to the fish tank. Her hours didn't accommodate having a cat or dog, but she needed something to take care of, hence Henry Cavill, her red-and-black betta fish.

Nate's chair was next to the tank, and Henry was at the edge of the glass, watching him. For some reason, Nate seemed to fascinate Henry. Taylor got that. The man fascinated her, too.

"Sprinkle some food in Henry's tank, please."

"Yes, ma'am." He trailed his finger across the glass, and Henry chased after it. It was a game they played, which Taylor found strange because she couldn't get Henry to follow her finger. "You hungry, Henry?" Nate said, picking up the food and sprinkling a few flakes into the water. The fish torpedoed to the top, snapping up the food.

She watched Nate watch Henry, taking advantage of Nate's attention on the fish to admire him. Because that was one of her favorite things to do. He'd told her that he was one-quarter Seminole on his mother's side, and his Native blood was there in his black hair—which he wore long and in a ponytail—and in his high cheekbones and olive skin. And lord, his black eyes, when he turned them on her, always made her feel gooey, like her insides were made of warm syrup.

She'd had an immediate reaction to him the first time she'd seen him. It had been at the beginning of her second week when he'd walked into the office for a meeting with their boss. *Want him,* her brain and girly parts had clamored. He'd both intimidated and fascinated her, but as a newbie agent and the first woman in their field office, she couldn't afford to make a misstep. She'd managed to keep her attraction to him hidden for an entire year.

Then she'd been assigned to him and his brothers, her job to assist however needed in their undercover investigations. Life had suddenly become considerably more interesting. Not only had she given up on trying to hide her attraction to him, but she'd gone and fallen in love with the man. She'd bet her one pair of Jimmy Choos that he was just as interested in her. Only problem: he was still doing his best to hide it.

"Stop staring at me," he said, still eyeing the fish.

"Make me." Sometimes she just couldn't resist poking the bear.

Those smoldering black eyes landed on her. "Careful, Taylor. You haven't a clue what you're asking for."

No, she probably didn't, but where he was concerned, she was willing to take the risk. She'd never asked him why he wore an "Off-Limits" sign, but she was feeling bold tonight. Maybe it was this case reminding her that there were no guarantees in life. One day she could be alive and breathing, and the next not. Rosie had taught her to go after what she wanted, and she wanted Nate.

"Then clue me in. Don't deny that you want me. I see it in your eyes. Well, I want you, too. So what's the problem?" With a heart trying to pound itself out of her chest, she went to him, leaned down, and put her hands on his knees. "Give me a reason good enough to make me stop wanting you in my bed."

His eyes darkened, his pupils swirling with the turbulence of a storm-tossed sea. His gaze fell to her lips, and then without warning, she was pulled onto his lap. When his mouth crashed down on hers, she had the passing thought that he'd been right. She hadn't had a clue what she was asking for.

It wasn't a gentle kiss. He possessed her, owned her, devoured her. His mouth was hot and hungry, and his tongue was relentless, tasting and licking as if she were his favorite candy. In her wildest imagination—and God knew she'd spent hours and hours imagining this moment—she'd been sorely lacking in envisioning how thrilling it would be to kiss Nate Gentry.

His mouth tasted minty, like the Tic Tacs he was always sucking on, and his masculine scent surrounded her, something spicy that was uniquely him. Just kissing him wasn't enough. She wanted all of him. "Nate," she whispered against his lips, following her plea with a moan.

He stilled, then pulled away.

"Don't stop." She brushed her thumb over his bottom lip, damp from their kiss. "Please don't stop."

"We can't do this," he said, picking her up with the ease he would a ten-pound sack of potatoes, and setting her on her feet. "I won't do this."

"At least tell me why." God, now she was begging. She never begged anyone for anything.

He stood, collecting his keys from the coffee table. "You want a reason? Here it is. You're my best friend, Taylor. If I give in to this thing between us, I'll end up hurting you, and then I'll lose you completely."

Well, as reasons went, it was a good one. She'd worried about the same thing, but they were both professionals. If they had a relationship and it ended, why couldn't they still be friends? But if she tried to argue with him now, he'd just dig in.

"Rosie's been asking why you haven't been to see her. Why don't you pick me up at seven, and we'll stop by on our way to the office? That way I can see the girls before they leave for school."

She could tell he was about to refuse, so she shook her head. "I've been ordered not to show up again without you. I think Rosie loves you better than me. See you in the morning." She gave him a smirk, then headed for her bedroom, leaving him standing at the door.

As soon as she heard the door close behind him, she returned to the living room. She bent down, brought herself eye level with Henry, and trailed her finger across the glass. The fish ignored her.

"What is it about him that fascinates both of us, Henry, my little man?" Henry had no answer. "Fine, ignore me like you always do." She slid the deadbolt closed, then turned off the lights. After a shower, she grabbed her cell phone, taking it to bed with her. If she didn't warn Rosie her favorite man was coming over in the morning so she could be pretty for him, Taylor would get a tongue-lashing.

CHAPTER FIVE

Nate loved Taylor's foster mother. He didn't want to think about how Taylor's life would have turned out without Rosie. He opened his arms for the hug Rosie would give him, whether he liked it or not. He did.

"You naughty boy. Avoiding your Rosie," she said, lifting her hands to their maximum reach to pinch his cheeks.

"Never," he said, meaning it. The woman was a tiny spitfire. The thing he liked the most about her was that she never saw him as a threat. Sometimes—most times—the people he came in contact with shied away. He cultivated a menacing persona, needed to be a mean-assed sonofabitch to keep the biker gangs frequenting Aces & Eights in line. But Rosie? She'd seen through him from day one. He just hoped she never told Taylor he was a softie.

Against his will, his gaze slid to Taylor, who was currently on her back on the floor, buried by six giggling girls, ranging in ages from two to nine years old. Girls who would be lost in the system without Taylor and Rosie. His damn heart skipped a beat, and then another one.

He'd kissed her, which had been the biggest mistake of his life. He'd not thought about anything else since their lips had touched. He'd not gotten a solid hour of sleep after returning home. *Why not have an affair? You know you want her,* the tiny, fork-wielding devil on his left shoulder had whispered in his ear. *Because you'll hurt her,* the angel sitting on his other shoulder had quietly said.

"When are you going to stop fighting whatever demon it is that's holding you back?" Rosie said, following his gaze. "You think I don't see how you look at her?"

He could thank his father for his demons, and he had no choice but to fight them. Especially where Taylor was concerned. He knew the statistics. Had looked them up years ago.

"Don't know what you're talking about," he said, extracting himself from Rosie's hold.

She snorted—actually snorted. "Sure you don't, but something's changed between you two. I knew it as soon as you both walked in. Just so you know, I'm betting on my girl."

And that was why he hadn't wanted to come today. Rosie had to be a witch, able to see things she shouldn't. And yes, something sure as hell had changed between him and Taylor. Namely, that kiss. Sweet Jesus. He'd been poleaxed. Sucker punched by a woman he'd promised himself he'd never touch. And that knowledge had him thinking of asking for a transfer. That and the fact that Taylor didn't have any intention of listening to him. He could tell her nine ways to Sunday that he'd only end up hurting her, but she'd stuffed her ears with balls of cotton.

Rosie slapped his arm. "Man up, Nathan. She'll either make you or break you."

"You're imagining things, Rosie. There's nothing going on between Taylor and me. You gonna offer me some of your delicious coffee or not?" She made the best *café con leche*, a Latin latte made with steamed milk and a shot of potent Cuban coffee.

"*Sí, sí.* I have it brewing. Come sit." She flitted off on size-four feet encased in pink-heeled slippers with pom-poms on them.

Instead of following her into the kitchen where she could start on him again, Nate moved to the sofa where he could watch Taylor and the girls. All but the two-year-old were dressed in their school uniforms. Most mornings, Taylor tried to be here to walk them to the Catholic school two blocks away.

Years earlier, Taylor and Rosie had managed to qualify as foster parents. Fortunately, Rosie had put her foot down, saying six was her limit, after the oldest girl, nine-year-old Brianna, had arrived. Otherwise, Nate figured if Taylor had her way, there'd be at the very least a baker's dozen living here. He also knew this was where a good chunk of Taylor's paycheck went, since what they received from the state wasn't nearly enough to cover expenses.

What Taylor didn't know, because she would have refused his help, was that he slipped Rosie a couple hundred dollars whenever he visited. Rosie, bless her little self, had no qualms about taking his money, telling him the first time he'd offered, "I have no pride where my babies are concerned." She also liked that they shared a secret from Taylor and had devised a scheme where he would slip the bills between the sofa cushions when Taylor wasn't looking. Rosie was a sneaky devil and had charmed the hell out of him from day one.

"Here you are," Rosie said, handing him the latte. She set the second cup down on the coffee table. "Girls, go make your lunches while Taylor has her coffee."

He listened as Rosie filled Taylor in on how the girls were doing in school and any problems that had cropped up. In her early sixties, Taylor's guardian angel had more energy packed in her small frame than most twenty-year-olds.

When Taylor and Rosie went into the kitchen to hurry the girls up, Nate pushed two one-hundred-dollar bills between the cushions before following them. He enjoyed watching Rosie and Taylor interact with the girls. This house was so different than the one he'd grown up in. There was love and laughter instead of yelling and beatings.

The only reason Taylor didn't live here anymore was because Rosie had kicked her out, believing Taylor needed a life away from the responsibilities of raising six children.

For the first few times he'd come here with Taylor, the girls had been afraid of him, and he hadn't wanted to come back. But Rosie wasn't having it, so he came with Taylor whenever he was invited. The girls had gotten used to him, but except for Annie, they were still shy around him. Each had a sad story that could break a heart, mostly from being abused in one way or the other by men.

The only one who seemed to like him was the baby, who was now trying to crawl up his leg. He leaned down. "What does Annie want?"

"Up, Nae," she said, tugging on his pants.

He picked her up. Her learning disabilities and poor language skills were a result of being born to a meth-addicted mother.

"Walk now."

"Yes, ma'am." It had become a tradition for him to walk with Taylor and the girls to school whenever he was here, him carrying Annie. She was a cute little thing with her big black eyes, curly black hair, and dark-brown skin.

She gave him a toothy grin as she patted his face. "Nae walk, Nae walk, Nae walk now," she sang, bouncing in his arms.

The trip to the school took about five minutes, and Nate trailed behind Taylor and the other girls, listening to Annie chatter away. He only understood half of her conversation, but she didn't seem to care as long as he said "Oh, yeah?" the few times she paused and looked inquiringly at him.

These mornings he spent with Rosie and Taylor's little family were weird. The other mothers and a few fathers would greet them, believing he and Taylor were a couple, and she never disabused them of that assumption. Too often, he let himself pretend they were, the little boy who'd never felt the kind hand of his father, longing to be a part of the loving family Taylor had created. He needed to cut that shit out. They didn't need him in their lives.

"Good morning," a woman with a little boy at her side said when they arrived at the crosswalk at the same time. At seeing Annie in his arms, she glanced from him to Taylor as if trying to puzzle out why they had a black baby. That happened sometimes, those odd looks, and he always found himself tightening his hold on Annie, while clamping down on his urge to say something snarky.

"Morning, Rhonda," Taylor said. She bent down. "How did you do on your spelling test, Jared?"

"C-A-T," Jared responded with a big grin on his face.

"Wow, that's very good."

"I can spell *dog*," Sarrie, Taylor's six-year-old, said. "And *cow*, and *house*, and *Rosie*, and . . ."

The group crossed the street, the kids tossing out all the words they could spell. Nate stayed at the corner with Annie, waiting for Taylor to return. He never went any farther than this. From here, he could keep an eye on her and the girls as they walked up to the school's entrance. There were too many mothers and their children on that side for his comfort.

"Bye-bye," Annie said, waving her little hand.

Brianna turned, walking backward, a grin on her face. "Bye-bye, Annie." She waved back.

"Nae walk." Annie leaned away from him, wanting to go with her sisters.

"You'll see them this afternoon, little girl." He turned her away from being able to see them disappear past those double doors, having learned that she would cry at losing sight of them. He glanced over his shoulder. "Here comes Taylor. Time to go home. Rosie's already missing you, you know."

"Rosie!" she yelled into his ear, forgetting she'd been ready to cry.

Taylor walked up to them, holding out her arms to take Annie from him. Usually, Annie went right to her, but for the first time, she shook her head. "No." She patted his cheek. "Walk, Nae."

"What do you know? The big, bad wolf isn't so unlovable after all," Taylor said, amusement in her voice.

He gave Taylor a smirk, but the heart that had turned into a solid chunk of rock the day his mother had climbed into Harmon Baker's truck suffered a hairline crack. He hid his face behind Annie, not wanting Taylor to see that something was going on in his head that even he didn't understand. Didn't want to understand, truthfully. He was perfectly fine with his life just the way it was.

"We need to get this little one home so we can get going." He pried Annie's hands from around his neck, then handed her to Taylor. "I'll wait in the car. If we both go in, we'll never make it to our meeting in time."

"True. Come here, sweet Annie. I think Rosie has your breakfast ready. Tell Nate bye."

"Bye-bye," Annie said, waving to him as she was carried away.

Nate waved back before sliding into his car. Coming here with Taylor was a bad idea, something he needed to put a stop to. It put silly ideas in his head, made him wonder what it would be like to have a family. He wasn't family material. What if the rage simmering inside him took control and he turned into his father? He'd looked it up. Twenty-five to thirty-five percent of abused children grew up to be abusers themselves. Although those weren't alarming odds, how did one know if they were going to be one of the twenty-five percenters? It was a risk he wouldn't take.

So he stuck to seeing women who wanted nothing more from him but a few hours of mutual enjoyment. Except it had been—he counted in his head—five or six months since he'd gotten laid. He tried to blame it on work. All the shit that had gone down with Alex's investigation into the Alonzo crime family, and if that hadn't been enough to worry about, Alex had fallen hard for Jose Alonzo's niece. Fortunately, that had worked out, and now Alex and Madison were married. But not before baby brother had gotten himself shot and almost died. Nate prayed he'd never have to stand over one of his brothers' hospital beds again.

In the middle of all that, a woman from Court's past had walked back into his life, bringing all kinds of trouble with her. After some tense times, Court had married his Lauren two days ago, and the two were honeymooning at some resort in Mexico.

From the day their mother had walked away, Nate had been responsible for his brothers, long used to putting their needs and happiness above his. He wouldn't have had it any other way. With all that had gone down the past year, though, he'd put his life—what little he had—on the back burner.

Taylor walked out, heading for the car. Even in what he thought of as her FBI uniform of dark pants, a cotton blouse—which she rotated between blue, red, and white—a jacket that hid her gun, and sensible shoes, she was still sexy as hell. And who was he kidding? It wasn't anything going on with his brothers or the job that had him being celibate for too many months. It was the woman. Her. Taylor Collins.

Not that he'd act on it. He was too afraid that it would only take one night with her and she'd become his drug of choice. She would stay off-limits, and he would keep on taking showers, just longer ones.

♠♠♠

Using a long-range lens, the man snapped pictures of his angel and the girls she often visited. When she came in the mornings, she walked them to school, but this was the first time the man was with her since he'd started watching them a few weeks ago. He'd seen the same man at her apartment last night, but he hadn't stayed long. Maybe he was just a friend, but even that made him angry.

She belonged to him.

He drove straight home, anxious to develop his newest photos.

♠♠♠

They were in yet another meeting, this time in the boss's office, trying to get a handle on their perp. "In his warped mind, I think he believes he's saving them," Taylor said. She'd given the wedding rings and white dresses a lot of thought, and to confirm that feeling, she'd called one of their profilers in Virginia. "Pauline agrees. She thinks, as I do, that we'll find out that his mother was a prostitute and that something happened to her." She glanced at Rothmire, getting a nod to continue. "The question is, is he putting the dresses and rings on them before or after he kills them?"

"I think after," Nate said. "I have trouble believing he convinced three prostitutes that he was marrying them. One maybe, not all three. And something else. Does he think he's really marrying them?"

"Good question." Taylor thought about it for a moment. "I'd say yes. I think our bad guy is one messed-up dude. I asked Pauline to work up a full profile. It will be interesting to see what she comes up with."

"So you both agree our subject is a male?" Rothmire asked.

Taylor nodded. "Absolutely."

"No doubt in my mind," Nate said.

She chewed on her bottom lip, nervous about telling them her idea. Nate's gaze lowered to her mouth, and she swallowed a grin. Chewing on her lip was a habit, one she unconsciously did when thinking, but she'd noticed lately how his eyes would darken when she did it. Since becoming aware of his attention, she would sometimes do it on purpose just to mess with him. This time, though, she wasn't trying to tease him.

"I've been thinking," she said.

Nate grunted. "Then stop it. I can already tell by the look on your face that I'm not going to like whatever's about to come out of your mouth."

She stuck her tongue out at him.

"Children, behave," Rothmire said.

"Sorry. Anyway, our victims are blonde and blue-eyed. I'm blonde and—"

"No." Nate shook his head. "No. No. No."

She bristled. "You think I can't take care of myself? I can put you on the floor before you can say 'jumping jacks.'"

"Let me think about it," Rothmire said. He eyed Nate. "She's exactly the look our man seems to be going for."

Nate didn't respond, just stared hard at her before standing. "We done here?"

"I think my ride just left," Taylor said after Nate walked out.

Her boss turned a curious eye on her. "Anything you need to tell me?"

Rothmire was too perceptive by far; one of the things that made him a good agent in charge. She considered her response, not sure how he personally felt about employee fraternization. Better to stay mum about her fascination with Nate Gentry.

She gave him her best innocent look. "Such as?"

A grin split his face. "Such as, should I warn my best *male* agent that he's lost the game before it even started?"

"Haven't a clue what you're talking about." Taylor stood, busying herself with collecting her folder and Nate's, all the while hiding her own grin. So her boss knew she had the hots for Nate and had just let her know he didn't have a problem with it. He'd also qualified Nate as his best male agent, a subtle emphasis on *male*, telling her he thought of her as his best female one. Although, as she was the only female agent in the Miami field office, maybe she shouldn't feel all that honored.

Since she knew Nate hadn't had his last word on the subject of her going undercover as a prostitute, she went to her cubicle to get some work done until he came stomping back. She made a bet with herself that it would take him about two hours at the gym with the heavy bag before he was calm enough to talk.

CHAPTER SIX

"What did that bag do to make you want to kill it?"

Nate kept punching the heavy bag. Maybe if he ignored his annoying baby brother, Alex would go away.

"What's got your panties in a twist?"

Apparently not. "Go find someone else to bother." He punched his way to the opposite side of the bag, out of sight of Alex. He'd been at it for a little over an hour. Doing his best to kill the bag, as Alex put it, usually worked to calm him down, but not so much this time. The thought of Taylor standing on a street corner waiting for a psycho to pick her up made him crazy.

Yes, she was highly trained, and yes, she'd be armed, and yes, a team would be watching over her from various places, but all those yesses could go screw themselves. As soon as he could think rationally again, he'd make a list of all the reasons it was a bad idea. She was a smart woman and would agree.

"It's Taylor, isn't it?" Alex said, poking his head around the bag. "You should just admit you're hot for her and stop fighting it, bro."

Nate dropped his aching arms to his sides. "Swear to God, Alex, one more word and I'll use you for a punching bag."

His idiot brother laughed. "You can try."

Unfortunately, that was true. Like Taylor, Alex was a black-belt Krav Maga master. Although Nate and Court had brown belts, their baby brother could take them down without breaking a sweat. He was that good.

"Don't you have someone else you can annoy?"

Alex shook his head. "Nope. Madison's at work and Court's on his honeymoon, so that just leaves you. Want to go a few rounds in the ring?"

"Lucky me. I need to head back to the office, so not today." He had a few things to discuss with his fellow agent. She'd make herself a target over his dead body.

"Anything I can do to help on the case?" Alex tossed him a towel.

"Yeah. You can start doing some searches, see if you can find any murders with a similar M.O." He scrubbed the sweat from his face. If Court were here, Nate would put him on that project, as Court was their computer geek. Alex could find his way around on a computer well enough, though, and hopefully it would keep his brother busy so he'd shut up and stop speculating about Taylor.

"I'm on it, but just so you know, I'm fully aware this is a diversion tactic. You'll never convince me you're not panting over Taylor."

Amusement danced in his brother's eyes. Nate barely resisted punching him. "Fuck off, Alex."

"And even after you saying that, I still love you, big brother." Alex walked away, trailing laughter behind him. Nate glared at Alex's back, debating whether to go after him or to take what was left of his frustration out on the bag. The way he was feeling right now, he might put a real hurt on his brother, so he lifted his boxing gloves, eyed the heavy bag, and went in for the kill.

♠♠♠

"You're not going to stand on a street corner and troll for our bad guy," Nate said, his gaze on Taylor as he slipped onto his chair. Their desks were next to each other's, although until being assigned as the lead on their case, he hadn't been here much to use his. Too risky to be seen entering the FBI building. His only rebellion against his new assignment was that he refused to wear a suit like the other male agents.

"You're so funny," she said, eyeing him as if he were a comedian telling jokes.

"Not being funny here. You are not going to put yourself in his sights." He clamped his mouth shut. What had happened to the rational reasons he'd come up with as to why she couldn't consider doing such a thing? He hadn't been able to think straight since he'd kissed her. That had been a big mistake. He'd been trying to teach her a lesson that she shouldn't play with fire. The only one burned, though, had been him.

She leaned forward, her blue eyes turning icy. "You don't get to tell me what I can and can't do, Nathan."

"Oh, but I do. You seem to forget that I'm the lead on this case." Not good when she called him Nathan. Time to retreat and regroup. Maybe Rothmire would see reason and put a stop to this foolishness.

He stood. "I'll be around if you want to grab some lunch later."

"I know what you're about to do, and you better not."

He paused. "And what is it you think I'm about to do?"

"You're headed straight for Rothmire's office to try to convince him I shouldn't go undercover. If you do, I'll . . . I swear, you'll never have a moment's peace."

Nate pushed his hands into his front pockets, narrowing his eyes at the woman who was determined to make him crazy. If anyone could make his life miserable, it was Taylor Collins. She already was, though. One kiss and his brains were now about as useful as scrambled eggs.

Since he already didn't have any peace because of her, what was one more reason to add to his sleepless nights?

"Do your best," he said, then headed straight for Rothmire's office. She might never be his, but he'd damn well make sure she stayed alive.

♠♠♠

"Shot you down, did he?" Taylor said, her eyes glittering with amusement when Nate returned to his desk.

Shot down faster than he could have drawn his gun. "If you're going to gloat, go do it somewhere else." Since Rothmire was going to sanction Taylor going undercover, Nate would go to plan B. Catch the sonofabitch before Taylor had a chance to play hooker.

Her lips curled into a pleased-with-herself-smile as she stood, slipping her purse strap over her shoulder. She leaned her mouth next to his ear. "Don't pout too long. I'm hungry." With that said, she trailed her fingers across the back of his neck. "I'll wait for you downstairs."

Nate pinched the bridge of his nose. "You're killing me, woman," he muttered. His neck tingled where she'd touched him and even her lemony scent lingered, as if she'd intentionally left it behind simply to torture him.

"Who's killing you?"

"Just talking to myself." Nate leaned back in his chair, glancing at Rand Stevens. "Want to go to lunch?" Wouldn't hurt to have Rand with them. It would keep him from getting into an argument with Taylor.

"I was coming to ask you the same thing." He looked around. "Where's Taylor? Maybe she'd like to join us."

"Downstairs, waiting on me."

"There's a new deli I want to try," Rand said as they headed to the elevator. "Supposed to have kickass hot-pastrami-on-rye sandwiches."

"Works for me." And Taylor loved matzo-ball soup.

♠♠♠

"When are you planning on talking to Linda Harding's daughters?" Rand asked Taylor after their food was served.

She lifted her spoon to her mouth and blew on the hot soup. "This afternoon. I doubt they can tell us much, but maybe they noticed something useful."

"Want me to go with you?" Nate said.

"No, but thanks. I think I can get more out of them if it's just me questioning them." She pointed her spoon at him. "You can be intimidating."

"Do I intimidate you?"

She rolled her eyes. "Not even."

"Too bad." Maybe if he did, he could intimidate her right out of her harebrained idea.

"I know you're adamantly against me going undercover." She pushed her empty soup bowl away. "Let me ask you a question. If it wasn't me but a different female agent, would you be taking the same stand?"

Would he? He wanted to tell her yes, but if there was one thing he hated, whether from him or someone else, it was lying. "I don't know." That was the most honest answer he could give her.

"You're going undercover? I hadn't heard that," Rand said.

"I am. And before you go all protective alpha wolf on me like Nate's trying to do, Rothmire signed off on it. So if you don't like the idea, keep it to yourself. I don't want to hear it."

Nate barely managed to suppress a growl.

Rand glanced between them. "What am I missing here?"

"Not a thing." He grabbed the check their waitress had set on the table before Rand or Taylor could. "Ready to go?" Her earlier question was bugging him. Was he treating her differently than he would another female agent? If so, that wasn't fair to her.

As he followed Taylor and Rand out of the deli, he decided that he wouldn't like putting any female in the sights of a serial killer, but he especially didn't like that it would be Taylor. Since he couldn't stop her, he'd just have to make sure she stayed safe.

♠♠♠

Taylor had asked Nate to drop her off at her apartment after lunch so she could pick up her car and go question Linda Harding's daughters. As she pulled into a parking space back at the office after talking to them, she debated turning around and going to Rosie's. The interview with Mellie and Becky had left her depressed, and the best medicine when she was down was spending time with Rosie and the girls. She turned off the ignition, leaned her head back, and closed her eyes.

Lost girls always broke her heart. No one knew better than she did what it was like to lose a mother, even one who was a prostitute. When the girls had cried, she'd cried right along with them.

Someone tapped on the window, and she opened her eyes to see Nate staring down at her. "Stay there," he said, then jogged around the hood.

She unlocked the door, and he slid onto the passenger seat. "Something happen while I was gone?"

"No. I saw you sitting out here and knew you were taking a little time to be sad."

Sometimes it was scary how well he knew her. She managed a smile. "It wasn't an easy interview."

"Tell me about it."

That was one of the many things she loved about him. He was a good listener. "It was hard, you know? They don't want to believe their mother's never coming back."

"Something we can both understand."

"Yeah. I didn't learn anything useful, unfortunately. When Linda would leave for the night, they were under orders to stay on the mattress. Because they were afraid of some of the people who called the building home, they obeyed. Mellie said she'd had to twice threaten to use the knife she kept under their pillow."

She stared out the window, thinking of how fierce Mellie had looked when she'd said that. "At least they're safe now."

"And you'll keep tabs on them."

"You know I will." She pulled the key out of the ignition. "Rothmire and I are going to try to track Hector Ramirez down in the morning. See if he'll admit to knowing Alana Gilmore."

"His club usually comes into Aces and Eights on Thursday nights. Will be interesting to see if he shows up with them."

"You've met him. Do you see him as our bad guy?"

"Not really, but we certainly can't rule him out. I'll be curious as to your impression after you talk to him."

"Want to grab some dinner tonight?" She really didn't want to sit in her tiny apartment alone with her thoughts. She could go over to Rosie's, but she wouldn't be good company for the girls tonight. At his hesitation, she said, "Please. I promise not to make you kiss me again."

"Swear?"

At least she'd gotten a slight lip twitch from him. She held out her finger. "Pinky swear."

"Seriously, Taylor? What are we? Twelve?"

"Don't be such a stick in the mud." She wiggled her finger. One way or another, she was going to teach him to play. He curled his pinky around hers, but the gesture came with an eye roll. "See, that wasn't so hard, was it?"

"Next you'll be wanting to play hopscotch."

"It could happen. So where do you want to go for dinner?"

"How about pizza and beer on my balcony?"

"That sounds perfect." And it did. Much better than going out and having to talk to people.

"We need to make it early. I have to head over to Aces and Eights no later than nine when the bikers start rolling in. Alex will be there by himself until then. Why don't you go home, change into something more comfortable? I'll meet you at my place around five or so."

"I think I will." When Nate opened the door, Taylor put her hand on his arm. "Thanks."

He paused, one foot already on the ground, his eyes searching her face. "Feeling better?"

"Yeah." And she was. Talking things out with him always made her feel better. "See you in a few."

He nodded, then exited her car. She watched him walk into the building, appreciating how his black T-shirt stretched across his broad shoulders. Her gaze roamed down to his very fine butt. The man definitely wore jeans well. She sighed, then put the key back in the ignition. As she drove home to change, she wondered if she'd ever be able to tear down that wall. Unrequited love sucked.

CHAPTER SEVEN

"He claims he hasn't seen her for three or four months," Taylor said.

"When we told him she was dead, his reaction seemed legit. He was shocked, and then his eyes teared up." Josh shrugged. "I'm leaning toward believing him."

Nate hadn't thought Hector Ramirez was their killer. Not that the man would hesitate to kill someone who did him wrong—even if he only thought they had—but he was a look-you-in-the-face-while-he-put-a-bullet-between-your-eyes type.

He glanced around the conference-room table where he, Taylor, Alex, Rand, Josh, and Rothmire were seated. The team assigned to this case was, in his opinion, the best of the best. The only one missing was Court. Besides being a wizard on a computer, he also had a talent for seeing patterns. Court and his bride would be back home Sunday night, and as soon as he was available, Nate would get him started on doing his magic.

Alex's strength was his ability to understand a killer's mind. His baby brother felt things too hard. Nate wasn't sure how else to explain it than that. He attributed Alex's compassion for suffering souls to the hurt their mother had put on Alex's heart the day she'd left them. How that understanding worked for Alex, Nate didn't have a clue, but that particular talent had helped them catch bad guys more than once.

As for Rand, his talent was his willingness to follow through on any task assigned to him, no matter how laborious, boring, or distasteful. Ask the man to interview one hundred subjects in a day and, by damn, somehow he'd get it done.

Then there was Josh Sheridan, their newest and youngest member of the team. He had a good head on his shoulders, but he was a little too eager to prove himself. He'd grow out of that soon enough, so it wasn't anything that was worrisome.

Nate had always been honest with himself, and if he were asked what he contributed to the team, he would say it was his ability to see the overall picture, along with getting each member to do what he wanted. He also had common sense, something he'd decided too many people didn't have, and if offered a choice between that and being the richest man on earth, he'd take the common sense.

Rothmire? The man was a people manager, one of the best Nate had ever known. Their boss recognized his agents' abilities and gave them free rein . . . within reason. He was also loyal to his people, the reason every agent in the Miami office prayed that the powers that be never decided to relocate him.

And then there was Taylor, the smartest and most dedicated, and as deadly as any of them. As a rookie, without blinking an eye in hesitation, she'd put a bullet through the brain of a pedophile she'd caught raping a six-year-old boy when the man had laughed as he'd held a knife against the boy's jugular. The woman was a true do-gooder, especially where children were concerned. She was Nate's personal hero.

"Are we all agreed then that Ramirez isn't our killer, although we'll keep him on the list?" Rothmire said, bringing Nate back into the conversation.

Everyone nodded.

"Our man is much like a cockroach," Taylor said. "He doesn't like the light of day, but in the dark, he scurries around, looking for his next crumb to feed on. Hector's a puppy dog compared to our killer."

Nate glanced at her. He'd discussed all this with her last night over pizza and beer on his balcony, all the while reminding himself he would not kiss her again. But he wanted to. That one kiss had slayed him. It had put a knife through his heart because he'd learned the second his mouth had touched hers that he'd want to kiss her every day until he took his last breath.

"Hector said that he stopped seeing Alana when she started talking about being in love with him," Taylor said.

Josh nodded. "He said that he didn't think she was really in love with him, but that she saw him as a way to get off the streets. He went on to say that when he first started seeing her she was pretty and fun, but then chasing the dragon became her life goal. When the heroin and crack she was addicted to made her"—he made air quotes—"'ugly,' he had no use for her."

"Nice guy," Alex said. "Did he try to help her?"

That was Alex for you, wanting to see everyone happy. Nate raised a brow at his brother. "You know Hector. Is he really a nurturing type?"

"Guess not."

Nate wanted to wipe that sad-dog expression from Alex's face with a hug, but touchy-feely was not in his DNA. His baby brother needed to toughen up. Life was a bitch, a lesson Alex hadn't learned.

Maybe that was his fault. He hadn't wanted either of his brothers to be as numb to life as he was, so he'd done his best to help them believe they deserved to be happy. He loved the hell out of them, and no one had been gladder than he was to see his brothers married to women who loved them.

And love was obviously too much on his mind, considering how many times he'd just thought the word. He blamed his lovesick brothers for that. Seeing them happily married was putting stupid ideas in his head.

He stole a glance at Taylor, only to see her watching him as if she could read his every thought. That was the problem with having a friend who knew you too well, maybe even better than his brothers did. He blanked his face.

"We should have Harding's autopsy report tomorrow," Nate said. "The first two victims had been thoroughly cleaned before being dumped in the Everglades. I'm sure we'll learn he did the same with her."

"Yeah, he's obviously bathing them to wipe away any DNA he might had left on them. If he had sex with them, he used a condom." Taylor chewed on her bottom lip.

Nate wished she wouldn't do that. For some odd reason, he found that sexy as hell.

She nodded, as if coming to some conclusion. "He's not having sex with them. He's purifying them."

"Meaning?" Rothmire asked.

"Saving their souls?" Alex closed his eyes for a moment.

When Rand started to speak, Nate shook his head. They sat in silence, waiting for Alex to speak.

"He couldn't save his mother, or sister, or maybe his wife . . . although that last one doesn't feel right. Anyway, he couldn't save someone close to him, so he's atoning?" Alex gave a little shake as he opened his eyes. "Which is why he's cleansing them and then marrying them, if only symbolically. Then he sends them off to heaven."

Taylor spread out the photos that had been taken before each victim was removed from the killer's dumping ground. "Look at them. He's made them brides. Their white dresses represent purity to him, and the wedding rings are symbolic. Marriage is a covenant based on religion. I think Alex is right. He believes he's saving their souls."

"We may find out differently, but my money's on issues with his mother," Alex said.

"Or he's playing us, and it's all just a game to him." Nate believed Alex and Taylor were probably right, but they couldn't get stuck on one theory and not consider all the possibilities.

"What do you want me to do?" Rand asked.

Rothmire stood. "I'll leave you all to hash out assignments. Keep me updated."

"Find any similar cases?" Nate asked Alex.

"Not yet, but I'm still looking."

"Taylor, this afternoon, you and Josh can canvas the areas our victims worked, see if you can find anyone who saw them get in a car shortly before they disappeared. Maybe we can get a better description on the vehicle. Rand, you can give Alex a hand on the searches until Court gets back, and then we'll put him on that."

"We're on it," Rand said. "Anything else?"

"Not at the moment." Alex, Rand, and Josh left, leaving him alone with Taylor. She lifted her arms in a lazy stretch. Involuntarily, his eyes strayed to her breasts, straining against her blouse. The woman was going to be the death of him.

Taylor hid a grin at seeing Nate swallow hard. She shouldn't tease him, she supposed, but it was downright fun. "I need a workout before I head out with Josh. Meet you in the gym in fifteen?"

"Better not," he muttered.

She stood, leaned across the table, and whispered, "Coward." She knew exactly why he was refusing, and she also knew he couldn't resist a challenge, so she walked out before he could respond. Lately, their workouts simmered with sexual tension . . . Well, they always had, but that tension had been growing.

After dropping her files on her desk, she grabbed her tote bag, then headed for the gym that was conveniently located across the street. Almost all the agents were members, and fortunately, Rothmire encouraged them to work out. He liked having his agents fit and healthy and considered their gym time a part of their working day.

When Nate stepped onto the treadmill next to hers twenty minutes later, she didn't gloat. Well, she did, but only to herself. They ran for five miles, and then headed for the heavy bags. Since Nate was obviously not in a talking mood, she left him to his thoughts while they did their best to punch their bags to death.

"Ready for some combat?" she asked thirty minutes later. Their martial-arts sessions were when things got hot and heavy between them. Krav Maga was a self-defense system that had been developed by the Israelis, a mix of aikido, judo, boxing, wrestling, and realistic fighting, focusing on real-world situations. She shouldn't find it sexy, and she didn't, except when she was going against Nate. And then . . .

When she and Nate went at it, he had the strength and she had the technique. It was a battle between brawn and brain that somehow turned into a sexual dance every time they went up against each other. She had a theory about that. There was already off-the-charts chemistry—at least in her opinion—between them. Add aggression and adrenaline to the mix, and you had a potent brew.

She and Alex often trained together, as they were on a higher level than Nate and Court, and with him it was never sexual, which she found interesting. That told her it was because she and Nate had feelings for each other, even if he refused to admit it. With Alex, it was all about the technique, and she always learned something from him, as he was the best Krav Maga fighter she'd ever gone against. With Nate, it was like having sex with their clothes on. She grinned at that thought.

"What's got you amused?" Nate said.

"You. Come on. I'm ready to put you on your ass."

"In your dreams, tiger."

He followed her to the private room they had reserved, both kicking off their shoes before they stepped onto the mat. "You're the bad guy first," she said. She pivoted, following his movements as he circled her.

Nate never came at her the same way in their sessions, always keeping her on her toes. Suddenly, he spun, kicking a foot out, doing his best to slice her legs out from under her. She did a flip, then rolled, coming up behind him and kicking the back of his knee. His leg buckled, but he managed to stay on his feet.

He faced her, narrowing his eyes. "What the hell was that?"

"Something I've been practicing." She'd bought some gymnastic tapes almost a year ago and had been teaching herself some of the tricks that might prove useful. Today was the first time she'd felt ready to incorporate the moves into her training. She grinned. "Impressed?"

"Always," he answered, and as she was preening he tackled her, taking her down to the mat.

"No fair. I wasn't ready."

"So the bad guy's going to wait until you are?"

Well, she had walked right into that one. She grabbed his finger, bending it back, and as he tried to pull away, she wiggled out from under him—not that she wanted to, since she rather liked his body pressed against hers—and before he could react, she straddled his back, hooking her arm around his neck.

She put her finger against his head. "Bang. Another bad guy bites the dust."

And just like that, he flipped her over his head. They fought and wrestled and did their best to kill each other for a good twenty minutes. When he had her pinned again, his body pressed hard against hers, she stared into his eyes, watching them darken.

"It's a draw," she gasped, sucking air back into her lungs. He was as turned on as she was, and although this was far from the first time that had happened, it was the first time he didn't push away as soon as the sparks started flying. His groin was pressed against hers, and she could feel him growing hard.

"Nate," she whispered.

His eyes glittered, anger dancing in them. "Damn you," he said, then covered her mouth with his. As with the first time he'd kissed her, he wasn't gentle. But she didn't want tender. She wanted him out of control, and he was. As he explored her mouth, his tongue dominating hers, he rocked his hips against her. Her sex wept with pleasure. She wrapped her arms around his neck, holding him to her.

When his hand covered her breast, over her T-shirt, she wanted to rip the shirt off so he could touch her skin. Needing to touch him, she trailed her fingers down his back, over his spine until she reached the top of his workout shorts. She tugged his T-shirt free, then slipped her hands under it. He was hot, a furnace, and she was going up in flames.

Suddenly, he stole his heat away. Taylor stared up at him as he stood over her, panting as hard as she was. Nate was her best friend, and she knew how his mind worked. If she said one word about that kiss or tried to convince him to take what she willingly offered, he would dig in, more determined than ever to draw a line in the sand that he wouldn't cross.

She scissored her legs around his, dropping him to the mat, then scrambled onto her feet. "I win." As she walked away, she said, "I need a shower. Meet you back at the office." With her back to him, she allowed herself a smile. She was breaking through his defenses, brick by brick by brick.

♠♠♠

Once back at work, she grabbed everything related to their case—which she'd started thinking of as the Everglades Girls—and took the files to the conference room. She and Josh wouldn't go out until later, when the creatures of the night started venturing out.

As she spread everything across the tabletop, she wondered what the press would call the murders when they connected the dots, realizing there was a serial killer walking the streets. It would be something sensational, like the Dead Brides or the Killer Groom.

Nate never returned, which didn't surprise her. He was off somewhere doing his moody thing, but he'd get over it. He always did. She'd had two boyfriends in her life, one who'd turned out to be a jerk, convincing her that he loved her, then disappearing after he'd taken her virginity. It had taught her a valuable lesson. She'd been almost eighteen then, and had learned never to trust a sweet talker.

Her second boyfriend had been a great guy. They'd met her second year in college and had been together for two years before the relationship began to feel more like they were just going through the motions. Their parting was amicable, and they still kept in touch with an annual Christmas email, updating each other with what was going on in their lives. He was married now, with two kids, and she couldn't be happier for him.

The one thing she'd promised herself was that she would never allow herself to be helpless like her mother, pushed to the point where she felt she had no other choice but to sell her body. She'd studied hard, gotten a partial scholarship, and had worked a part-time job to get her degree in criminal justice. Her goal in life was to put away bad guys like the one who'd killed her mother. Someday, if luck was on her side, she'd find her mother's murderer. Until then, substitutes would do.

So she'd loved a douchebag, and she'd loved a really nice guy in her twenty-eight years, but neither one had ever felt like her soul mate. Nate, though? He was a man she respected more than any other, and she could love him real hard if only he'd let her.

All she had to do was find out why he was resisting what was obviously between them.

CHAPTER EIGHT

Tonight belonged to the Cubanos Motorcycle Club. Nate sat at the Aces & Eights bar, nursing a beer while listening to the rumble of a few dozen bikes pulling into the parking lot. He hoped Hector Ramirez was with them.

As he waited for them to come in, he read the text from Taylor for about the tenth time.

> Alex invited me to go riding with you guys on Sunday. Sounds like fun. What time should I come over?

Damn his matchmaking brother for sticking his nose where it didn't belong. Unless it was raining or too cold, every Sunday he, his brothers, and their wives would ride somewhere for lunch. Court and Lauren wouldn't be home until Sunday evening, so Nate hadn't planned to go, giving Alex and Madison a day alone.

Taylor had hinted in the past that she'd love to go with them sometime, but he'd never invited her. There wasn't any question in his mind that he'd like having her ride behind him too much. Better to just avoid the temptation. Now Alex had gone and taken that decision out of his hands. Baby brother was going to get an earful when he showed his face, which should be any time now.

Nate had avoided Taylor for the past three days, only talking to her on the phone when they needed to discuss the case, which left him feeling like a coward for hiding out. He had needed a little time to put that kiss out of his mind, but so far avoidance wasn't working. All he'd thought about, night and day, was how much he wanted to kiss Taylor Collins again. And that was just for starters.

He sighed in defeat, then texted her back.

Be at my place at 10

Awesome ☺

Like an idiot, he smiled back at the smiley face.

"Bro, what's up?" Alex said, coming up behind him and slapping him on the back.

"Besides your murder?"

Alex slid onto the barstool next to him. "If you'd stop being so stubborn, I wouldn't have to arrange a date for you with the lady of your dreams. You'd be doing it yourself."

"Alex?"

"Yeah?"

"You pull another stunt like that, and your lovely wife will be without your services for the next year."

His idiot brother laughed. "You can try, but I feel compelled to remind you that I'm a black belt and you're not."

"Which is why I'm going to kill you while you're sleeping." He eyed the door. "And the gang's all here." Hector Ramirez was one of the last to come in, and while most of the club made a beeline for the pool tables, Hector headed for the bar, choosing a stool next to the far wall.

"I'll get him a beer," Nate told Riker, their bartender. He poured a draft, then took his bottle of beer and the mug over to Hector. "Dude, you look like you could use a beer. This one's on me."

"Thanks, man." Hector lifted the mug to his mouth, downing half the contents.

"Want to talk about it? I'm a good listener."

"No." He drained the rest of the glass.

Nate refilled Hector's mug. "Heard you had a visit from the FBI about a girl you dated. She was murdered, huh?"

"How'd you hear that?"

"You know these club dudes gossip worse than a pack of twelve-year-old girls. I had a girlfriend who was murdered." A lie, but who was counting? "We'd broken up, but for a long time I thought I should have done something to save her."

"You ever stop thinking that?" Hector said, his gaze intent on Nate.

"Not really." Nate shrugged. "But she should have been smarter about who she hung with."

"Yeah. She should've been."

"Are we talking about my ex-girlfriend or yours?" Nate said, fully aware they were talking about Hector's.

"She could've been my number-one bitch, ya know? All she had to do was quit the crack and whatever other shit she was taking. I told her that. Didn't do any good."

"That sucks, man." Nate already knew that Hector's mother had been an addict who'd overdosed when he was eleven years old. "I take it you don't indulge?"

"Weed, booze, a little coke now and then, shit yeah. The hard stuff? Nope. I like keeping my teeth in my mouth."

"Can't argue with that." Nate refilled Hector's mug a third time. "When was the last time you saw her?"

"I dunno. Maybe two months ago? Like I keep a calendar of events."

"So she leave you for some other dude?"

"How the hell should I know? The woman sold herself to any man with a few bucks in his pocket." He looked up at Nate, suspicion in his eyes. "Why all the questions? You're starting to sound like the fucking FBI, asking questions like I did her in. The blonde bitch was hot, though. Wouldn't mind doing her."

Since Nate was a lawman, he didn't kill Hector on the spot for that last bit. The man was a douchebag, but he wasn't their killer. "Yet you're hanging over here by yourself, feeling guilty that you didn't somehow help your ex-girlfriend." Nate leaned toward Hector. "You got a tender heart, dude, but don't worry. Your secret's safe with me."

"Fuck you, Gentry."

Nate laughed. "No thanks." As he walked by Riker, he said, "He pays for his next one." Alex seemed to have everything in control for the time being, so Nate made a detour to the office. Normally, he would call Taylor, but now that they had an official date—thanks to his butthead brother—he wasn't sure what to say to her. Instead, he logged on to the computer and typed her an email, recapping his conversation with Hector and writing that he agreed with her assessment that they could eliminate the man as a suspect unless some new information turned up linking him to the murders.

He hovered the cursor over Send, paused, sat back, and stared at the screen. She was his best friend, and he was treating her like she had the plague or something. He deleted the email, then called her.

"Hey, what's up?" she said on answering.

"Just had a conversation with Hector Ramirez." He filled her in, thinking as he did so that he was glad he'd called her. The thing he liked about Taylor, one of the many things, she never made it into a big deal whenever he was a jerk. She should, but he was glad she didn't. Because of that, he tried not to be an ass too often.

"I got the profile back from Pauline," she said. "I'll shoot it over to you when we hang up."

"You going into the office tomorrow?" She usually went in for a few hours on Saturday.

"Yeah."

"Then hold on to it. I'll stop by and read it there."

"Great. I'll see you in the morning, then. Oh, and Nate?"

"Hmm?"

"I'm glad we're friends again."

She hung up before he could answer. "Yeah, me too," he said to dead air.

♠♠♠

Taylor arrived at the bureau after spending the morning having breakfast with Rosie and the girls. She'd promised to be back by three to take them to the library to turn in their books and check out new ones.

Not one of them had liked to read when they'd first come to her and Rosie, but that was one thing Taylor was determined to teach them to enjoy. Reading made them smart and introduced them to worlds they'd never known. Her hope was that they'd want more out of life than working some job for minimum wage or, God forbid, deciding to drop out of school as soon as they legally could.

They could check out whatever they wanted, and right now the older ones had discovered the Harry Potter books and were devouring them. Once they finished a book, Taylor would have discussions with them about what they'd read. Annie loved any book with pictures of animals in it, frogs being her most favorite thing. For some reason, frogs made her giggle.

When Taylor had first started taking them to the library, they'd dragged their feet and fussed about having to go. Now, it was the highlight of their week. Each of their grades had remarkably improved in the past year, and she couldn't be prouder of them.

"What're you daydreaming about?"

Taylor tore her gaze from the window, her girls forgotten because of the man standing in front of her desk. He wore what she thought of as his Aces & Eights uniform, a black T-shirt with the bar's logo on it, topped by an ace of spades card. Each of the brothers had their own card above the Aces & Eights logo on their work T-shirts. Nate was the ace, Court the king of clubs, and Alex the jack of hearts.

"You need a queen of diamonds," she blurted.

"You asking for the role?"

That had sounded almost flirty, something new from her moody man. He never flirted. "And if I were?" One side of his mouth twitched, and she knew she shouldn't feel so smug in being able to make him almost smile.

His gaze swept over her, and his eyes darkened. "You'd be a top contender."

Well, just wow, the reticent Nate Gentry really was flirting.

"But the role's taken. Aces and Eights is the queen," he said.

Just go and burst my bubble, Nate. He stepped to his desk, lowering his beautiful body—one she craved more than iced mocha coffees, her honest-to-God weakness—onto his chair.

"You got that profile?" He popped one of his wintergreen Tic Tacs into his mouth.

Back to business, then. She handed it to him, watching him as he read. The man was too freaking hot for his own good . . . Or maybe more like for *her* own good. How was she supposed to stop wanting to pull that leather band off so she could run her fingers through his long black hair?

She could totally see him with a sword strapped to his waist and armor covering his body, while the wind from the moors blew his hair around his head. Or better yet, bare chested, wearing nothing but leggings and leather boots. Just imagining how hot he'd be dressed like that, long hair falling over his shoulders, sent a lightning bolt straight to her stomach and parts below. She picked up a folder and fanned herself.

"Pauline says pretty much what we're already thinking about our bad guy," he said, handing the report back.

"Let your hair down." Well, that had slipped out. But now that the fantasy was there in her mind, she wasn't going to be able to quit thinking about it. In all the time she'd known him, she'd never seen him without his ponytail. He looked at her as if she were a green alien that had just stepped out of a spaceship.

"Seriously, I want to see your hair loose."

"No."

"That just makes me more determined, you know?" He knew how stubborn she was when she made up her mind she wanted something.

He tilted his head, studying her. "You smoke a joint or something? You're talking weird and fanning yourself."

"Funny." If he only knew where her mind was, he'd be fanning her, too. She slid the report she'd already read several times back into its folder. "Want to have dinner with us before you head over to Aces and Eights tonight? Rosie's making spaghetti."

"I'll have to take a rain check." He pushed away from his desk, swiveling the chair so that he was facing her. "Listen, about you going undercover—"

"Don't start, Nate. This creep's going to strike again if we don't stop him. The women he's choosing have no one to fight for them." If someone had cared enough, maybe her mother would be alive. And if anyone in law enforcement had given a damn about a dead prostitute, her killer would be in prison.

"They have you," he said, softly.

"And you, along with everyone else here."

"And we'll catch him. What I was going to say before you bristled—"

"I don't bristle."

He grinned. "Yet, you did."

It took every ounce of her willpower not to do a fist pump at seeing his mouth curve into the sexiest grin ever. *Get his lips to twitch. Check. Get him to grin. Check. Get him to laugh. Working on it.*

"Did not." She put her foot on his knee and pushed, sending him rolling away. "Shut your mouth if you don't want to have your manly self crying uncle."

His eyes, already black, turned even blacker, and how was that even possible, she wondered. They smoldered as he stared at her with an intensity that almost had her climbing onto his lap. She might have if she hadn't spied Rothmire coming down the hall, reminding her they were at work.

"Incoming," she muttered, whipping out Pauline's profile report.

"Boss man?"

She nodded.

He grinned again, a very devilish one this time. "I think I should tell him you have the hots for my body."

What in the world had gotten into him? Whatever it was, she liked it, but Rothmire was only seconds away. "I swear, Nate, if you do, I'll kill you," she muttered.

His grin grew wider. "Hey, Rothmire," he said without looking behind him. "Taylor has the—"

She kicked him.

". . . profile of our killer back from Pauline." He smirked at her, then popped a Tic Tac into his mouth.

She glared at him before lifting innocent eyes to their boss. "Pauline agrees that our bad guy is trying to atone for something in his past. He's thirty-five to forty and probably lives alone. He has a job that is detail oriented, something along the lines of a technical writer or something in the finance area. He is or was very close to his mother. She thinks his mother is probably dead, most likely murdered. What's new here is that she says we should watch for someone who grew up in one of the towns near Tamiami Trail, considering his familiarity with the area."

"Was she a prostitute?" Rothmire asked.

"Pauline believes she was, or possibly the mistress of a married man," Nate said. "If the latter, she feels the woman was abused and probably the son, too."

Rothmire frowned. "Assuming Pauline's right, does she have a guess as to how old our man was when his mother died?"

"No, unfortunately," Taylor said. "If we knew that, it would narrow down our search for a murdered woman who lived somewhere along Alligator Alley. I wouldn't be surprised if we find out the case was unsolved." It was possible Pauline was completely wrong, but all her profiles in the past had been spot-on.

Nate flicked the button on the pen he held, making clicking noises. "Court will be back Sunday night. I'll put him on looking for women who were murdered during the past thirty years or so in that area. It's a lot of years and a lot of ground to cover, but that kind of thing is right up his alley. I want Alex to start reviewing all the files on our victims, see if he can find anything we missed. You and Josh can keep looking for witnesses who might have seen our three victims get in a car right before they disappeared."

"A definite description of the car he uses would be a big help." Taylor pulled out Pauline's profile, scanning it. "There's one other thing of interest. She doesn't think he knew Linda Harding had children, that he would have picked someone different if he had. In talking to her daughters, they said that their mother kept them hidden in the building when she was working, so he probably didn't know."

She'd given that some thought, wondering how they could use it. Nate and Rothmire watched her expectantly, both of them knowing that her brain was in high gear and that she had more to say. That was what she loved about the Miami office. She didn't know if it was the same for female agents elsewhere, but her boss and male counterparts respected her opinions, and best of all, they treated her as their equal. Not one of them had ever asked her to get them a cup of coffee. Of course, if they had, they'd have gotten it dumped on their heads, which they knew, so they weren't stupid . . . Another thing she liked about them.

"I'm wondering if we should release a statement to the media that Linda was survived by two daughters. Pauline believes he would have picked a different prostitute if he'd known Linda had children. What does that mean, exactly? Would knowing that send him spiraling into a guilt trip, maybe cause him to make mistakes? Or would it send him into hiding, making it harder to find him? Or worse, up his game?"

"Your mind is a wicked thing, Taylor."

There was admiration in Nate's voice, which she soaked up like sunshine on a winter day. "How so?"

"I read that and didn't think anything of it. So, he would have chosen someone else if he'd known about her daughters? I didn't question that, and I should have."

Rothmire stared at the two of them, the hint of a smile on his face. "I'm not going to tell either one of you that you're my best two agents. It might be true and it might not. My vote's for releasing a statement to the media, but don't let that sway you just because I'm your boss. Keep me informed."

Taylor laughed as he walked away. "I guess we need to write a statement."

"Once we do, the media's going to connect the dots, realizing we have a serial killer on our hands." Nate scooted his chair back to his desk, close enough for her to catch his scent, which was definitely a distraction.

Why did he always have to smell so good, like pure male musk and something earthy combined with a hint of something spicy? "Yeah, but they're going to catch on sooner or later. Probably sooner."

"True, so we might as well control the narrative. Include all three women." He stood, pushing his chair back under his desk. "You want to write up the release?"

"Sure. Still no on Rosie's spaghetti dinner?"

"Still no." His shoulder lifted in a shrug. "It's just me and Alex at Aces and Eights until Court gets back. See you in the morning?"

"I'll be there." It wasn't a date, since he hadn't been the one to invite her, but it felt kind of like a date. She tried not to be too excited about spending the day with him outside of work. As she tidied up her desk before heading over to Rosie's, she mentally reviewed the clothes hanging in her closet that would be suitable for a day on the back of a motorcycle, smiling when she thought of the perfect outfit.

CHAPTER NINE

Whoa! Nate stopped in his tracks, his gaze traveling over Taylor. She stood next to his bike, talking to Madison and Alex. Because she hadn't noticed him, he took the time to appreciate how sexy she looked in a pair of white jeans that hugged her hips and long legs before disappearing into a pair of mid-calf-length red boots. His eyes roamed back up her body to the red silk camisole, the length of which stopped about an inch above the waist of her low-riding jeans, showing a tantalizing hint of skin. And was that silver flash a belly ring?

He'd always thought her sexy, even in her plain blouses, loose black pants, and sensible shoes, but eff him. This Taylor was mouthwateringly hot, and his mouth was definitely watering.

She held a plastic cup containing her favorite drink, an iced mocha coffee piled high with whipped cream. Arousal stirred as he watched her suck on the straw, which sent his mind straight into the gutter. He very much feared he was going to spend an extremely uncomfortable day on his bike. And she hadn't even touched him yet. How was he supposed to curb his desire for her when she was hugging his back, her arms around his waist and her thighs pressed against his?

Alex noticed him practically drooling over their fellow agent, and Nate had the urge to wipe that smirk off his brother's face. He settled for glaring at Alex, the little Cupid dumbass. Taylor looked over at him, and her happy smile at seeing him about stopped his heart. "Damn," he muttered to himself. Today was going to be pure torture.

He took a deep breath, then headed to his bike. "Morning," he said, coming to a stop on the opposite side of the motorcycle from her.

"Good morning."

There was that smile again. "Have you ever ridden on a motorcycle before?"

"No, but I've always wanted to."

Pleasure filled his chest that she'd never been on the back of a bike with another man. There was nothing he loved doing more on his off day than riding. Would she get it once they got on the road? True bikers understood that, along with the pure fun of it, the cliché was true . . . Nothing could compare to the freedom one felt with a powerful machine between their legs while riding the open road, the wind blowing in your face and hair.

"Okay, here's what you need to know. I don't have a backrest, so keep your arms around my waist. When I lean the bike, your instinct is going to be to resist and lean the other way. Don't. Just keep your body against my back and lean with me."

"Okay, got it."

He grabbed his helmet and a spare from the hooks on the wall. She put on the one he handed her, but fumbled with the snap. "Here, let me do it." Standing this close, her lemony scent floated up, and he caught himself leaning closer. Yep, today was definitely going to be torture. "There, all buckled up."

She picked up a black jean jacket from the seat of his motorcycle, slipping it on.

"You look nice," he said. That was a lie. She didn't just look nice. She looked stunning. And really, really sexy.

She beamed at him. "Thank you."

While he'd given her instructions and gotten her helmet on, Alex and Madison had put on their helmets, and Madison was already on the bike behind Alex. Nate slung a leg over his, lifting it upright.

"Put your foot on the peg, then climb on." Once she was settled behind him, her arms circling his waist, he started the bike. Having her wrapped around him was as torturous as he'd thought it would be. Her breasts were pressed against his back, the insides of her legs were aligned alongside the outside of his, and her palms rested on his shirt, right over his belly button. As he pulled away, he tried to decide whether he was in heaven or in hell.

Once they were on the road, he put his hand over hers to make sure she didn't let go, then accelerated. She laughed, the sound of it pure joy. He should have known she'd love riding on a motorcycle. It had been a long time since he'd had a woman behind him, and he'd forgotten how much he liked it. Even more so this time because it was Taylor.

He glanced in his rearview mirror to make sure Alex was behind him, then headed north on A1A. After learning Taylor would be riding with them today, he'd decided to take the beach road to Pier 66 in Fort Lauderdale. There was a nice poolside restaurant at the pier, and after eating they could walk along the docks, playing tourist while gawking at all the huge yachts.

It didn't take long for Taylor to get the hang of being on the back of a motorcycle. A few miles down the road and she was leaning with him, not holding on for dear life or constantly bumping the back of his helmet with hers like so many passengers did their first time on a bike. That didn't surprise him. When she made up her mind to do something, she invariably succeeded. They'd traveled another mile before he realized he had his hand on her knee. When had he done that?

Then she started playing with his ponytail whenever they stopped at a light. Between her legs pressed alongside his, her breasts bouncing against his back, and her fingers combing his hair, he thought he might go insane. Or be permanently aroused, never able to walk normally again.

And he still had his hand on her knee. He snatched it away, putting it back on the handlebar. To counter the effect she was having on him, he turned his mind to their case and what they knew so far. As yet, they had very little except for assumptions. Although most of those would probably prove true once they found their killer, Nate wanted facts. Thinking of their victims dumped in the Everglades in their white dresses, gold bands on their ring fingers, should have been as good as a bucket of ice dumped down his pants.

But by the time they pulled into a parking space at Pier 66, he needed to cross his hands in front of him to hide his erection. *Note to self: next time you have Taylor on the back of your motorcycle, wear the longest shirt you own.*

"That was awesome," she said as she hopped off his bike. "I want a motorcycle." She eyed Madison. "Wouldn't you like to have your own bike?"

"Nope, I like riding behind my man." Madison gave her husband a sexy smile. "It's a total turn-on to ride pressed all up against him."

Taylor glanced at him, mischief dancing in her eyes, and he braced himself for what was about to come out of her mouth. "I totally get that now that I've ridden behind Nate, but still. Being in control of all that power between your legs? Man, the thought of that makes me hot."

The air left his lungs at thinking of her straddling a motorcycle in that outfit. He bent over, more than was necessary, to lock the bike's fork, while at the same time pulling his T-shirt out of his jeans in an attempt to cover his zipper area. It wasn't damn long enough.

Alex grinned, ambling over while the girls busied themselves with removing their helmets. "Should I just shoot you now? Put you out of your misery?"

"Bug off, Alex." Alex laughed so hard that Nate thought he might have to give his baby brother CPR.

"What's so funny?" Madison asked, joining them.

"Nothing. Nothing's funny." Nate glared at Alex, daring him to open his mouth one more time.

Taylor came up on the other side of him. "Can we go look at the yachts after we eat?"

"Sure," he said, a little surprised that his voice hadn't sounded strangled.

She handed him her denim jacket. "Hold this for me, okay?"

As he took it from her, holding it in front of him, he glanced at her, getting a sly smile. She knew what was going on below his belt and was helping him hide the evidence. His heart took a disconcerting leap, something that had never happened with another woman. He didn't like it.

Liar, a voice whispered in his ear. He ignored it. "We're eating at the Orchids Bar and Grill. It's a poolside restaurant." He glanced at Madison. "They have fish tacos."

"I knew I loved you," she said, racing ahead, then turning and bouncing on her feet, her eyes on Taylor. "If Nate hasn't told you, I would leave Alex for fish tacos."

"Hey," Alex said. "I feed you fish tacos every chance I get. Get back here, woman."

Madison danced back to her husband with a big smile on her face, and Nate tried not to envy that his little brother was ridiculously happy for finding a woman who loved him unconditionally. When she reached Alex, she tucked herself under his arm, both of them staring at each other as if they were the only two people left on earth and they were good with that.

The temperature was perfect for a day out on motorcycles, his brother and sister-in-law were flirting as if they were still on their honeymoon, and Nate had the one woman he could love, if only he knew how to accomplish such a feat, walking by his side. It didn't get much better or much worse than that.

After a great lunch, they strolled down to the pier, Alex and Madison walking ahead, their arms around each other's backs. Taylor slipped her hand in his, and he glanced at her, his brow raised. She was staring with wide eyes at a yacht that had to be close to two hundred feet long.

Nate had never held hands with a woman. Because he had no intention of ever marrying, he didn't have relationships. He wasn't a monk, far from it, but the women he took to bed knew the score. He made sure of it. They wanted nothing more from him than a few hours of pleasure, and at the first sign of interest in spending time with him outside of the bedroom, he backed off.

He was thirty-three years old, on his first real date, and holding hands with a woman he'd desired for a long time. This wasn't good. Not how much he liked her hand in his and not whatever the hell it was in his heart that felt like some kind of happy bubbles. Damn Alex and his meddling.

A small fishing boat pulled up to the stern of the yacht. A man in a white double-breasted chef's jacket appeared on the wide back deck. They stopped, watching as the fisherman handed up several large groupers.

"Wow, that's so cool." Taylor eyed the fisherman. "Fresh fish delivered right to your door."

"I guess if you can afford that kind of boat," Madison said, "you can afford a personal chef and all the fresh seafood you want."

Alex smirked at his wife. "The little thing bobbing behind is a boat, Mad. The big thing is a yacht. There's a definite difference."

She punched his arm, then hopped away, laughing. "Boat, yacht, whatever. Make fun of me and see if you get any tonight."

"Get back here, wife," Alex said.

She jogged backward down the pier. "Nope. I'm going to find a sea captain and sail away with him . . . Or is that yacht off with him? Oh, wait. I think I'll just boat off with him." Alex took off after her, both laughing as he chased her.

"They're adorable," Taylor said.

"Yeah, they're a Hallmark movie come to life." He glanced at her, struck by the longing in her eyes as she watched his brother and Madison. Tearing his gaze away, he swallowed the question hovering on his lips. *Is that what you want, Taylor? Someone to love you that way?* He'd thought she only wanted an affair, a little fun to work off the chemistry between them that sometimes felt like an out-of-control wildfire. That he might be able to handle, as long as they came to an understanding that they were taking their relationship to no more than friends with benefits.

The idea of it had been brewing ever since he'd kissed her. He'd even made a mental list of his conditions before he'd agree: the most important one being that either could call it quits and there wouldn't be any hard feelings. Once the heat between them dimmed, they would still be best friends.

The longing he'd just seen in her eyes, though, had him putting the brakes on any thought of taking their relationship to the next level. If she wanted someone to love her the way Alex did Madison, he wasn't that man. She was the last person in the world he wanted to hurt, and he would if she was looking for more than a fling. That was a given.

Yet he didn't let go of her hand.

Taylor sensed the change in Nate. That was how well she knew him. She doubted any other woman would have noticed the slight loosening of his hand around hers or that he'd withdrawn into his moody self. But she did, so what did that say about her? That she was yearning for a man who didn't believe he deserved to be loved?

She wasn't sure that was exactly his problem, but based on his history—rejected by his mother, abused by his father—who wouldn't think that? It was enough to bring tears to her eyes at thinking of him as a boy, unloved but struggling to be both mother and father to his brothers. She quickly blinked her tears away. He would hate knowing she hurt for him.

Sometimes she let herself imagine being with him, wondering what he was like in bed. Skilled, for sure. Was he dominant? She liked to think he was. Hoped he was, if she ever got time in his bed.

She spent all day in a man's world and had to come across as strong, always a step ahead if she wanted to keep from getting walked over. It would be exciting to let go with a man she trusted to take charge of her and her body in the bedroom. She believed Nate could be that man.

"See those two dudes over there?" Nate said, breaking into her thoughts.

She followed his gaze, spying two oversized men standing at the bottom of stairs leading up to a yacht bigger than the one they'd just walked by. "Bodyguards?"

"Yeah. And they're carrying."

"Wonder who the yacht belongs to?" She scanned the deck. There wasn't anyone moving about, but there was a helicopter sitting on a landing pad. "Someone famous, or there'd be no need for the muscle." Both guards' attention was focused on them as they approached.

"Good name for it," Nate said.

She smiled at seeing *Escape* in script across the back. "I could definitely escape in that."

Nate nodded to the guards as they walked past. Neither responded, only watched them through mirrored sunglasses. He glanced at her. "Would you like having that kind of money?"

"Not even. Sure, I'd love to have enough money to open a home for girls, but the kind to buy a yacht like that? It would be too much of a burden. I'm just a simple girl, Nate. I don't need much." She grinned. "Well, maybe enough to buy a few more pairs of Jimmy Choos, but

I'll get there. Anyway, I just want someone—" She snapped her mouth closed. She'd almost said she just wanted someone—namely him—to love her the way Alex and Court loved their wives. Someone she could trust enough to hand him her heart.

"I'm not that man, tiger," Nate said, letting go of her hand.

How had he known what she'd been about to say? She stood on the middle of the pier, watching him walk away.

"I think you could be if you'd only let yourself believe," she whispered to his retreating back.

CHAPTER TEN

"I talked to Rothmire this morning," Taylor said. "As soon as we get a better idea of who we're looking for, I'll be going undercover. We need to get some kind of description of our man and one of his car, otherwise it's a no-go."

Nate squeezed his fingers around the pen in his hand. His team, with the addition of Court—back from his honeymoon, looking tanned and absurdly happy—sat around the conference-room table early Monday morning. The day after his first and last date with Taylor.

She glanced at his hand. "You're going to break that in half if you squeeze it any harder."

He'd like to break Rothmire in half for agreeing to the undercover plan, but at least the boss had qualified his approval. "Alex and Josh will be out on the streets tonight, looking for any witnesses who might have seen someone suspicious or a description of a car that caught their attention."

Alex was decent at disguising himself, and since the case against Madison's uncle was closed, he was getting antsy. Sitting around staring at a computer screen wasn't Alex's thing, so Nate was letting him out of his cage.

"Prostitutes have a sixth sense for danger," Taylor said. "I'm sure there's at least one out there who either encountered him or noticed something that made her uneasy. We just have to find her so we can get a line on this bastard before victim number four turns up."

Taylor passed around the press release that would air on the evening news on all the local stations. Nate read it over again. He hoped it would bring their man out of hiding, but it could just as easily send him deeper underground.

"We purposely didn't mention that the three women were prostitutes, although that will come out soon enough," Taylor said. "As for Linda Harding, Nate and I decided to say that she was a single mother of two young daughters, struggling to make ends meet."

Nate slipped his copy of the release into his folder. "We don't think he knew she had children. Learning that she did will upset him." He glanced around the room. "Anything else? No? Okay, we'll meet back here in the morning." Until their man was behind bars, the team would meet each morning to review their findings and make decisions on how to proceed.

Alex and Josh walked out together, making plans for meeting up that evening. "Stay a minute," Nate said when Court and Rand rose. "You too," he told Taylor. She'd been sitting at the other end of the table but moved to the chair next to him and across from Court. Close enough for Nate to catch her scent.

He'd been something of an ass on the way home yesterday, for which he was sorry. That longing in her eyes had slayed him. He wanted to be the man who put stars in her eyes. But he was his father's son, and he didn't trust himself. What if the day came when he couldn't control the rage that simmered deep in his bones? It had gotten loose once, almost twice, proving that he couldn't be trusted.

Even though he had been quiet and moody riding back to his condo, she was her usual happy self today. It only made him feel worse. She should call him out on acting like a jerk. When they'd arrived home, he'd barely said good-bye before heading for the elevator, leaving her with Alex and Madison. He could always count on his brothers to speak their mind, and Alex hadn't hesitated to call him an ass first thing this morning.

"I need you both to concentrate solely on trying to find similar murders," he told Court and Rand. "These three kills are too clean and organized. I'd bet my paycheck that he's killed before. If so, he obviously wasn't caught, so they'll be unsolved." He glanced at Taylor. "Fill them in on what our profiler said so they'll know where to start looking. I'm going to go call that police chief . . . What was his name? The one we met in the Everglades?"

"Grant. I think his first name was Boyd."

He nodded. "Sounds right."

♠♠♠

"Did Chief Grant have any useful information?" Taylor asked.

"Nothing we don't already know. He was more interested in what it took to be an FBI agent."

Taylor grinned. "Aren't they all?"

They were sitting at a back table in a piano bar close to the office, Taylor sipping a glass of wine and him nursing a beer. He'd left right after he'd talked to Grant, heading over to the police station in Liberty City's jurisdiction.

Taylor probably wasn't going to be happy that he hadn't invited her along, but he'd needed to do some thinking. He'd decided to put his cards on the table and explain to her where he was coming from, and he owed her an apology. So he'd called her, inviting her for a drink after she got off.

Business first, though. "I also talked to the Liberty City detectives. They knew Linda Harding, had busted her a few times, but they hadn't heard she was dead. They also haven't had any complaints from their known prostitutes about anyone suspicious."

"Like any of them would go to the police," she said.

"Yeah, I didn't figure they would, but it was worth a try. They're going to keep an eye out and let us know if anything catches their attention."

"Based on their arrest records, Alana worked out of the Hialeah area and Stacy downtown."

"Unfortunate that our man doesn't stick to the same hunting grounds." She'd surprised him again by not busting his chops for taking off without including her.

"Yeah, it is. Harder to predict where he'll pop up next."

He pushed his beer aside and leaned forward, resting his arms on the table. "I owe you an apology."

"For?"

"For being an ass yesterday."

She laughed. "That's pretty much your usual self. No reason to apologize."

"If that's true, why do you even like being friends with me?" He'd never given it much thought, but no matter how moody he got, it didn't seem to bother her. She was always her happy self, mostly ignoring his grouch. That was one reason he liked her. She let his shit roll over her, and more times than not, he forgot to be grumpy when he was with her. But what did she get out of their friendship? He couldn't think of much.

"Because someone needs to be your friend." She smiled as she reached across the table and touched his arm. "Because I like you. Other than your brothers, I'm probably the only person you don't scare. I don't know why. Just one of the mysteries of the universe, I guess. Because I think you need me in your life."

"I don't even know what to say to that." He hadn't even cried when his mother had left, but this woman's words had him blinking his eyes against the sting in them.

"You don't have to say anything." She took her hand away from his arm, and he wanted to grab it back. "So when are you going to agree to have an affair with me?"

He choked on the beer he'd just swallowed. "Just get that right out there, why don't you?"

"Well, when it's what we both want, why not?"

"Yeah, why not?" He stared into blue eyes that he could drown in. "Because I'll only end up hurting you."

"I won't let you."

"You can't know that." If he could believe she wouldn't let him hurt her, he'd scoop her up this very minute and take her straight to his bed.

She peered at him over the rim of her wine glass. "And if I do? Then what's stopping you?"

His integrity, what little he had? "I'll never marry. If you fall in love with me, that's what you'll want. Since I can't give that to you, I'll hurt you."

The biggest grin he'd ever seen on her face appeared. "Already you're refusing a proposal I never asked for or wanted. Another reason why I like you, Nate. You're amusing even when you don't mean to be." Her smile faded. "So here's the thing. I'm not husband shopping. I just lust over your body."

"You're testing my limits, tiger. You know what they say. Be careful what you ask for."

She sighed as if he were clueless. "I've had two boyfriends in my life. One turned out to be a total douchebag. The other one I'm still friends with."

He narrowed his eyes. "Yeah?" He didn't like that at all. Did she still have feelings for the dude?

"Oh, drop the snarl. He's happily married with kids. The thing is, neither one had what it took to send me into the stratosphere. I think you can do that."

"Christ, Taylor." Did she even have a clue what she was doing to him?

Taylor was trained to observe, and observe she did. Why else would he be squirming in his chair if she weren't making him hot and bothered? She swallowed a smile. "Just putting it out there. If you were like any other man, I could be all coy"—she fluttered her eyelashes—"and girly." Ah, the ghost of a smile, there and then gone, flitted across his face.

"Please don't ever go all girly on me."

"I wouldn't know how if my life depended on it. Give me one good reason we shouldn't give in to this thing between us? And don't say you're afraid of screwing up our friendship." She believed that was a part of it, but there was more to his reticence than that.

"Isn't that a good enough reason? It's one you should be worried about."

"But I'm not. It's chemistry, Nate, nothing more. We're consenting adults, intelligent, and all that. There's no reason we can't enjoy each other for however long we want and still be friends when it's over." And yes, she was saying what she thought he wanted to hear. If she told him she loved him, he'd probably ask for a transfer to the other side of the world. She waited, watching him spin his beer bottle, sensing that she was finally going to find out why he'd always held back.

He lifted his eyes to hers. "What if you fall in love with me? I'll never marry, and I won't ever change my mind about that."

"Not a problem, but why not? What if you do eventually meet someone and fall in love?" And that would kill her.

"I won't." He stared at her with the kind of intensity that was so him. "When you say not a problem, how can you know that for sure?"

She didn't. "I'm not looking for a ring on my finger. There's too much on my plate as it is what with my job and the girls. The last thing I need is a man wanting me to take care of him, too. Or, God forbid, trying to tell me what to do."

"And you think I would?"

No, he was a man who wouldn't make those kinds of demands from her. He was also the one man she thought she could love for the rest of her life. But she'd cut her tongue off before ever admitting that to him.

"I don't intend to find out whether you would or not, since I'll never give you that kind of power over me." He still hadn't explained why he was so adamant that he'd never marry, but she'd drop it for now. "So, what do you say?" She reached across the table and trailed her finger over his arm. "Are we going to do it or not?"

He laughed. Actually freaking laughed. She felt like she'd just won the lottery, but she didn't make a big deal over it. Knowing Nate, if she did, he'd never laugh again. Her heart pounded as she waited for his answer. She hadn't intended to push the issue tonight, but she only had so much patience. If he said no, it would be the last time she'd ask. If nothing else, she had her pride.

"Well?"

Without answering, he pulled a twenty out of his wallet, dropped the money on the table, and then grabbed her hand, tugging her up with him. Mere seconds later, they were outside. He kept walking, not saying a word, and even with her long legs, she had to jog to keep up with him. She figured one of two things were about to happen. First option, he was going to put her in her car, tell her to stop asking to have sex with him, and then send her on her way. What she hoped would happen was that he'd finally cave.

When they reached her car, he backed her against the door, put his hands on the roof, caging her in, and said, "I give up."

Then his mouth came down on hers. Like the first two times he'd kissed her, this one was possessive, demanding, and hungry. But so much more, as if now that he'd agreed to this, he was all in. He tasted like malt beer and wintergreen. Tangy and delicious.

Her legs lost the will to hold her up, only the car at her back and Nate pressed against her front keeping her on her feet. When he pulled away, she growled in displeasure, and another ghost smile curled his lips, gone as fast as it had appeared.

"Go home, tiger."

What? "But I thought—"

"And we will." He trailed his thumb over her bottom lip, damp from his kiss. "But not tonight."

Staring into his eyes, she sucked his thumb into her mouth. She wasn't above using all her tricks—although her arsenal was sorely lacking. When she licked his finger, he groaned.

"Not tonight," he said again, pulling his thumb out of her mouth. "Will you go out with me Sunday? Dinner and dancing."

The vulnerability she saw in his eyes made her sad. Did he not realize any sane woman would gush an excited yes at that question? "You don't date." Why had she reminded him of that? *That was just stupid, Taylor.*

"Not until you." He stepped away. "Wear something sexy."

"Bossy man." Inside, though, she was a quivering mess. She'd probably spend every spare minute between now and Sunday night trying on everything in her closet in an effort to find the perfect seduction dress.

"I have a feeling you're going to like me bossy." With that said, he walked away. Before he reached his car, he pivoted, walking backward. "No falling in love? We're straight on that?"

"Yeah, we're straight." Or not, but that was her problem.

♠♠♠

"Alex told me Nate asked you out on a date," Madison said.

Taylor grinned. "Yeah, he did." It was Friday night, and she, Madison, and Lauren—only a few days back from her honeymoon—were having drinks and then dinner. She'd been surprised when Madison had called to invite her, since she'd never socialized with either woman before.

It had been a nice surprise, though. She didn't have any female friends. Between her job and the time she spent with Rosie and the girls, she didn't have the energy or opportunity to cultivate friendships. And when all your coworkers were male, where was she supposed to find friends, even if she'd wanted them?

She liked both women, and she could see why their husbands had fallen hard for them. Madison was gorgeous with her red hair and mischief-filled green eyes. It was easy to see why she'd caught Alex's attention. She was fun to be around; they both were.

Lauren wore her hair short and spikey, the ends pink-tipped. Taylor couldn't imagine wearing her hair like that, but it totally worked on Lauren. She was the more serious of the two, but she'd been terribly abused by her ex-husband, and Taylor thought she was still fighting her way back from that. It was obvious by how her eyes softened whenever she mentioned Court that she was head-over-heels in love with him.

"I've never known Nate to date," Lauren said. "Although maybe I haven't known him long enough to say that."

"As far as I know, he doesn't." Madison grinned at Taylor. "Until now, anyway. Alex always said the two of you had the hots for each other."

"I haven't tried to hide that. It was always Nate holding back. But it's just a date. Don't be expecting wedding bells."

Madison waggled her eyebrows. "You never know. His two brothers have wedding rings on their fingers. No reason Nate shouldn't be next."

"Court said Nate swears he'll never marry," Lauren said.

"Did he say why?" She could make some educated guesses, but she'd like to know the real reason.

Lauren shrugged. "No. I don't think guys talk about stuff like that, even brothers."

"You know they were abused pretty badly growing up?" Madison said. "That might have something to do with it."

"Yeah, Nate told me their father was, in his words, 'an effing son of a bitch' and that the happiest day of his life was when he died."

"I think they all felt like that." Madison picked up her wine glass. "But we're here for a fun girls' night out, so enough about all that. It makes me too sad."

"Me, too," Lauren said. "So, where are you going on your date?"

"I don't know. All Nate said was to wear something sexy." Taylor grinned. "The guys won't be home until they close the bar. Want to go shopping with me after dinner, help me find a sexy dress?"

"Oh, yeah," Madison said, clicking her glass against Taylor's.

Well, this should be interesting. She'd never gone shopping with girlfriends before. By the time the mall closed for the night, she had her dress, along with some sexy panties and bras they'd talked her into buying. Having girlfriends was expensive.

CHAPTER ELEVEN

Nate was nervous as hell, which was stupid. Taylor was his best friend. He'd spent more hours with her than he could count, so why was his heart beating as if it might go into cardiac arrest as he walked up to her door? He hadn't lied when he said he'd never been on a date. No proms or school dances, as there had never been extra money for nice clothes and other date-related expenses.

Then he'd held down two part-time jobs through college, and what spare time he had was dedicated to studying and raising his brothers. Sometimes he'd been jealous of his classmates when hearing them talk of their dates for football games or other school events, but he'd shaken the envy off by burying his nose deeper into his textbooks.

After graduating, he'd managed to achieve his goal, landing a job with the FBI. His experience with women consisted of hooking up for a few hours of pleasure. Now here was Taylor, shaking up his world. He wasn't sure how he felt about that. A part of him was excited, but the other part wanted to know just what he thought he was doing.

He popped a Tic Tac into his mouth and then knocked on her door. When she opened it, whatever words he'd been about to say disappeared. The woman standing in front of him in a killer black dress was the most gorgeous, sexiest thing he'd ever seen. He swallowed hard as all the blood in his body took a direct route south. Instead of telling her to wear something sexy, he should have told her to wear a burlap bag. Although she'd probably manage to look great in one of those, too.

"Here," he finally managed, pushing the bouquet of red roses wrapped in tissue into her hands. Along with her being his first-ever date, she was the first woman he'd ever given flowers. He'd spent an hour in a florist shop debating what to buy, until the owner had assured him he couldn't go wrong with roses.

She lifted them to her nose, inhaling deeply. "They're beautiful. Thank you. Come in while I put them in water."

Tell her she's beautiful. He stood inside the door, watching her fill a vase. He could have taken her straight to bed the other night when he'd finally given in to what now seemed inevitable. She'd made it clear she would have been fine with that. But she deserved more than a quick roll in the sack. He snorted. There would be nothing quick about it.

"That dress is a killer. You look beautiful, Taylor." The black dress hugged every curve, the hem stopping about two inches above her knees. He particularly liked the bodice, his eyes falling on the hint of breasts visible above the straight line of material. The two-inch-wide straps fell over the tops of her arms, giving the illusion that the dress might slide down her body at any moment. He was good with that.

But it was the back of the dress—or the lack of—that had him thinking he might need oxygen if he wanted to continue breathing. It ended in a *v* at her lower spine, and his hands itched to touch all that creamy skin. His gaze lowered to the strappy black heels and her cherry-red painted toenails. He was going to enjoy peeling her out of that dress later, but he might let her keep on the do-me shoes.

She glanced over at him, a shy smile on her face. "Thank you."

He liked how she accepted a compliment. No trying to deflect it, or no coy eyelash fluttering as if she'd expected him to pay homage to her beauty.

"You clean up pretty nice, too."

"I try." Although he preferred jeans and T-shirts, he owned a few suits, mainly worn to weddings, funerals, and the few times Rothmire made him attend a meeting with the brass. He'd spent more time than he ever had before on deciding what to wear, finally settling on a suit and dress shirt. That was it, other than his ruby earring, a watch, and his hair banded in a ponytail. No tie. He hated the damn things.

Taylor carried the vase to her minuscule living room, setting it on the coffee table. His eyes tracked how her body moved in her dress. He tore his gaze away before he started panting like a Saint Bernard in the middle of August.

"There you go, Henry," she said. "Something pretty to look at while I'm gone."

Nate eyed the fish that had his nose pressed up to the glass. "I didn't buy the flowers for the damn fish, Taylor."

"No you didn't." She walked to him, her hips swaying in a seductive way that he'd never known she had in her. "The flowers are all mine, Nate." She slipped her finger inside the *v* of his shirt, giving a little tug. "I'm just letting him enjoy them for a while." She gave another tug, lifted onto her toes, and bit his bottom lip. "I might even sleep with my flowers after I get home . . . Unless something better comes along."

He grinned. Who was this woman? Taylor had never been shy about speaking her mind, but she was blowing his tonight.

"Ah, you can smile." She let go of his shirt, walked to the door, glanced over her shoulder, and said, "Coming?"

"You can count on it." With that one word, she'd put an image in his head that did nothing to help him get blood circulating back into his brain. He'd known Taylor for two years. She'd been his best friend for the past year, and he'd always liked her. He really liked this new version.

After she locked up behind them, he put his hand on her lower back, not because she was incapable of walking by herself, but because he absolutely had to touch her. Her skin was soft and silky, and her body heat seeped into his fingers, warming his palm. When they reached his car, he opened the door for her, then before she could slide in, he kissed her. Because he absolutely had to do that, too.

"Mmm," she murmured when he lifted his head. "I don't usually kiss on the first date." Then she smiled. "But for you, I'll make an exception."

He cocked a brow. "Any other rules I should know about?"

"Yes, as a matter of fact. No checking out other women when you're with me."

"Trust me, tiger, you have my undivided attention." He closed the door, and as he walked around the car, he frowned, wondering why she'd said that.

"I have one question," he said after sliding into the driver's seat.

"What's that?"

"You told me once that you've had two boyfriends. Did one or both have a roving eye?" Even as he asked, his eyes roved right to her legs as she settled into the seat, causing her dress to slide up her thighs. But she hadn't said there was a rule against checking her out, so he should be good there.

"One did. How did you know?"

"I'm an officer of the law, ma'am. I'm trained to pick up on things."

"Are you now? Then what am I thinking, Officer?"

He tilted his head and studied her. "Well, you're wondering if I'm going to frisk you." She laughed, and it hit him that he liked making her laugh.

"Yeah, you nailed it."

"I also have one rule for tonight." He turned the key in the ignition. "No work talk."

"Definitely a good rule. Where are we going?"

"Told you when I asked you out. Dinner and dancing."

"Awesome."

The idea of a date had been a spur-of-the-moment decision simply because he couldn't bring himself to think of her like one of his usual hookups. She deserved better, and what would a few dates hurt?

♠♠♠

Taylor tried to remember the last time she'd enjoyed herself this much as Nate led her around the dance floor of South Beach's hottest club. He was an amazing dancer for a man who didn't date, possessing a natural rhythm that she lacked. He kept his hand firmly on her back, and once she'd relaxed and let him lead, she'd stopped worrying about her lack of dancing skills. Or maybe it was the two glasses of wine at dinner that had her feeling limber and mellow. Or it could have been the way he slid his thumb in a circular motion on her back, right above the cut of her dress, that had her practically melting in his arms, so much so that the mechanics of dancing was the last thing on her mind.

Whatever the reason, she was newly in love with dancing, at least as long as it was with him. He pulled her against him, their bodies now touching breasts to chest, hips to hips. She rested her head on his shoulder with her face nestled into his neck. He smelled so good that she wanted to lick him.

When he'd arrived to pick her up, she'd almost forgotten how to breathe. He wore jeans and T-shirts—almost always black—very well. He'd looked delicious in a tux at Court's wedding. But standing there in a charcoal-gray suit and pale-gray silk shirt, his hair in a ponytail, a ruby earring in one ear, he'd looked like a cover model for a men's magazine. She wasn't sure there was another man on the planet who could pull that look off as well as Nate, the mix of business suit and bad-boy long hair and earring.

By the end of the night, she hoped to have that pony-tailed hair loose and falling around his shoulders. The slow song ended, a faster one following it. Instead of letting her go, he kept her against him, only picking up the tempo of their steps. He pushed his leg between hers, his muscled thigh rubbing against both her weapon and her sex. She swallowed a moan as need shot straight to her core.

He chuckled, his warm breath tickling her ear. "Never considered I'd find a gun strapped to the inside of your leg sexy, tiger, but turns out that's pretty hot."

"With this dress, it was the only place I could think of to put it." They both were armed, a requirement even when off duty. His was in a holster under his arm.

"I'll have to take a closer look later," he murmured.

"Yes, please."

He laughed, only the second time she'd ever heard him do so, and she smiled against his neck, very pleased with herself. The man needed her in his life as more than just a friend, and she hoped he was beginning to realize that.

"I've always wondered. Why do you call me 'tiger'?"

He stepped back, lifted their joined hands, and spun her under his arm. Then he pulled her back to him, tucking her against his body again. It happened so fast, and he'd performed the move so expertly, that she hadn't had time to stumble like an awkward teen on her first date.

"Because tigers are fearless. They're passionate and elegant. That's how I see you."

After that dance maneuver and his answer murmured into her ear, she was toast. If he'd told her right then to wrap her legs around his waist so he could give her what she knew they both wanted, she would have willingly obeyed.

Nate was a tortured soul. She knew that. Although he'd shared much of his life with her, she didn't doubt there was more that he'd left unsaid. The parts that even he couldn't bear to revisit. Why he was the one man she craved, she didn't know. He just was. She longed to soothe his pain and to heal his heart. It hurt that he probably wouldn't ever allow her to be the one thing that could make him happy.

That was okay, though. It was a given that he would likely break her heart, and she could live with that. She'd survived a life of living on the streets as a child, had kept breathing after her mother's death, and had been like the phoenix, rising above the ashes to make a life for herself that she could be proud of.

She was strong and Nate wouldn't break her. But she was willing to let him try.

♠♠♠

"Henry's agitated," Nate said as he peered into the fish tank.

"What?" They'd just arrived at her apartment. While she'd headed to the kitchen to get him a beer and her a glass of wine, Nate had walked over to see Henry.

She rushed to the tank. Henry was a calm fish, and she'd never seen him agitated, whatever that meant. He seemed to be trying to suck in air the way someone would who couldn't breathe.

"What's wrong with him?" She'd had Henry for almost four years and was attached to him, even if he did refuse to follow her finger the way he did Nate's.

"Looks like he's having trouble breathing. How long do betta fish live?"

"Three years on average, I think, but sometimes up to five years." Was that it? Henry had grown old and had come to the end of his life? Suddenly, a shudder traveled through him, and then he turned onto his side, floating to the top.

"Oh, Henry," she said, swiping at the tears falling down her cheeks.

Nate put his arm around her shoulders, tucking her against him. "I'm sorry. He was a very good fish and had a great life with you." He stroked a finger down Henry's little body. "Rest in peace, Henry."

She giggled, even as her lips trembled and the tears still fell. "That sounded like a eulogy." How many men would comfort her at the loss of a fish instead of thinking she was silly for being sad? He was downright sweet, but she didn't tell him that.

"I assume you don't want to flush him down the toilet?"

"God, no." Henry had given her too many years of enjoyment to do that to him. "I don't know what to do with him, though. I'd like to think of something special."

"I have an idea. Change into something comfortable for a motorcycle ride." He put his hands on her shoulders, turned her to face him, and then brushed his lips over hers. "I'll be back in thirty minutes."

She stood next to Henry's tank after Nate left, unable to help comparing Nate to her only two boyfriends. Neither one would have gotten how much losing Henry hurt, but the bad-boy biker guy had understood. After one last sad glance at Henry, she went into her bedroom and changed into jeans, a black turtleneck sweater, and a pair of black boots.

Only twenty-five minutes later, there was a knock at her door. After peering through the peephole to see that it was Nate, she let him in. His gaze skimmed over her, and if the heat in his eyes was any indication, he liked what he saw. The emotions swirling inside her were a strange combo. Her sadness over Henry, while at the same time wanting to drag the man standing at her door straight to her bed, left her standing speechless in front of him.

He'd changed into what she was used to seeing him in. Black leather pants, a black T-shirt, a black leather jacket that looked well used and butter soft, and heavy black boots. Just stick a fork in her and call her done.

"Hi," she gushed, as if she hadn't just seen him mere minutes ago.

He grinned. "Hi yourself." He handed her a small wooden box. "I didn't know if you had anything to put Henry in, so I stopped at a drugstore and picked up this."

There went her heart again, giving him another piece of itself. That was a dangerous thing to do with this man. She knew that, but was helpless to stop.

"Want me to do it?" he asked when she stood over Henry's little body, trying to decide how to pick him up.

"No, he was my fish." She scooped her hand under him, lifted him, and then gently laid him in the box. "I'll miss you, Henry," she said as she lowered the lid.

Nate took the box, slipping it into the inner pocket of his jacket. She followed him to his bike, and once they were helmeted and seated, he reached for her hands, pulling them around his waist.

"If you're going to spend time riding with me," he said, "we need to get you a leather jacket."

"It's not cold." Between her sweater and the heat from his body, she was nice and warm.

"No, you need one for safety purposes. Protection from road rash, should the worst happen."

"Oh, okay." She liked that he seemed to think she would be taking future rides with him.

The night wasn't turning out the way she'd imagined, and she had no idea where Nate was headed, but she was touched that he was going to all this trouble because of her fish. Although it was really more that he understood she was sad than anything to do with Henry. She leaned against his back, letting her mind go blank and just enjoying the ride.

A few miles later, he pulled into a parking space at South Pointe Pier. "I thought we'd return Henry to the sea," he said after stepping off the bike.

She swung her leg over the seat, and after removing her helmet, lifted onto her toes and kissed him. "That's perfect." And it was. Nate slipped his hand around hers as they walked to the end of the pier, soft lights along the rail lighting their way.

When they reached the end, he handed her the box. "Did you want to say something?"

"He deserves a few words." She took it from him, opening the lid. "You were a very good fish, Henry. I'm going to miss you." She tipped the box, watching as he fell into the sea. Tears burned her eyes at seeing him disappear.

"Bye, Henry," Nate said quietly.

Her heart melted a little at his gentle voice, and again, she was touched that he'd taken Henry's demise and her sadness over it seriously. She leaned her head onto his shoulder, looking out at the ocean. It was a clear night with a half moon, and she wished she could see all the stars, but the lights of Miami made that impossible. Only the very brightest of them were visible.

"Thank you," she said.

He wrapped his arm around her, pulling her close. "You're welcome."

And it was that simple with him. No wanting to hear how great he was for what he'd done for her, no belittlement of her being silly for mourning a fish.

"Ready to head back?"

"Yeah, it's getting late." As they walked back to the bike, her hand in his, she said, "I guess this date isn't turning out to be what you expected."

He chuckled. "I told you I've never dated before. For my first one, it's been . . . Um, let's say unusual. I'm really sorry about Henry. For a fish, he was a cool dude."

"He was that."

When they reached his bike, Nate handed her the helmet. "Ready?" he asked after she'd buckled the strap.

"Yep." She climbed on behind him, once again wrapping her arms around his waist. That was her favorite part of riding with him. Too soon, they were back at her place. He parked next to her car, and when he cut off the engine, it seemed too quiet.

"You should wear ear protection before you lose your hearing," she said as she hopped off and moved to face him.

"I usually do." He leaned forward, draping his arms over the handlebars. "I should probably go home."

"Why? I thought . . ." She trailed off, not sure what she should say. Had he changed his mind?

He captured her gaze. "Are you sure it's a good idea? You and I?"

She pulled off the helmet. "I do, but you seem to be having second thoughts."

"Our friendship means a lot to me. I don't want to screw that up."

"I thought we'd settled this. The minute either one of us wants to call it quits, we do, and it has nothing to do with our being friends." She sighed. "Nate, I'm a big girl. I'm going into this with open eyes, okay? Whatever this is between us isn't going to go away. If we don't douse the fire, we're both going to end up combusting." And far back in the recesses of her mind, so deep that she only got occasional glimpses, was the idea that someday, he might fall in love with her.

He laughed. That was the third time, and yes, she was counting. Hopefully with practice, he'd do it more often. "Come in with me."

"For the purpose of fire prevention, then."

"Well, listen to that. Nate Gentry made a joke."

"Don't get used to it," he said as he swung a leg over his bike.

"Act tough all you want, but I saw that smile you just tried to hide." After his bike was locked up, she slipped her hand into his as they walked to her apartment. "Why don't you laugh? Is life really that terrible?"

"It made our old man mad if we laughed. If we were having fun, then we weren't doing our chores."

"What would he do?"

"Beat the ever-living daylights out of us."

He'd been conditioned not to be happy, and that was sad. Sometimes he would open up about his childhood, and each time he did, it made her want to cry for him and his brothers. But she never let that show. He'd hate it if he thought she pitied him, and if he knew she did, he'd clam up and never share again. So she kept her pity to herself.

She handed him her door key. "You should start laughing just to piss the bastard off."

He grinned as he pushed her door open. "That's why I like you, tiger. Always ready to spit in the face of all the bad guys in the world."

"I'd spit in his for sure." Now that she had Nate in her house, nerves struck. When they'd returned from dinner and dancing, the sexual tension between them had been palpable, and then Henry dying had cooled them down. Should she take him straight to her bedroom? Let him take the lead? She hated being unsure of herself.

CHAPTER TWELVE

"I see the wheels spinning," Nate said. "Stop thinking." He backed Taylor up to the wall, cradled her cheeks with his hands, and lowered his mouth to hers, nibbling his way across her lips. They were delicious lips, full, soft, and sweet tasting. He might never get his fill of her.

On the ride back, he'd come to his senses, but now he'd lost them again. This was not a good idea. A relationship wasn't in the cards. The rage burning deep inside of him was his alone to bear. Although he'd learned to control it, it was always there, threatening to erupt under the right—or, more accurately, wrong—circumstances. If he doubted that could happen, he only had to remind himself that he'd once almost killed his father. He would have if Court hadn't pulled him off the bastard.

But he wanted her, apparently too much, since it didn't appear he was going to do the right thing and walk away. She'd said she wouldn't let whatever happened between them ruin their friendship, and he was going to trust her on that.

"Nate," she murmured, putting her hands on his waist and trying to pull him closer.

That needy rasp in her voice did him in. He scooped her up, carrying her to the bedroom. When he reached her bed, he dropped her legs, letting her slide down his body. He wasn't sure which one of them he was trying to torture with that move. Letting go of her, he sat on the bed, removed his boots and socks and then his shirt, carelessly tossing everything on the floor.

She stood in front of him, her gaze on his chest, her eyes turning a captivating smoky blue. "Have you changed your mind?" He needed to be sure this was what she wanted. "Say it," he said when she shook her head.

"I haven't changed my mind. I want you." The ghost of a smile appeared on her face. "Very much so."

"Then come here."

"Take your hair down first."

He pulled the band from his ponytail.

"Now fluff it out."

"What's this fixation you have with my hair?" he asked as he obeyed.

"God, that's as sexy as I imagined it would be."

"You've been fantasizing about my hair?"

She nodded, licking her lips. "I have."

That hunger in her eyes was sure as hell turning him on. "Come here, Taylor." He spread his legs. When she stepped between them, he pressed his knees against hers. She reached for the hem of her sweater, but he swatted her hands away. "No, I'll undress you."

"Bossy man."

"Mouthy woman." At hearing her giggle—something so not Taylor—he swallowed a smile. She was nervous, which was something new and interesting. His usual hookups didn't have a nervous bone in their body. They knew the score, and were only looking for the same thing as he was. A few hours of pleasure, nothing more. He had a feeling just a few hours with Taylor wouldn't come close to satisfying him.

"This off first." He pulled the hem of her sweater up, pausing at the sight of her belly ring. "Well, look what I found." It was another thing he'd fantasized about since seeing glimpses of it on their ride to Pier 66. It was sexy as hell. Unable to resist, he leaned forward and sucked it into his mouth, giving a little tug.

"Ahhh," she murmured.

He was pretty sure that little tug had sent a charge down to her core. To test his theory, he did it again, getting a soft moan this time. Yep, she liked that. He filed that information away for later.

"Off." When she pulled the sweater over her head, he huffed a drawn-out breath. "Leave the bra on," he said, his voice sounding raspy even to his own ears. "Damn, tiger, you're just full of surprises." Did her panties match the transparent, lacy red bra? Only one way to find out. He unbuttoned her jeans, then pulled the zipper down. Red lace peeked back at him. "You're killing me, woman."

"I aim to please."

He laughed. "You're nailing it."

"Four."

Puzzled, he glanced up at her. "Four what?"

"Nothing. I was just thinking out loud." She put her foot on his lap. "Boots next? They have to come off before the jeans can."

Forgetting about strange numbers, he went back to undressing her. When she was standing in nothing but her sexy bra and panties, he twirled his finger. "Turn around." Thongs were the greatest invention ever. He'd always known she had a nice body, even when she wore her work uniform of loose pants and buttoned-up blouses, but his imagination on how she would look naked had failed him. Forget nice. She had a killer body.

Why, he wasn't sure, but the sexual tension that had sparked between them earlier, before the demise of Henry, had eased somewhat. When they'd first arrived back at her place, he hadn't been sure they'd get all their clothes off, much less make it to her bedroom. Now, it seemed the edge was off and neither wanted to rush things. That was good, because he planned to savor every minute with her.

"Do you wear a thong every day? Because if you say yes, that's all I'm going to think about, and I'll be one useless FBI agent."

"Should I lie, then?" She looked over her shoulder, a flirty smile on her face.

"God, yes. Lie." It wouldn't matter, though. Her perfect ass was seared into his brain, and yes, he was an ass man. Breasts were great, legs were worthy of attention, but a woman's ass did it for him every time. He hooked a finger into the waistband of the thong, pulling her to him.

She landed on his lap, and he put his hand under her chin, tilting her face up. As he kissed her, he vaguely wondered if he was going to be the one who wouldn't be able to walk away.

"What's this?" she said, her finger pausing from caressing his shoulder, then circling over one of many such scars.

"Nothing." The burn mark from a cigarette wasn't something he wanted to talk about.

"He did this to you, didn't he?" Her fingers went on a quest, stopping for a moment on each one she found.

"Don't go there, Taylor. He doesn't belong here with us. Not tonight." There were even more than the ones she'd found. His father hadn't spared his legs either, but if she persisted in wanting to know the reason for the burn marks, he'd walk right out the door before he'd tell her they were in retaliation for trying to kill his father.

She smiled up at him. "You're right, he doesn't. Tonight it's only you and me in this bed."

"Yeah, just us." He brushed her hair away from her neck, then pressed his mouth to the sensitive spot below her ear. She let out a little gasp when he nipped and sucked on her skin, the sound going straight to his groin. He closed his eyes. It didn't seem real that she was on his lap, in her bra and panties. He'd dreamed of her like this so many times that he wouldn't be surprised if he opened his eyes to find this was just another dream.

She ground her bottom against the zipper of his jeans, and he slid his fingers under her bra, flicking her nipple with his thumb. When she fumbled with his belt buckle, he stood with her in his arms.

If he didn't get his jeans off, he was going to bust right out of them. He dropped her on the bed, smiling when she bounced and giggled. Her eyes followed his hands as he pulled the zipper down. After removing a condom from his pocket, he pushed his pants and boxer briefs down his legs, kicking them aside.

"God, you're beautiful," she said.

For her, he wanted to be, which was new. He'd never much cared what women thought of him before. He had a moment of worry about that. They were friends first, above all else, and he didn't want to screw that up. The last thing he wanted to do was hurt her, and he was bound to do that. This really wasn't a good idea.

"Don't."

He didn't have to ask what she meant. The light in her eyes dimmed as she watched him, probably expecting him to get dressed and leave. And he should. She pushed up onto her knees, reached behind her back, and unhooked her bra, letting it fall to the bed.

"Don't think," she said.

He'd stopped thinking the moment she kneeled in front of him and bared herself. If they wanted to argue beautiful, she'd win, hands down. Her nipples pebbled from him only looking at them. He didn't know why she wanted him, but since he was no longer thinking, his male brain moved on to more interesting things. Like touching her breasts and tasting those pretty pink nipples. And that was just for a start.

"You're making me crazy, Taylor. I'm going to taste you from head to toe."

"Yes, please."

He laughed as he fell onto the bed, bringing her down with him. "That's much too polite for what I have in mind for you."

"Do tell." She rolled over and straddled him.

"You can be in charge later." He flipped her onto her back. "This time I am. Should I start tasting you here?" He palmed a breast, circling the nipple with his thumb.

"Yes. And that wasn't polite. I left off the please."

"So you did." He kept his word, tasting her from head to toe. Sometime later, he crawled up her body. "I could spend hours touching you, finding all your sensitive places, but I need to be inside you."

Nate loved women. Loved their minds, their smells, their soft bodies. He couldn't say how many women he'd been with. But he'd never felt like he was where he belonged the way he did now, joined with Taylor. He stared down into her eyes and swallowed hard. He wasn't supposed to feel this way, like he'd come home, wasn't supposed to want what he couldn't have.

"You got any moves in you, or are you just going to stare at me all night?" She waggled her eyebrows, wrenching a smile from him.

"Oh, I got moves, baby. Hold on tight, and I'll show you a few."

Whatever worries his mind was trying to stir up, he'd think about later. She felt too damn good to resist. He withdrew, then slid back in, slow strokes at first, until her whimpers and moans drove him crazy, and he couldn't hold back.

He loved her until they were both too exhausted to move. When she cuddled up to him, he expected to feel caged. He wasn't a cuddler. Surprisingly, he liked having her wrapped around him. Another thing he should worry about. But not tonight.

"I concede that you got moves," she said, sounding half-asleep.

"Told ya." He smiled against her hair, laced his fingers around hers, and allowed himself to enjoy the soft press of her body against his. With her as his inspiration, he could probably move mountains.

"Go to sleep, tiger."

"Kay."

And just like that, she was out. He should be sleepy, but left alone with his thoughts now, his mind was busy thinking again.

♠♠♠

The man punched his steering wheel so hard that a sharp pain shot up his arm. He wanted to destroy the motorcycle parked outside his angel's apartment. She belonged to him, but he would forgive her since she didn't know that yet. It was obvious the longhaired man was spending the night. As much as he wanted to tear the motorcycle apart with his bare hands, he resisted. Someone would hear him and call the cops.

The piece on the news informing him that his last angel had been a mother to two young girls had sent him into a rage. Mothers were sacred. They didn't need saving. The bitch should have told him she had daughters. He wouldn't have taken her away from them the way his mother had been stolen from him. It had taken hours to regain his control after the news story, and if there was anything he hated, it was losing control. That happening was unacceptable. Mistakes were made that way.

The woman inside the apartment was his true angel, not like the others. The girls under her care weren't her real daughters, so they didn't count. They didn't make her a mother. He'd tried to save Raisa Collins, but she'd rejected his offer of marriage, hadn't understood the honor he was bestowing on her, that he'd chosen her to love. When he'd followed her back to her pitiful room, it was with the intention of making her understand that he was her savior, there to take her away from the squalor and the life of a whore.

She hadn't wanted to listen, was furious that he'd followed her. He hadn't meant to kill her, but she wouldn't stop screaming. To get her to shut up, he'd wrapped his hands around her throat. It wasn't until she'd taken her last breath, finally going quiet, that the roaring in his ears had cleared and he'd heard a child crying.

When he'd seen her, so beautiful in her innocence, he'd stroked her face and neck. Her skin had been soft and flawless, her blue eyes wide and frightened. He'd known then that it wasn't her mother he was meant to save, but her. He would take her with him, raise her to be pure and untainted. She would be his perfect little angel, and he would give her the chances his mother had never had.

Then that bitch had come in with her baseball bat, and he'd fled. But he'd only gone down the hallway, where he hid around the corner. After the woman had taken the girl across the hall to another room, he'd gone back to Raisa's to make sure he hadn't left any evidence behind. While wiping his fingerprints from anything he thought he might have touched, he'd found an old Polaroid camera. Without stopping to think why he was doing it, he'd taken pictures of her body.

After he left the building, he'd waited across the street in the alcove of a closed neighborhood grocery for the police to arrive. But they never did. Instead, a short time later, the woman and girl had come out, carrying bulky trash bags. He'd followed them to a motel a few blocks away. All it had taken to learn their names was a few bucks handed over to the motel clerk. From then on, it had been easy to keep an eye on them.

As time passed, he often looked at the photos he'd taken of Raisa Collins. Then six years ago, on the anniversary of his mother's death, while looking at the pictures of Raisa, so pure in death—a beautiful angel like his mother—it had come to him, his life's work. He had been too young and helpless to save his mother, but he could save others like her by making them angels. He hadn't been able to make Raisa his bride, but his angels would arrive in heaven as brides, pure and virtuous. The way his mother had. He'd chosen his first angel the same night.

As for Taylor Collins, she belonged to him. He'd known that from the moment he'd seen her. It was time for her to come home. He needed to get her attention, and he knew just how to do it. Before going, he left her a little present.

♠♠♠

Nate lay on his side, watching Taylor sleep. The low glow of the lamp cast a golden light over her—he'd insisted they leave it on so he could see her face when she came. She was so beautiful. What would it be like to wake up to her smile every morning?

She was pleasured, sated, and sleeping. This was when he left a woman's bed, dressing in the dark and then tiptoeing out. Always. But he couldn't bring himself to slide out from under the covers, careful not to wake her so he could make his escape without awkward words. So he stayed. This time.

At the sound of Rothmire's ringtone, he came instantly awake. A call from the boss at this time of night wasn't good. He grabbed his phone from the nightstand, eyeing the clock. They'd only been asleep two hours, and it was likely the only sleep they'd get tonight.

"Yeah?" He listened, then said, "I'll collect Taylor, and we'll head that way." She was already up and dressing by the time he hung up. "A prostitute was murdered. Some kids found her body."

"I guess we're headed to the Everglades, then."

"No, she was found behind a grocery store in Hialeah. She's ours, though. She's wearing a white dress and there's a wedding ring on her finger."

"Damn."

That about summed it up. "We'll have to take your car," he said as he pulled on his clothes. He gave her a summary of his phone call with Rothmire.

Although the night hadn't ended the way he'd wanted it to, he'd enjoyed their date more than he'd thought he would. But he suspected that was because of her. She was a happy person, and he liked being around her. Dancing with her, holding her slim body against his . . . He was getting aroused just thinking about it. Unfortunately, duty called.

"I'll make us some coffee to go."

He yawned. "That would be great. I'm going to check my bike, make sure it's locked up good."

At his bike, he took a ball cap with the FBI logo on it out of the saddlebag and put it on, then slipped a lightweight FBI jacket on over his gun and holster. After working undercover for so long, it went against everything ingrained in him to advertise that he was an FBI agent.

After making sure his alarm was on, he walked over to her car. The woman who exited her apartment was all business now, her walk and expression her FBI persona. She'd put back on the jeans and black sweater from earlier, but had added a jacket with "FBI" emblazoned on it, under which he knew she had a holstered gun.

When she neared the driver's door of the car, she paused, glancing down, and then bent over and picked up something. "Someone dropped their good-luck angel." She held up a small angel on a chain, the kind he'd seen people hang on their rearview mirrors.

"Do people really believe those work?" To Nate it seemed silly to think a plastic replica of an angel would protect you.

"Maybe it's a question of faith." She dropped the angel into her pocket. "I'll put it in the lost-and-found box in the complex's office."

After she hit the remote, unlocking the car's doors, he slid into the passenger seat. "Start it up, and I'll put the address in the GPS," he said when she was seated next to him.

"It doesn't make sense that he's suddenly changing his M.O., leaving a victim behind a grocery store." She glanced over at him. "Unless he was scared off. If so, we might have a witness."

"Or the newscast messed with his head." The piece about Linda Harding having two daughters had run on the evening news.

"That's a possibility, too. We need to catch this guy, Nate. His kills are getting closer together. He's losing it."

"Which means he'll start making mistakes. That's what we want."

Her fingers curled around the steering wheel. "Not at the cost of another woman's life."

He got that. Their job was to save lives, but it worried him that Taylor was letting this case get to her. He needed to have a talk with her, judge for himself how much of a problem that was going to be. He'd do that tomorrow.

A police car was parked close to the body, the officer leaning against the hood, guarding the scene. On the other side of the crime scene tape, a group of kids milled about, laughing and pushing each other around.

"No respect for the dead. The little buggers should be home in bed," Taylor grumbled as they exited the car.

The area behind the store was well lit, so Nate took out his phone and snapped pictures of those standing around. While Taylor headed for the body, he made a wide circle, taking more pictures, watching for anyone who seemed nervous. Movement at the corner of the lot caught his attention, a man standing in the shadows. The man pulled the ball cap he was wearing down over his forehead. Nate took another photo, and just as he did, the man slipped around the building adjacent to the grocery store.

Was that their killer, or just a curious bystander? Nate ducked under the crime scene tape and jogged over to the other building. The man wasn't in sight, but halfway down the block, a car pulled out of a parking space. Because of the pinkish glow of the streetlights, it was hard to tell the color of the car other than it was something dark. He snapped several more pictures as it drove away, hoping Court could pull up the license plate.

A van pulled up next to Taylor's car, and two crime scene technicians got out. Nate walked back to where the man had stood, turned on the light in his phone, and searched the ground, seeing two fresh cigarette butts and what looked like a photo folded in half. He took a picture; then, not wanting to leave possible evidence unattended, he called Taylor.

"Send one of the techs over here," he said when she answered her phone.

She lifted her head, searching for him. At seeing him, she said, "Find something?"

"Not sure. Maybe."

After saying something to one of the techs, she came back on the phone. "I have something to show you when you're done there."

When their tech walked up to him, he said, "Hey, Laura. How's Daniel?" Her son had suffered a severe concussion in a high school football game.

"Much better, but now he's mad at me because I said no more football. Seeing him lying on that field, not moving? Not going there again."

"Can't say I blame you." Although if he were Daniel, he wouldn't be happy either, so he could sympathize with both sides. "A man was standing here, watching us when we arrived. As soon as I spotted him, he took off. Might be nothing, but let's bag these butts and whatever that is."

She took some of her own pictures, then snapped on a pair of rubber gloves and pulled a baggie out of her jacket pocket. "It's from a Polaroid. Who even has one of those anymore? Do you want me to open it?"

"Yeah, let's see if it's anything of interest."

After dropping the two butts into a bag, she picked up the photo, prying it apart. He leaned over her shoulder to see the picture. "Shit," he muttered. This wasn't the first time he'd seen the woman staring up at him with dead eyes.

Laura frowned up at him. "What?"

He glanced over at Taylor. He'd been worried about her taking this case too much to heart, and now, she was going to have every reason to.

"That's her mother." He'd pulled up the police files of Taylor's mother's case. Had seen the crime scene photos. The file had been thin, as apparently the police at the time hadn't cared about a dead prostitute.

"No," Laura gasped. "Oh my God, we can't show this to her. This woman is dead."

Not just dead, but murdered. Which raised a new question. What was the connection between Taylor's mother and their case? "We don't have a choice."

"Oh, Jesus," Laura said.

Nate swallowed bile as another thought entered his mind. What if the killer knew who Taylor was? He was going to find the man and kill him. "Hold that up." He took a picture of the Polaroid and then emailed it to Court, following it up with a text that he wanted a meeting in the morning before the one already scheduled with the team. That done, he strode over to Taylor. "What did you want to show me?"

Taylor frowned at the sharp edge in Nate's voice. She narrowed her eyes as she studied his face. Rage vibrated from him. "What happened?"

"I think our man was watching us."

"Seriously?" She didn't like how his eyes shifted away from her. He was hiding something. "And?"

He leveled his gaze on her. "And we need to talk, but not here." He glanced at the car coming around the corner of the store. "That's the M.E. Show me what you found and then let's get out of here."

Something about Nate's demeanor made her nervous, but she shook it off. "Look here." She knelt next to their victim's head, picking up a section of hair shorter than the rest. "Someone cut off a piece of her hair. I almost missed it."

The M.E. walked up, and Taylor switched her attention to him. "Hey, Reg. Check this out. We need to know if the other women had any hair cut off. It would have been easy to miss since we didn't know to look for it. If we find the same thing, then he's keeping souvenirs."

"The first body was claimed by the family and cremated, but the other two are still in the morgue." The M.E. bent over, studying the hair Taylor held. "Sorry for missing that."

"I only noticed because of the way her hair had parted." Taylor stood. "Give me a call tomorrow and let me know what you find." She tugged off her rubber gloves. "We need you to put a priority on the autopsy."

"Of course."

"Thanks." She glanced over at Nate, not liking his troubled eyes. "Ready?" When his gaze flicked to Laura, she caught some kind of message passing between them. What the hell was going on? She waved to Laura and Jerry, the other crime scene tech, then followed Nate to her car.

♠♠♠

"Okay, spill," Taylor said when they were at her place. Nate had refused to tell her what was on his mind on the drive back—had, in fact, gone into silent-brooding mode.

He glanced at the empty fish tank. "Let's talk in the kitchen."

"You're scaring me, Nate."

Instead of reassuring her, he poured a glass of wine, setting it on the table. "Sit," he said, pulling a chair out for her, and then taking a seat across from her. He clasped his hands, resting them on the table.

"Stop staring at your knuckles and start talking." She'd never seen him like this. Yeah, he was sometimes a moody man, but whatever this was, it had to do with her, something he dreaded telling her. She couldn't imagine what would have him this rattled, but his silence sent her heart to pounding, and not in a good way.

Black eyes lifted to hers, pity swirling in them. "Our killer left something at the scene. A picture . . . a Polaroid, to be exact."

"And?" she said when he paused. She still didn't know what this was about, but suddenly, she was sweating. Realizing she still had her FBI jacket on, she tugged it off, tossing it on the chair next to her.

"I should have called Rothmire with this first." He motioned at her wine glass. "Maybe you should drink some of that."

"Dammit, Nate, I'm about three seconds away from shooting you. Talk. Now."

"Yeah, it's just that I don't know how to tell you this." He scrubbed his hand over his face, already showing the beginning of a beard.

When he'd picked her up—how many hours ago? It seemed like days now—she'd noticed that he'd shaved, but she liked his scruffy-faced look best. And why was she even noticing that his beard was already growing back in when she was sure he was about to turn her world on its end? Why else was he having trouble looking her in the eyes if that wasn't the case?

"Nate," she practically growled.

He reached over, putting his hand on top of hers. "He left a photo of your mother."

She stared for a moment at his big hand covering hers—as if in some kind of protective gesture—confused as to what he was trying to say. "I don't understand."

"I'm sorry, tiger. It must have been taken right after she was murdered. I think our bad guy was your mother's killer, or he's been in touch with whoever was."

His voice was so soft, so filled with compassion, that in that moment she hated him. She yanked her hand away, resenting his pity. "I don't believe you." It wasn't possible.

"I'm sorry."

"Stop saying you're sorry." She pushed away from the table, and in six steps she was standing in the middle of her living room. The walls were closing in around her, and for the first time, she wished she had a bigger apartment. Enough room to pace, to breathe. Nate walked up next to her, but as if he understood she couldn't bear it, he didn't touch her.

"I want to see the photo."

"No, you don't. You're going to have to take my word for it, at least for tonight. When you're calm, if you still do, then I'll show it to you."

"That's not your decision to make." She poked him in the chest, fury burning a searing path through her. "I'm a part of this investigation, and that's evidence, which I have a right to see."

"I'm sorry, Taylor, but I'm taking you off the case."

She stared at him in disbelief. "The hell you are."

CHAPTER THIRTEEN

Nate wanted to punch something. The rage that lived inside him burned hot, threatening to consume him. From the moment he'd seen that Polaroid, it had been bubbling like molten lava, ready to spew.

He walked away, not wanting to give Taylor even a glimpse of what he was capable of. On the pretense of getting a glass of water, he sought calm. Using a trick that sometimes worked, he imagined the rage was a ball of fire in his stomach. Then he visualized it traveling up, past his chest and into his throat. He opened his mouth, giving it an escape hatch. He let out a sharp breath, and the fire with it, and then took several calming breaths. Once he was sure he was in control again, he drank the water. At the sound of her footsteps coming up behind him, he inhaled one more deep breath before facing her.

"Please, Nate. Don't do this." She steepled her hands, touching her fingers to her lips as if begging him.

He leaned back on the counter, and as much as he wanted to give her anything she asked for, he refused to let those pleading blue eyes get to him. "Consider it done. And there is no way in hell you're going to pose as a hooker. Not now."

She lowered her hands, fisting them at her sides. "I hate you." She pressed her lips together, her jaw clenching after slinging those words at him.

Hearing her say that cut like a knife straight through the center of his heart, but he managed not to flinch. "Better you hate me than I mourn you." Yeah, she was pissed, but he didn't care. Whatever it took to keep her safe, he'd do.

"I want you to leave." She walked to the door, opening it. "Now."

Why couldn't she understand that the game had changed? First thing in the morning, he'd call their profiler, but for now, he'd give her time to think things through. She was a smart woman, and once she calmed down, she would see that he was right.

"And just so you know," she said as he walked past her, "I'm going to Rothmire in the morning. We'll just see if I'm off this case or not."

He stilled, a thousand responses running through his mind, heavy with regret that what had been one of the best nights of his life was ending this way. He doubted she would ever forgive him.

Keeping his back to her, he said, "I'm the lead on this, and my word is final. I'm sorry, Taylor, but that's just how it is." He left it at that, although he could have reminded her that going over her team leader's head was never a good idea. Or that if the situation were reversed, she would have done the same thing. Or that he knew—and had ignored his own warning to himself—it was a mistake for them to get involved. Yet, even though he should, he didn't regret that last one.

He walked out to the door slamming behind him. As he unlocked his bike, he made a mental list of things he needed to do before the morning team meeting. High on that list was to call Rothmire, get to him before Taylor had a chance to.

He rode to the entrance of her complex, pulling into a parking space. There was no way he was leaving her unguarded now if there was even a remote possibility that Taylor could be a target. But sitting on his bike the rest of the night wouldn't fly. He called Alex.

"Yo?" Alex said, his voice rough with sleep.

"Need you to bring me the car and then ride my bike home."

"It's four-fucking-o'clock in the morning, bro."

"I know what time it is. Get your ass out of bed and just do it. I'm at Taylor's. And bring me a thermos of coffee." He hung up.

Never a patient man, he paced while waiting for Alex. The rage was still there, and with it came the memories. He'd gotten good at keeping them at bay, except when the fire burned. And right now, the fire was out of control.

He'd learned about pain and disillusionment at an early age at the hands of his sire. The old man was a master at teaching his boys those things. Nate never once regretted pulling as much attention as he could onto himself and away from his brothers. Yeah, there were days he could barely walk after a beating, days he seriously considered running away. He would have if not for Court and Alex, too young to take with him and too helpless against their father's heavy hand to be left alone with the bastard.

Then the day had come when he'd almost killed the old man. Not that he'd never fantasized about it. He had. Many times. But when he'd come upon the son of a bitch beating Alex with the buckle end of his belt—the scars from that day were still on Alex's back—his baby brother unconscious, his skin a bloody mess, Nate had lost all reason. If not for Court trying to pull him away, and then Alex coming to, bleeding like a stuck pig as he wrapped himself around Nate's leg, begging Nate not to go to jail while tears stained his cheeks, Nate would have killed his father without remorse. But Alex's words had penetrated the red haze. If he went to juvie, possibly even prison if tried as an adult, his brothers would have been sent to foster homes.

He'd been sixteen at the time, already bigger than his sire. That didn't stop his father from getting his revenge. Taylor had wanted to know about the burn marks on his shoulders, and she'd made no comment about the ones on his legs, but he'd felt her touch, knowing the moment she'd discovered them. Fact was, he was ashamed to admit that his drunk, lousy excuse of a father had managed to tie him to his bed while he was sleeping, catching him unaware. No, his father hadn't let his oldest son's rebellion go unpunished. He'd had his fill of fun with the burning end of a cigarette.

The boy he'd been had learned to hate, had welcomed the rage, had let it consume him. No, he didn't trust himself to have a wife or children. If he ever lost his temper around his own child so badly that he used his fists, he'd put his gun in his mouth and pull the trigger. Better not to even go there. But if the man who'd left that Polaroid for them to find was standing in front of him right now, he'd have no problem tearing the bastard apart limb from limb. That he could live with.

Headlights from an approaching car landed on him. He stepped in front of the black SUV that he recognized as his, the vehicle coming to a stop six inches from his knees.

"Dude, you have a death wish?" Alex said, sticking his head out the window.

He did, but not for himself. "Back it in next to my bike." Once the SUV was parked, he slid into the passenger seat, knowing Alex wouldn't leave without an explanation.

"Why are we sitting outside Taylor's apartment?" Alex asked.

"We aren't. You're going home."

"Not until you tell me what's going on."

"Our man struck again, only this time he left the body behind a store in Hialeah." He brought Alex up to speed, the fury that had been riding him since finding the photo still running high.

"Man, that's not good. Not good at all," Alex said when he finished. "You're gonna pull her from the investigation, right?"

"Already did, and she's not a happy camper right now. She can still work on the case behind the scenes, but that's it." He opened the container of coffee, pouring some in the cup. "You can go home now."

"Nope, I'll hang for a while." Alex took the cup out of his hand. "You've been up all night. Grab a catnap, and I'll keep watch."

Baby brother was as stubborn as they came, and knowing it would be useless to argue, Nate reclined his seat. "Wake me in an hour." Although he was tired, he doubted he'd be able to sleep, but he'd give it a go.

♠♠♠

"Up, Sleeping Beauty. Your woman's on the move."

Nate yawned as he blinked his eyes open. "What'd you say?"

"Taylor's backing out of her space."

"This early, she's probably heading over to Rosie's." He and Alex slid down in their seats as she drove by. His bike was fortunately parked on the far side of his car, out of sight. The sun was just now coming up, so she was heading out earlier than usual. It didn't take much thinking to know she wanted to be at their field office before Rothmire arrived so she could ambush him the minute he walked in the door.

"Out," he said.

"I saved you some coffee." Alex handed him the container. "You're welcome."

"Sorry. Thanks." He jogged around to the driver's side, but paused. "Seriously, thank you, brother." Nate tossed him the bike keys.

Alex saluted him. "Anytime."

It didn't take long to catch up with Taylor, and she was definitely heading to Rosie's. He pulled over a block away, and while he waited for her to come out, he called Rothmire. The conversation went the way he'd expected. The boss agreed that she needed to stay in the background and would back Nate up on his decision.

Taylor was going to be royally pissed, but Nate could live with that. He couldn't live with anything happening to her.

♠♠♠

The bag swung back her way, and Taylor punched it again—a hard one, two—visualizing that it was Nate. Still furious after her meeting with Rothmire, she figured she had two choices. Go on a rampage at the office or head straight for the gym, taking her frustration out on the heavy bag.

How could Nate do it? Even though he knew how much this investigation meant to her—that catching the bastard killing these poor women, and who had maybe killed her mother, was something she needed to do—he'd pulled her off the case. And worse? He'd gotten to Rothmire before she could, convincing their boss that her butt should be parked behind a desk for the duration.

She was a highly trained federal agent, perfectly capable of taking care of herself. Apparently, it didn't matter that she could outshoot most of her fellow agents, could physically fight them and win, and could outthink them. Nope, she was just a silly girl who had to be protected by the alpha men in her life. Well, they could just go eat dirt.

She'd been too young to save her mother, but she could save women like her who had no one else who cared enough to fight for them. The bag came her way again, and Taylor twisted in the air, back kicking it, sending it soaring in the opposite direction. *Take that, Nate.*

"Impressive."

Taylor eyed the man standing off to the side. She'd seen him at the gym a few times, mostly walking on the treadmill. He was maybe ten or fifteen years older than she was, and his hazel eyes were kind.

She smiled. "Thanks."

"You need a sparring partner?" he asked, his voice gravelly.

Her gaze slid over to Nate, leaning against the wall as he watched them. It was as if they had some kind of psychic connection; she knew when he was within fifty feet of her. If looks could kill, the nice man talking to her would fall over dead this very second. She tore her gaze away from Nate.

"Not today, but thanks for the offer," she said, offering her hand. "Taylor Collins."

He stared at her outstretched hand for a moment, as if surprised. "Wade Tillman." He wrapped his fingers around her hand, giving her a firm shake.

She liked that about him, that he wasn't afraid of hurting her like some men whose handshakes were limp, as if she were a breakable doll. Little did they know. From the corner of her eye, she caught Nate's scowl. Well, screw him.

"Nice to meet you, Mr. Tillman. See you around." She walked away, needing to get out of Nate's line of sight. Even furious with him, his eyes on her sent a jolt of desire streaming through her body, her girly parts not caring one bit about his betrayal.

Last night had been amazing, right up until Rothmire had called, telling them another woman had been murdered. It went downhill from there, and she wasn't ready to face Nate after he'd gone behind her back.

And that hurt. He could have at least told her he was going to talk to Rothmire. The fact that those hours he'd spent in her bed were amazing—mind-blowing, if she were honest with herself—no longer meant anything to her. And she'd keep telling herself that until she believed it.

How was she supposed to act around him now? Pretend last night had never happened? If nothing else, she'd learned a valuable lesson. Never fall in love with one of her fellow agents. Even if it wasn't an office rule, it was now one of hers.

In the gym's shower, she scrubbed herself raw, ridding herself of all traces on her skin that Nate had left behind. And when the last scent of him was gone, she leaned her forehead against the tiles and cried. Her tears were for her mother, for the women left with no choice but to sell their bodies, and for something she couldn't name, only that it had to do with Nate.

When her tears ran dry, she turned off the faucet, then grabbed the towel she'd draped over the hook right outside the door. After drying off, she slipped on her clothes. And lo and behold, a very moody-looking FBI agent was waiting for her when she walked to the lockers. Ignoring him, she retrieved her badge and gun.

"We need to talk."

"If you say so." She was tempted to walk away, but Nate would just follow her. And yes, she was acting bitchy, could hear the petulance in her voice. That was so unlike her, but she couldn't seem to care. Dressed in his usual black jeans and black T-shirt, he stood in front of her with his fingers stuffed into his front pockets. She loved men's arms, his in particular, and against her will, her eyes lingered on his forearms, the ones that had held her with such tenderness last night.

"Not here."

She jerked her gaze up to his. "Fine. Text me when and where."

"Taylor." He put his hand on her shoulder.

Any other time, she'd love his hand on her, but right now it felt condescending, as if she were someone he was trying to calm down. She stepped out of his reach. "Yes?"

He sighed, regret, maybe even sadness, in his eyes. "Nothing. When you're ready to listen, we'll talk." He walked a few feet away, then paused. "You missed the team meeting this morning. That's your one pass."

"I thought I was off the case."

"If you'd been at the meeting, you might have learned different."

When he turned to leave, she grabbed his arm. "I'm still a team member?" He stared down at her hand, then lifted his gaze to hers. It was at that exact moment—when those same eyes that had darkened with desire for her last night turned cold—that she felt like she'd lost her best friend.

"Like I said, let me know when you're ready to listen."

"What? You want me to crawl back, begging forgiveness?" Her mouth needed to shut up.

"No." He tapped her forehead. "I want you to use that brain I know you have and look at the situation objectively. I get that you're mad. I probably would be, too, in your place, but with that Polaroid, the game changed."

"I know that, but—"

"This isn't the place for this conversation," he said when two men walked up to the lockers. "Come with me."

Back at the office, she followed him into the conference room. "Look, I'm sorry I missed the meeting, but I really did think I was off the team. That's what you said last night."

He closed the door, then gestured for her to sit. She felt like a kid who had been called to the principal's office, and maybe she had a lecture coming, but it still rankled. There was no hint of warmth in his eyes as he sat across from her. It was as if last night had never happened, that they hadn't laughed together, shared passionate kisses, hadn't made love, hadn't explored each other's bodies for hours.

If she hadn't gotten her crying done in the shower, she'd probably burst into tears right now because his indifference hurt. But she refused to let him see her wounds. He wouldn't see one damn tear leak from her eyes.

CHAPTER FOURTEEN

Nate hated how Taylor had closed in on herself, hated even more that he was the cause. Her face was a blank page, not a hint of emotion showing. But she'd let the situation affect her judgment, and he couldn't allow that to pass. This would have been easier to deal with before last night. Now all he wanted to do was drag her onto his lap and hold her close, giving her whatever she wanted.

There was a wall between them that had never existed before, and that was his greatest regret. He'd lost his best friend. Although too late in coming where she was concerned, lesson learned. Never let his desires come before the job. She was a fellow agent, and he should have never given into temptation. It might be different if something could come of it, but he had nothing to offer her, even though the idea of a life with her sent a longing through his heart that he was having trouble ignoring.

"Tell me something," he said. "And be honest. If you were the lead on an investigation and you learned one of your team . . . let's say Rand. If Rand had a connection with the bad guy, but you didn't know who your suspect was, didn't know if he knew where Rand lived, the places he went, who his family was, or what your bad guy's intentions were, what would you do?" He held up a hand. "Before you answer, add to that mix that the case, for whatever reasons, turned personal for Rand, which would mean that you couldn't predict his behavior. Now you can answer."

Anger flashed in her eyes. "Are you implying that I won't do my job? That I can't be trusted?"

"We're not talking about you yet." He scrubbed his hand over his jaw, which was in much need of a shave. With everything that had happened since Rothmire had called with the news of another body, he hadn't even made it home to shower and change the clothes he'd been wearing since yesterday. He resisted the urge to sniff under his arms.

"Answer the question, Taylor," he softly said. There was no reason to remind her to be honest. He knew she would be, and hopefully, her answer would sink in and the proverbial light bulb would go off.

She made circles on the table with her finger. He waited her out, letting her work his hypothetical question from all the angles. Taylor Collins was one of the smartest people he knew, and if she could separate her emotions from her brain, she'd realize he had no choice in his decision.

Finally, she sat up straight, looked him in the eyes, and said, "I'd put him at a desk, out of sight. Is that what you plan to do with me?"

"Yes. You'll still be involved with the investigation, but behind the scenes." He let out a relieved breath, thankful that they'd successfully jumped the first hurdle.

"I'm not happy, but I understand. It's better than being taken totally off the case, I guess."

He hated that defeated voice. She wouldn't be any good to them if she didn't believe that she was a valuable member of the team, so he needed to restore her confidence in herself. But first, he had some more heavy shit to drop on her.

"It's likely that our killer knows who you are. And if so, he might know about Rosie and the girls."

Her face paled. "Oh, God. I should have considered that."

"Yes, you should have. That's why you need to step back and regroup." He leaned forward, resting his arms on the table. "You have to stop seeing your mother in each of these dead women. It's clouding your vision."

She covered her face with her hands. "I think I'm going to be sick."

"Look at me, Taylor." When she raised her eyes to his, he said, "No, you're not. What you are going to do is your job. I want you to work with Court on searching for similar murders. Also, I want you to work closely with Pauline on keeping her profile updated as we get new information. I was going to call her this morning with what we learned last night but haven't had a chance. You need to do that as soon as we're finished here."

"What about Rosie and the girls? We can't leave them unprotected."

"We're not. Josh is sitting in front of their house right now. But I think we should send them on a vacation so we don't have to worry about them. We have a safe house in Jersey that's only a few blocks from the beach. The girls would love it there. You on board with that?"

"What about school?" She shook her head. "Don't answer. That was a stupid question. Their lives are more important than anything else."

"Nothing's going to happen to them, Taylor. That's one thing I can promise you." The gratitude shining in her eyes, as if he were some kind of hero, made him uneasy. He wasn't anyone's hero. Not his brothers', as he hadn't been able to protect them from their father's fists and worse, and not hers. Not when he'd crossed a line he shouldn't have.

"Thank you. I'd die if they were hurt."

"I know. So you're on board with sending them away until this is over?"

"Absolutely. I'll go see Rosie as soon as we're done here." Her eyes shifted away, then landed back on him. "I was out of line, but it won't happen again. As for my new assignment, you know I'll give it my all."

"I do know that. There's one other thing you're not going to like. You don't go anywhere without a partner." When she opened her mouth, he was sure intending to protest, he shook his head. "That's not negotiable. This is no reflection on you or your abilities. We don't know what this clown is capable of or what he has planned. I'd put the same rule in place if it was any other member of the team."

"Okay. Just do me a favor and catch this bastard fast so I can get out of jail."

"That's the plan. Let me know what Pauline has to say after you talk to her." He pushed away from the table.

"Nate?"

"Yeah?"

"What about us?"

"There is no us." He walked out, unable to stay and see her reaction to his words. Nor did he want her to see the regret on his face.

♠♠♠

"I want you to dig into Taylor's mother's murder," Nate told Court. He'd called Court and Alex to meet him at his condo so they could talk privately. "The file is thin, but work on running down any of the cops or detectives involved and see what they can add to it. Get Rand to help you. Alex, I want you to personally interview anyone they think might have information."

Court frowned. "So, these killings really do connect to Taylor and her mother?"

"I think the Polaroid is evidence of a connection of some sort. The question is exactly how? Did he accidently drop the photo, or did he want us to find it? And if the latter, why? Did he kill her mother, or did he somehow come into possession of the photo? Does he know who Taylor is? It all seems like too much of a coincidence. Too many fucking questions that we need answers to ASAP."

"We're going to keep someone on her at all times, right?" Alex said.

"Yeah, and we're sending Rosie and the girls to a safe house in New Jersey. Taylor's not happy about either of those things, but she understands."

"You think this dude might come after her?" Court said.

"Who knows, but I have a bad feeling about this one."

"Why don't you just move in with her, or better yet, bring her here?" Alex leaned back in his chair, giving Nate a thoughtful look. "Don't tell me you wouldn't like that."

"For the last time, there is nothing going on between Taylor and me."

Alex snorted. "Right, but your nose is growing, Pinocchio."

"I'm going to miss you, baby brother, when he kills you," Court said, laughing.

"Nah, he loves me too much to put a hurt on me."

"Don't count on it." Nate put his foot on Alex's chair, pushing him away from the table. "Go do something productive, both of you." His brothers exchanged a look that he didn't like, much less trust. "Whatever's about to come out of your mouths, I don't want to hear it."

"Why are you being so hardheaded about Taylor?"

"Alex, shut it. We're not talking about this." He'd never told his brothers that he feared being like their father, and he wasn't about to start now.

"We just want to see you happy, brother," Court said.

"I am happy."

Alex stood, staring down at him. "Liar."

He didn't like the worry in either of his brothers' eyes, didn't want their pity. Just because they were married and ridiculously happy didn't mean he should run out and find a wife. But he had been happy for the few short hours he'd spent with Taylor. He'd had a taste of what it would be like to be with someone special, and that had been a mistake. Because now he wanted more.

♠♠♠

There is no us. Those words reverberated in Taylor's mind like a broken record. Their friendship was broken, and she didn't know how to fix it. That hurt as much as knowing that he'd never fall in love with her.

She didn't do hookups, had never gone out looking for one night of pleasure. Doing that felt too much like her mother's life. But being with Nate had seemed so right, as if they were meant to be. She didn't regret it, not for one minute. Her only regret was that it would never happen again.

"You're awfully quiet today," Rand said as he pulled into Rosie's garage.

"Just have a lot of things on my mind. You coming in?"

"No. I want to talk to Josh, see if he's noticed anything unusual."

"Okay. We won't be long." She glanced at the car parked across the street and waved at Josh—assigned to keep an eye on Rosie and the girls—then headed inside. Not being able to go anywhere without an escort was wearing on her already, and it was only the first day. It was also unnerving that there was an agent parked in front of Rosie's house, but she wasn't complaining about that. She wasn't about to risk whoever this creep was getting to her family.

The plan to secretly get them out of town that Nate and Rothmire had devised was probably more elaborate than necessary, but the girls would probably see it as a grand adventure. It hadn't been a problem getting approval from the girls' case worker to take them out of state, since the request had come from the head of the FBI's Miami field office.

When she walked into the house, she found Rosie in Bri's room. "Need any help packing?"

"No, this is the last of it." Rosie huffed out an annoyed breath. "Your phone call was very mysterious. What's going on, and why do we have to go away? And exactly where are we going? All you said was pack their bathing suits."

Taylor sat on the edge of the bed. "Is there anything about my mother's murder you've not told me?"

"What? Why are you asking this now?" Rosie sank onto the mattress, the suitcase between them.

Taylor probably should have eased into that question, but they didn't have much time. "Someone's murdering prostitutes, and at the last crime scene, he left a photo of my mother, taken right after she was killed."

When Rosie gasped, Taylor reached across the suitcase, putting her hand over Rosie's. "We think he knows who I am, and that's worrisome. I doubt he knows about you and the girls, but we're not taking any chances. So you're going to a safe house in New Jersey until this is over. The house is only a few blocks from the beach, thus the bathing suits."

"Of course we'll go. We can't stay here and take a chance they'll be harmed. You need to come with us until this is over."

In Rosie's eyes, she was still a little girl needing taking care of. Her foster mother preferred to believe that she sat behind a desk, answering phone calls or some such. Taylor had never disabused her of that notion. Rosie had no idea she knew how to kill a person nine different ways. Actually, more than that.

"I can't. I'm a part of the team to catch this creep. I understand your concern, but this is my job, Rosie. You didn't answer my question."

Rosie deflated right before her eyes. "I knew you would say that. Why couldn't you grow up to be a schoolteacher or something that wasn't dangerous like this job?"

Taylor chuckled. "These days, being a schoolteacher isn't all that safe." She squeezed Rosie's hand. "Stop avoiding my question. You know something."

"I don't think it's anything that will help in your investigation, but there was a man she told me about right before . . . You know, before." Tears pooled in Rosie's eyes.

Raisa Collins and Rosie had been best friends, both prostitutes until the day her mother was killed. On that horrid day, Rosie's world had changed as much as Taylor's had. She'd changed her life to raise Raisa's daughter. As far as Taylor knew, Rosie had never had another man in her bed. If not for this woman, Taylor firmly believed she would have gotten lost in the system.

She pushed the suitcase behind them, scooting next to her savior. "What did she say, Rosie?"

"That there was a man who scared her. He was one of her johns, but then he started getting jealous of the other men. He asked her to marry him, told her he would save her from the life she led."

"Did you ever see him?"

"No. Right before she died, she told him to leave her alone. She said he got angry when she refused to see him anymore."

"Did she tell you his name?"

"Not that I remember."

That was unfortunate. A name right now would be handy. Those early years with her mother were fuzzy. For the life of her, she couldn't remember her mother's face, although Rosie often said Taylor looked just like Raisa.

She did remember that they lived in a room in a run-down building. Whenever her mother went out for the night, she made sure the door was locked behind her, always reminding Taylor not to open it for anyone. She couldn't think of one single time her mother had brought a man home to their room. But the night her mother was killed was a black hole in her mind.

"We've never talked about what happened that night, Rosie. I've read the police reports, what little there are of them, but I don't remember anything." Had she seen her mother murdered and blocked it out?

"Oh, *chica*, it's best that you don't know."

"Possibly, but with what's happening, I do need to hear what you saw. There might be something that can help us." She squeezed Rosie's hand. "I know it's hard, but take me through that night." At her foster mother's hesitation, she said, "It's important. Just start from the beginning. Were you working that night?"

"Yes, we both were. We walked out together. Raisa was seeing one of her regulars. I didn't have anyone scheduled, so I headed to my usual corner."

"Do you know who her regular was and where they met?"

"I only knew his first name. Paul. There was a little motel where he'd reserve a room, but it was torn down years ago. I don't see how any of this can help you."

"Maybe, maybe not. What time did you come home?"

"Around midnight. I was walking down the hall to my room when I heard you screaming. Your door was cracked open, and I knew that wasn't right. Your mother was very protective of you. I . . . I . . ." Rosie covered her face with her hands. "If only I'd come home sooner."

Taylor put her arm around Rosie's shoulder. "You can't blame yourself. So, you came in to see why I was screaming?"

"I started to, but I had a bad feeling. I hurried into my room to get the baseball bat I kept. You know, just in case. We didn't live in such a good neighborhood, so it was best to have a weapon handy. Your mother kept one next to her door, too."

"I remember." Funny that she'd forgotten that until now. "And then what happened?"

A visible shudder passed through Rosie. "The first thing I saw . . . You don't want to hear this. You don't need to."

"Yes, I do. I know it's hard, but you have to tell me everything." Truthfully, she didn't want to hear it, but she needed to know anything that would help them find their killer, no matter how close to home it hit.

Rosie took a deep breath, her heaving chest proof of her misery. "Okay. I eased the door open. The first thing I saw was your mother. She was on the floor, not moving. I started to go to her, then I saw the back of a man. You were in bed, but you'd stopped yelling. He was leaning over you. I . . . I screamed at him and slammed the bat down on his legs. I should've bashed his head in."

Taylor rested her cheek against Rosie's hair. "My vicious Rosie. What was he doing?" It confused her that Rosie's story wasn't tearing her up inside, but nothing Rosie said triggered any memories of that night. It was strangely as if they were talking about people she didn't know.

"He had his hands on your throat." Rosie squeezed her eyes shut. "I thought he was trying to kill you, too."

How could she not remember that? Not even a flicker of a memory from that night came to mind. Had she been so traumatized that she'd blocked everything out? All Rosie had told her before now was that her mother had died. It wasn't until she'd joined the FBI that she'd searched for information on her mother, shocked to learn that she'd been murdered. When she'd tried to question Rosie about it, her foster mother had refused to discuss it—until now.

Taylor pressed her fingers against her throat. She should remember almost dying, if Rosie was right and the man was strangling her. "Did you see his face?"

"No. I raised the bat to hit him again, but he ran away. I only saw the back of him. All I can tell you is that his hair was blond—dishwater blond I think they call it. I was more worried about getting you away before he came back."

"Was it Paul?"

"No, I'd seen him several times. He had dark-brown hair."

"Please don't cry," she said when tears rolled down Rosie's cheeks. "You were so brave."

"I had nightmares for a long time about that night."

"I'm sorry to make you relive it, but I needed to know. If you remember anything else, call me, okay?"

"Of course. I called the police. After I got you to the motel and asleep, I went to a pay phone and called them, told them where to find your mother. When they asked my name, I hung up. I was afraid he'd find us."

Taylor's phone buzzed. At seeing Nate's name on the screen, her heart did a little dance. "Hey."

"The men are here."

"Okay, we'll seen you soon." He disconnected. She hated the tension between them. Even over the phone she could feel it.

She stood, pulling Rosie up with her. "Thank you for telling me. Go get Annie ready while I load the suitcases in the car."

"Are we picking up the girls now?" Rosie asked.

"Not yet. My boss has a friend who owns a security company, hires only former SEALs. K2 Special Services, I think is the name. Anyway, Rothmire says they're the best there is, and his friend sent two of his men to us. They're going to stay with you and the girls until this is over."

"Oh, I don't know about going off with strange men. Why can't that nice Josh go with us?"

"With this case and a few others going on right now, we're stretched thin. Rothmire trusts these men, and I trust him. It will be okay, Rosie. Besides, I understand their nicknames are Doc and Saint." She smiled at her foster mother. "How can you not trust a man his friends call Saint?"

CHAPTER FIFTEEN

Nate eyed the two men from K2 Special Services. They were big and intimidating. The dudes were going to scare the hell out of the girls. After introducing Jamie Turner and Ryan O'Connor, Rothmire had left for a meeting, leaving Nate alone with them while they waited for Taylor and Rosie to arrive.

"Did my boss tell you that you'll be babysitting six girls, ages two to nine?"

"Yeah. Scariest assignment ever," the green-eyed one said.

"You're O'Connor?" Nate asked the man sporting a grin.

"Yeah, but the team calls me Doc." He pointed a thumb at his friend. "We call him Saint, and trust me when I say the moniker suits."

"Just try not to scare the hell out of the girls, okay?"

The one called Saint cracked a smile. "We're teddy bears at heart."

"You should know that these girls come from homes where they were either neglected or abused. They're afraid of men."

Both men frowned. "Don't like hearing that," Doc said. "No one will hurt them under our care, I promise you."

"If I didn't know that, those girls wouldn't be going anywhere with you. Rosie, their foster mother, is a tiny little thing, but don't let that fool you. She's as fierce as a mother lion when it comes to her babies."

"Good for her. Your boss explained the situation," Doc said. "We'll take good care of Rosie and her babies, but I gotta tell you, we'd rather be here helping you catch your bad guy."

"Truth," agreed Saint. He walked to the glass door leading out to Nate's balcony. "Nice view you got here."

"Thanks." His doorbell chimed. "That will be Taylor and Rosie." He let the women in, following behind them as they walked to the living room. Taylor had barely nodded when he'd greeted her, and he hated how she'd avoided looking at him. Somehow, he had to find a way to repair their friendship. He missed her.

"Where's Annie?"

"With Rand. He's moving the car seat to the van and getting her buckled in," Taylor said.

He was going to miss the little girl. "Taylor, Rosie, this is Jamie Turner and Ryan O'Connor."

"I'm Jamie, but my friends call me Saint," the blue-eyed one said. He shook hands with Rosie first, then Taylor.

"And I'm Ryan. My friends call me Doc."

"Are you a doctor?" Rosie asked, staring at the men with a gleam of appreciation in her eyes.

"No, but I am a medic. You and your girls will be in good hands."

Nate scowled, not liking the matching gleam of appreciation in Taylor's eyes. Both men wore wedding rings, but he still had the urge to growl *Mine!* "Let's get this show on the road." At the odd look Taylor darted at him, he headed for the door before he made a fool of himself.

In the underground garage, he helped Rosie into the van they'd rented. "Are our suitcases in here?" Rosie asked, peering around.

"Rand loaded them in the back."

"Nae!" Annie reached for him.

"Hey, sweet girl. You be good for Rosie, okay?"

Taylor opened the opposite door, leaning in and giving Annie a hug. Nate slipped away while Annie's attention was diverted. He faced the two K2 men. "Rothmire said he gave you both mine and Taylor's numbers. You call one of us if anything—"

"We will," Saint said. "Here're our cell numbers." He handed Nate a card. "Hopefully you'll be calling us in a few days, telling us to bring the girls home."

That was the plan. He nodded, then headed for his car. The van pulled out first, and a few minutes later, the car with Rand and Taylor left, Nate following behind them.

His job was to watch for anyone following the car Rand and Taylor were in. It wouldn't be unusual for Taylor to visit the school, and by now if their man was watching her, he had to be aware that she had someone with her wherever she went. What he wouldn't expect was a van parked behind the school, waiting to whisk Rosie and the girls away.

The drive to the school was uneventful, and when Rand pulled up in front, Nate kept going. At the end of the block, after making sure no one was following them, he turned around. As soon as Taylor was safely inside the school, he drove to the back.

It would take a few minutes for Taylor to talk to the principal and then collect the girls. He parked next to the van. Rosie stayed in the back with Annie, but the K2 men exited, taking up positions behind the van, their alert eyes scanning their surroundings.

Although no weapons were visible, Nate didn't doubt they were armed to the teeth, which was reassuring. He walked inside the school, finding himself in what appeared to be a supply room, where he waited for Taylor and the girls. Hopefully, they'd see this as an adventure, but he was worried about their reaction to the men from K2. The girls were only now getting used to him, no longer giving him suspicious glances or shying away from his touch.

Each one had a story that had broken his heart when Taylor had shared their histories. The only one seemingly unaffected was Annie. She was blessedly too young to remember how horribly she'd been neglected by her meth-addicted mother the first year of her life.

Would the men sent to guard the girls appreciate how fragile these six children were without knowing their backgrounds? He strode back outside, stopping at the back of the van. "I trust that you both have the ability to guard Taylor's girls," he said at their raised brows. "But to understand why they fear people and places they aren't comfortable with, you need to know each have tragic pasts. They're especially afraid of men."

"We'll do our best not to scare them," Saint said.

Doc gave a firm nod. "And we'll guard them with our lives."

"Why don't you come inside so I can introduce you to them? Having two strangers sitting in a van about to carry them off to parts unknown might frighten them." And these two dudes were big and intimidating, the kind of men that Taylor's girls wouldn't want any part of.

"Let's do that in shifts," Saint said. "One of us needs to stay out here to keep an eye on things. Doc, you go first."

Nate arrived back in the storeroom with Doc in tow just as Taylor and the girls walked in. At seeing the stranger, all five girls came to a stop, crowding in behind Taylor. Nate had anticipated that reaction, but it still made him sad that they expected the worst to happen at any given time.

"Girls, I want you to meet a friend of mine."

Doc squatted down, putting himself at eye level to the girls peeking around Taylor. All but Bri. She'd totally disappeared behind Taylor's back. Doc glanced up at him, his eyes filled with compassion. Robin seemed the most curious, so Nate reached for her hand as he squatted next to her.

"His name is Doc, you know, like one of the seven dwarfs."

"The dwarfs are little," she said.

Doc smiled. "Well, that's true. My mama made me eat my broccoli, so I grew up big and strong."

"My mama's in prison."

"But Rosie told me on the way over here that she writes you every week, so that means she really loves you. I have a baby girl. She's only two months old. Would you like to see a picture of her?" When Robin nodded, Doc pulled out his wallet, opening it up and handing it to her. "Her name's Skye."

"That's a funny name," Sarrie said as she inched up to see the photo.

"My wife is a pilot. The sky is her favorite place to be, so we named our baby Skye."

"She has pretty eyes. They're just like yours," June said, joining her sister and Robin. "I wish I had green eyes."

"And I wish I had beautiful brown eyes like yours."

At the big smile appearing on June's face, Nate exchanged a relieved look with Taylor. It appeared that at least one of the K2 men would be able to win the girls over. Even Bri was now peeking around Taylor.

"I want to be a pilot," Bri said, almost whispering.

That was news to Taylor. Bri had never hinted at such a thing. Taylor put her hand on Bri's head. "Would you like to go for a ride in a plane someday?"

"Can I?"

Ryan O'Connor glanced up at her. "If you ever get to Pensacola, let me know. Charlie will be glad to take her up."

"Who's Charlie?" Elle asked, edging up to the other girls.

Well, that was interesting. Elle was shyer than a mouse and never talked to strangers. Taylor wondered who Charlie was, too.

"Charlie's my wife."

"But that's a boy's name," Robin said.

"Her real name's Charlene, but we all call her Charlie."

"Do you have a picture of her?" Bri asked, moving out from behind Taylor.

Taylor stepped away, letting her girls quiz the man squatting in front of them. She'd been worried about sending them off with strangers, men they didn't know. Except for Annie, they were like cats. If it hadn't happened at least three times before, they didn't like anything new and unexpected. It seemed like that wasn't going to be a problem where Ryan was concerned. She hoped it would be the same with Jamie Turner.

"Have you told them yet that they're going away?" Nate quietly asked, moving next to her. The first thing to hit her was the heat from his body, the second his scent. He smelled like soap and spices. She wanted to lick him. She already knew how delicious he tasted, but their one time together had done nothing more than leave her wanting a repeat. Lots of repeats.

"No. I haven't had a chance. I'm hoping they'll be excited about spending a few days at the beach with no school." His gaze was on the girls, and that he cared for them was obvious by the way his eyes turned soft when he looked at them. She loved that about him. Not that she had a lot of experience with men, but most would probably run fast and far from a woman responsible for six kids.

"I have a friend I want you girls to meet," Ryan said. "I'll send him in. We call him Saint, and he's a real nice guy."

Ryan stood, giving her a smile as he left. The K2 men were gorgeous specimens, real easy on the eyes, but in her opinion, they didn't come close to being as hot as Nate. Right now, though, she'd give up any hope of being with him again in return for having her friend back. She missed the easy rapport they'd had with each other, hated that she was carefully measuring her words around him.

"Does his friend have green eyes, too?" June said.

Taylor knelt, pulling her girls close. "No, sweetie. Saint has blue eyes, but they're just as pretty. Listen up. All of you and Rosie are going on vacation to the beach. You're going to have so much fun playing in the sand and in the water. I bet Doc and Saint would help you build a sandcastle if you said please."

"Are you coming with us?" Bri asked.

"I wish I could, but I have to work. Promise me you'll be good for Rosie, but most of all, promise that you'll have a really fun time, okay?"

Bri frowned. "But we want you to come with us." She shyly looked up at Nate. "You could come, too."

"I'd love to, sweetheart, but I have to work, too," Nate said, kneeling.

Taylor didn't miss the flash of pleasure in Nate's eyes at Bri's invitation. It was the first time she'd spoken directly to him, which Taylor considered a huge step for Brianna.

Saint walked in, crouching down a few feet from the girls. "Are we having a powwow?"

"What's a powwow?" Sarrie asked.

"It's what Native Americans call a meeting. I'm Saint, by the way. It's very nice to meet you lovely ladies."

Elle giggled. She tugged on Taylor's hand. "He said we're lovely."

"And you are," Saint said, smiling.

"You have pretty eyes, too," June said. "But I like the other man's better. I wish I had green ones."

Saint laughed. "Doc's eyes are pretty, but I'd rather have brown eyes like you. Yours remind me of chocolate, and I love chocolate."

Taylor stood, stepping away to let the girls get acquainted with their protector. They'd all surprised her with how easily they'd accepted the two men. Maybe they were finally starting to feel safe, ready to start trusting again.

Nate moved next to her. "I'm kind of jealous. They're just now starting to acknowledge my existence, yet they seem fascinated by these two strangers."

"Well, they both do have pretty eyes." She almost laughed at the scowl on his face.

"You're noticing eyes now?"

Was he actually jealous? A little thrill went through her, and she couldn't resist testing this new revelation. "How could I not? I just can't decide which are sexier. Ryan's green ones or Jamie's blue ones."

He wrapped his fingers around her arm, pulling her further away. "We have an investigation going on. You don't have time to be noticing any dude's eyes."

She gave a mental high five. He was jealous. That was good intel. "What about yours? Am I allowed to notice them?"

"Always."

CHAPTER SIXTEEN

"What?" Nate shifted his gaze to his brother.

"Where the hell's your mind?" Court sighed. "You haven't heard a word I said."

His mind was on Taylor. Where else would it be after having her stare into his eyes, asking if she was allowed to notice them? After experiencing his first-ever streak of jealousy—an emotion he'd never expected to feel in his lifetime—because she apparently had it in her to appreciate a man, or men in this case, who wasn't him. They were surrounded daily by men, other agents, and she'd never once indicated that she thought their eyes were sexy.

Court snapped his fingers in front of Nate's face. "Yo, dude, what's wrong with you? You're spacey. You're never spacey."

"You think my eyes are sexy?" Hell! Did that really come out of his mouth? "You say one word right now, I'm going to put you on your ass."

His douchebag brother's lips twitched, then furiously twitched. Then laughter burst out of his mouth. He laughed so hard that his face turned red and tears rolled down his eyes. Nate considered the ways he could get away with fratricide.

"What's so funny?" Alex said, walking into the Aces & Eights office.

"Nothing," Nate said, shooting Court an I'm-going-to-kill-you-if-you-open-your-mouth glare.

"Didn't you once tell me you thought our big brother had sexy eyes?" Court said, between gasps.

Alex dropped onto the opposite end of the couch from Court. "I did?"

"You're a walking dead man," Nate said to Court.

Court grinned. "Probably, but I'll go out knowing I've never been more entertained."

"Asshole," Nate growled, which sent his idiot brother into more laughter.

"Feeling like I walked in on the end of a movie here." Alex darted glances between him and Court. "One of you needs to share before I decide to make you."

"Since Alex could put both of us on our backs without half trying, I'll—"

"Shut the hell up, Court." Nate pushed his chair away from the desk. "I'm out of here for the night. You two can close up." He picked up the plastic bag filled with water he'd set under the desk earlier.

"What's up with the fish?" Alex asked.

Nate walked out without answering. Court would tell Alex why he'd been laughing, which only proved why Nate rarely shared. Swear to God, he loved his brothers, but sometimes he was positive their development had hit a snag somewhere in their teens. The stupidest, most juvenile things amused them.

The door hadn't yet closed behind him when he heard Alex's belly laugh. Nate shook his head with a sigh. He'd be hearing about sexy eyes for the next month. He couldn't stop a smile. Dumbass brothers. He reached the door to the garage behind Aces & Eights before remembering that he'd walked out without getting Court's update on his research into murders with a similar M.O. Letting out a long sigh, he did an about-face, heading back to Comedy Central.

♠♠♠

"I wasn't expecting you," Taylor said after opening her door, wearing nothing more than a pair of boxer shorts and a cropped T-shirt. She peered out at the parking lot. "Is Rand still out there?"

Nate's mouth dried up, his eyes automatically sliding to her little silver belly-button ring. She was the queen of his best dreams. And he had dreamed of her, often and erotically. Before their night together, it had only been his imagination fueling the dreams. After that night, after he'd mapped her body with his eyes, his hands, his mouth, his tongue . . . Eff him. He hadn't been able to think straight since the best night of his life.

"Earth to Nate." She snapped her fingers in front of his eyes. "Is Rand still here?"

People really needed to stop snapping their fingers in his face. He tore his gaze away from her stomach and that sexy-as-all-get-out belly ring, clearing his throat so he could talk. This woman was his heaven and his hell.

"Rand? No. I sent him home. You know we've been keeping an eye on you?" Taylor snorted, then walked back into her apartment. Since she'd left the door open, Nate took that as an invitation to come in.

"You want a . . ." Her gaze fell to the plastic bag he held. "What's that?"

He held it up, eyeing the contents. "A fish?"

"I know it's a fish. What are you doing with it?"

"It's for you." He held out the bag. "I know you miss Henry, so I brought you another Henry." Why was she blinking her eyes so hard?

"Sometimes I don't know what to do with you, Nate Gentry." She took the bag from him.

What did that mean? And why did she swipe at her eyes as she turned away? "Did I do something wrong? I thought you'd like the fish."

"He's beautiful." She turned on the air pump. "I love how blue he is."

"He matches your eyes." Henry had been red and black, and he'd thought a different color wouldn't make her think of Henry every time she looked at it, so he'd gone with the blue-and-white one. And the color did remind him of her eyes.

After dropping the fish into the tank, she stepped back and watched him familiarize himself with his new home. "I think I'll call him Henry Too." She glanced over her shoulder. "Thank you."

"You're welcome. What did you mean by you don't know what to do with me?"

She put her finger in the water, flicking it. The fish swam up, circled her finger, then nibbled on it, causing her to laugh. "That tickles, Too."

"Are you calling him the number 'two,' or 'too' as in 'also'?"

"Henry Too, as in 'also.'"

"Cute." Since it appeared she was going to ignore his question, he went for a beer. "Want anything?" When she didn't answer, he glanced back, frowning at seeing an empty room. "Guess not," he muttered. He poured her a glass of wine anyway.

Returning to the living room, he set his beer and the glass of wine on the coffee table, then walked to the fish tank. Henry Too didn't chase his finger like Henry the First, which was disappointing. Too many things had been disappointing Nate lately, namely himself. As much as he'd sworn he wouldn't screw up his friendship with Taylor, he had. He'd sent her girls away, watching her cry as the van disappeared from view. He hadn't put his arms around her, comforting her, even though he'd longed to.

For the first time since he'd joined the FBI, he didn't know what he wanted anymore. The day after he'd almost killed his father, he had gone into town, an angry boy on the cusp of manhood. The only future he could visualize for himself was more of the same, ending up like his father, trying to scratch a living out of their nothing piece of dirt, raising pigs and chickens. If a bit of luck was on his side, maybe he'd land a job as a mechanic at Hank's Garage.

Rage had still burned in his blood as he'd headed to the drugstore to get something to treat Alex's shredded back. There wasn't money for a doctor, and the few dollars in Nate's pocket wouldn't buy much, but maybe it was enough for a jar of salve. After finding a generic brand he could afford, he went to the end of the line to pay. As he waited, he read the instructions.

"Something stinks. Smells like a pig farmer."

Nate recognized that voice. Reese Dagger was the captain of the football team, one of the popular kids at their school.

"Yeah, stinks like shit around here."

That was Reese's best friend, Carter Milliard. Nate pretended not to hear them.

"Think the Gentry boys get it on with those pigs?" Reese said.

Carter laughed. "Probably. That's the only way they're gonna get any."

"Maybe those boys get it on with each other," Reese said.

Blood boiling hot streaked up Nate's neck and face. "Shut the fuck up."

"You gonna make us, pig boy?" Reese nudged his friend with his elbow, imitating a squealing pig. They both laughed as Carter joined in, making his own pig noise.

Nate lost it. He stepped toward them, all reasoning gone, one word hanging black and heavy in his mind. *Kill.*

A firm hand clamped down on his shoulder. "Easy, son."

It was only the strength in the hand holding him back that kept him in place. He glanced behind him to see Sheriff Buddy Burton. The sheriff had paid numerous visits to the Gentry home back when Nate's mother still lived there. Each time he'd thrown Gordon Gentry in jail for a few days for beating up his wife and/or kids. Unfortunately, that had never cured Nate's father from doing it again.

Still keeping his hand on Nate's shoulder, the sheriff said, "Reese, Carter, you boys have five seconds to disappear before I let go of him."

Reese puffed up his chest. "He puts a hand on me, my dad will sue him to hell and back."

The sheriff snorted. "What, you have a hankering to own a few pigs of your own? You boys should be ashamed of yourselves. Go on, get out of here."

"But we haven't paid—"

"Don't care. Put those rolls of toilet paper on the counter. You're not papering anyone's house tonight."

With the rage that had blinded his vision, Nate hadn't noticed that Reese's and Carter's arms were loaded up with packages of toilet paper. What would it feel like to have no problems bigger than did you have enough rolls to do a decent job of papering someone's yard?

"Spoiled rich kids," the sheriff muttered after Reese and Carter slammed their packages down on the counter and then stomped out. "Come with me."

Nate held his ground. "I have to buy this."

The sheriff eyed the jar. "What's that for?"

"I just need it." Nate kept his gaze on the floor, wishing it would swallow him up. Sheriff Burton hadn't been out to the trailer since Nate's mother had left. He was embarrassed to admit his father was still using his fists and belt.

"Who'd he hurt this time, son?"

"Alex," Nate muttered, knowing the man wouldn't relent until he had a name.

Somehow, in the next twenty minutes, Nate had a better brand of salve to smear on Alex's back and a job. He was to report for an hour after school—the sheriff understanding that was the most Nate could get away with before his father would get suspicious of where he was spending his time—to the sheriff's office to do whatever Sheriff Burton directed. Most of his small weekly paycheck went toward groceries, and since his brothers liked the improvement in the food that appeared on the table, they worked harder to compensate for the time Nate spent on his new job.

During Nate's senior year of high school, Sheriff Burton groomed him for a career in law enforcement without Nate catching on to the devious man's plan. The first week, Nate swept floors, made coffee for the sheriff and his deputies, learned how to file reports in the gray metal cabinet behind his mentor's desk, all the while listening in as Sheriff Burton conducted business.

As each day passed, Nate grew more interested in the goings-on of law enforcement. His mother had instilled in him the importance of an education, and the man he grew to love, the man who'd probably kept him from going to prison for killing two high school jerks, had given him hope for a better life. When a group of Miami cops got together and offered a scholarship to a worthy recipient for a degree in criminal justice, without telling him, the sheriff had sent them Nate's name.

His mentor had never shared what he'd written on the application, but against all odds, Nate was selected to win the scholarship. As soon as he learned of it, he'd made a promise to himself. He would never let Sheriff Burton down. The best way he could do that was to control the rages he still had when someone made him angry. He'd learned how to walk away from assholes like Reese and Carter.

What scared the hell out of him were women and children. What if he had it in him to hurt them, to be like his father? The only solution was to never marry or have children.

His next piece of good luck was when an FBI recruiter came to Florida State during Nate's junior year. After talking to the man, Nate made up his mind. He would become a special agent for the FBI. The recruiter made him a list of the best classes to take, but most importantly, he gave Nate his card, telling him to call after he graduated with a degree in criminal justice.

Because a sheriff had believed in him, and with the financial backing from a group of cops, along with his own stubborn determination, he'd achieved something he wouldn't have dared to dream before that day in the drugstore. What really made him proud, though, was that his brothers had followed in his footsteps. He'd been satisfied with the life he'd mapped out.

Then along came Taylor. Lately he'd been feeling like a cartoon character that had jumped off a cliff without knowing how far he'd fall. If there was one thing he disliked more than any other it was not being in control, and he'd lost that the moment he'd first kissed her.

He trailed his finger over the aquarium's glass again, but Henry Too didn't seem impressed. "You match Taylor's beautiful blue eyes, but you're not as smart as your predecessor."

After putting on jeans and her favorite baseball jersey, Taylor stood in the hallway, watching Nate. He seemed to be in deep thought, and she wondered what was going through his mind. It touched her deeply that he'd shown up with a replacement fish. The man might not like admitting it, even to himself, but he had a soft heart. She smiled, listening to him talk to the fish, especially liking his comment about her eyes.

"You'll just have to train him to follow your finger," she said, walking into the living room, stopping a few feet away. Why was he here? She'd thought just to bring her Henry Too, but the beer and glass of wine on the coffee table indicated he planned to stay a while.

Facing her, his gaze skimmed over her. "You changed."

He sounded disappointed. "Very observant, Mr. Gentry." Wearing only a pair of boxer shorts and a cut-off T-shirt when she didn't know where she stood with him had made her feel vulnerable. He had something on his mind, and if it was another lecture as to why they couldn't be together, she'd rather hear it fully clothed.

"I sense sarcasm there, Ms. Collins."

His expression was stern, but his eyes twinkled with amusement. "Is there a reason for your visit, Mr. Gentry, other than to deliver a fish?" she said, continuing the game. "Which was really sweet of you, by the way."

"I'm not sweet." The humor faded from his eyes. "We need to talk."

"Ruh-roh." She glanced at the glass on the coffee table. "Apparently, I need wine for this conversation?" Now she was sad, knowing what was coming. He'd no doubt come up with a long list of reasons they couldn't have a repeat. That was too bad, but his loss. She just had to figure out how to stop loving him.

"Well, let's get this party started." She sat at the end of the sofa, curling her legs under her. He picked up his beer, then settled in *his* leather chair. "So, let's hear it."

"Court's turned up some similar murders, fifteen to be exact, going back forty years."

Okay, this wasn't about them. She relaxed, comfortable with talking business. "What was his criteria?"

"Strangled prostitutes with blue eyes and blonde hair. There was only one, though, prior to our three, who had on a white dress and a gold band."

"How long ago?"

"Six years. So, odds are our man killed her. Of the other fourteen, until we look closer, there's no way of knowing which of those could belong to him, but they don't fit his M.O."

"And considering some small-town police departments might not have entered their cases into the data bank, there could be others Court hasn't turned up."

"Exactly. But we've got these to start with. I'm going to have Alex and Rand interview each of the detectives assigned to the cases."

Her blood raced with excitement. "I can—"

"Don't even think it. You're not taking off for parts unknown to interview anyone. He's watching you, Taylor."

"You don't know that."

"No, but I feel it. For whatever reason, I think he's fixated on you. From what Rosie said, he was trying to kill you when she came in. Although, I wonder if she saw it wrong."

"What do you mean?"

"I've been thinking about everything Rosie told you. Maybe he was going to take you with him, but then ran away when she started beating on him with the bat. I called Pauline, told her what you'd learned. We agree that we have to consider that he's kept an eye on you all these years, and now he's decided to come for you."

Okay, now he was creeping her out. "But why wait all this time? And how did he know who I was?"

"A lot of possibilities. He was married, but recently divorced. Or his wife died. Or he's been in prison. As for knowing who you were, I wouldn't be surprised if he followed you and Rosie to the motel that night."

"I'm not liking this conversation at all. You were right. I need wine." She drained what was left in her glass. "Why can't I remember that night?"

"My guess is you blocked it out. What child wouldn't be traumatized if their mother had been killed in front of them?" He stared at the beer bottle he held for a moment before moving to the sofa, angling his body to face her. "I'd like you to consider hypnosis. You were there that night and saw him, so somewhere in your mind is a description of him. You might even know his name if your mother happened to mention him."

Her first reaction was a firm no. But what if she held the key to finding her mother's murderer? If she could describe him, it would go a long way in helping them find him. She set her glass down, then stood and went to the fish tank. Henry Too was still exploring his new home, and she watched him for a few minutes.

To relive that night? Once she remembered, it would be in her mind forever. Could she deal with that, seeing her mother murdered in front of her eyes? Did she have a choice?

CHAPTER SEVENTEEN

"I'll do it."

Nate had known she would, but he didn't like it. He'd argued with Pauline when she'd suggested it. He also didn't like the dread he saw in Taylor's eyes. "Why don't you think about it overnight before making a decision?"

"No. I need to do this." She came back to the sofa. "The sooner the better."

"I'll set it up."

"Will you come with me?"

"Of course." There was no way he'd let her go through that alone. Surprising him, she stretched out her legs, resting her feet on this thigh. "Looking for a foot rub, tiger?"

She smiled. "That would be nice."

The tension that had existed between them the past several days had eased in the last few minutes, but there was more they had to talk about. What he had to say would probably put them back on edge, and he almost let it go. He didn't want to be at odds with her, but he owed it to her to tell her why they couldn't be anything more than friends.

"I missed that, you know."

"What's that?" He stroked his thumb along the bottom of her foot, eliciting a moan from her that sent his blood streaming straight south. She had pretty feet. The skin was soft, and her cherry-red toenails drew his attention. He'd never in his life sucked on a woman's toes, had never wanted to. Inexplicably, he wanted to lick hers.

"You calling me tiger."

He gently set her feet aside. "I can't . . ." How did you tell a woman you wanted her but you couldn't let yourself have her?

"Call me tiger?" She pulled her legs up under her. "Fine then, don't."

He was screwing this up. "That's not what I meant." He swiped his hand over his face. "I'll never marry." There, he'd said it.

"Me either, but what does that have to do with anything?"

"It's why I don't do relationships. Women fall in love. They want to get married. They want children."

"Okay." She scrunched her brows together. "Out of curiosity, why?"

"Won't I ever marry?" She nodded. "Because . . ." Man, this was hard to admit. He stood, going to the fish tank. Maybe that was why she kept a fish. So she'd have something to look at when she said things she'd never dreamed of talking about. "Because I'm afraid I'll lose my temper someday and hurt my family. If I had one."

"Nate?"

"Yeah?"

"Turn around and look at me."

He obeyed, pushing his fingers into the pockets of his jeans.

"Have you ever lost your temper enough to hurt your brothers? Have you ever hit them in anger?"

"No."

"Have you ever hit anyone?"

Instead of answering, he said, "Did you know that around thirty-five percent of abused children grow up to be abusers? It's what we know, Taylor. All we know about how to behave in a relationship."

"I don't believe you'd hit anyone in anger."

He snorted. "Shows what you know. I almost killed my father."

"If that's true, then you had a good reason." She patted the sofa's seat. "Come here."

"I'm fine where I am." If he got close to her, he wouldn't get the rest of it out. "The only reason I didn't was because of my brothers. But make no mistake, I wanted to."

"What did he do?"

"I should have killed him when he broke Court's arm, making sure he would never play baseball again. He was good, Taylor. Could have made it to the majors."

"I would kill him for that myself, but Court seems pretty happy to me."

"Sure, now he is. Back then, he was crushed. Our father stole his dream."

She drew her knees up, hugging them. "But that wasn't when you lost it, right? What did he do to drive you over the edge?"

Why couldn't she just accept what he was trying to tell her without asking him to bare his soul? The bad guys didn't stand a chance against her. She'd just sit there, looking at them with those big, understanding blue eyes, and she'd stay that way until she'd wrung every last secret out of them.

"I walked in to find him shredding Alex's back with the buckle of his belt. The fucking reason?" He pulled his hands out of his pockets, fisting them. "Alex didn't get him a beer fast enough."

"You should have killed him." She got up, came to him, took his hand, and pulled him back to the sofa with her.

He let her.

"I would've helped you hide his body. Your father was a bastard, no mistaking that. But you're not him, Nate."

"You don't know that. I don't even know that."

She smiled sadly. "Then you're deluding yourself."

"Perhaps, but I won't risk it."

"So, what? You're afraid you'll hurt me?"

"You're a beautiful woman. You'll want to fall in love and have babies."

She stared at him for a moment, then burst into laughter.

Okay, not the reaction he was expecting.

"Do I look like I need more babies? I think six is more than enough."

"Someday, you'll want your own."

"We've known each other for two years, been best friends for almost a year now, yet we've never talked about this. I wonder why." She leaned forward and put her hand on his knee. "Here's the thing. I will never bring a child into this world. There are too many kids out there who need someone to love them. Any babies I had would be one less lost child I could rescue. As for a husband, I have no use for one. I have enough on my plate between my job and my girls."

He blinked, his mind trying to comprehend what she'd just said. Didn't all women want candy and flowers, a man to stare into her eyes with worship in his, cute babies to cuddle and giggle with?

"Is that the truth, not something you're saying because you think that's what I want to hear?"

"I just want a man to play with, Nate, and I want that man to be you." Her hand traveled a few inches up his thigh. "Of course, if you're not interested, I guess I'll have to find someone who is."

"Like hell you will." He scooped her up. "Bedroom," he said.

She rested her head on his shoulder. "We should have had this talk months ago."

"Yeah, look at all that time we wasted." At the door to her room, he paused. "No falling in love, right?"

"Not a chance on my part, but your brothers fell fast and hard. Maybe that runs in the Gentry blood, so you might be the one we have to worry about. I am really hot, you know."

"Understatement there, tiger."

Taylor nuzzled Nate's neck, loving the taste of him. He'd broken her heart with his secret fear that he could hurt a woman or child. He was so full of it. The man had a bigger heart than either of his brothers', and theirs were pretty big. It was sad that he didn't know that. She hadn't lied to him. Long ago, she'd decided to save children instead of having them, she wasn't looking for a husband—not today, anyway—and she wasn't going to fall in love with him because she already was.

"I'm going to buy you a bigger bed," he said after removing his boots and then stretching out next to her.

She lifted onto her elbow, glancing at the end of her bed to see his feet hanging off the end. "Well, I wasn't thinking ahead when I bought it. That I'd have an overgrown man in it someday."

"Overgrown, am I?" He flipped her onto her back.

"Yeah, but trust me. I'm not complaining." She'd baited the lion when she'd threatened to find another man to play with if he wasn't interested. The way his eyes had gone midnight black and possessive had sent a thrill through her. There was no other man she wanted, but she'd keep that fact her secret.

"I want your hair down." She hooked a finger in the leather band, dragging it down his ponytail. Once freed, she combed her fingers through his hair so that it fell around his face and shoulders. There he was, her warrior man.

Except he was clothed. "Shirt off."

Amusement glimmered in his eyes. "You have a bossy mouth."

"That's not my mouth's only talent."

"Dammit, Taylor," he growled, yanking his T-shirt over his head. "Keep talking like that and—"

She leaned up and latched her teeth onto his nipple. His groin jerked against her, then settled in the *v* of her legs. "You were saying?" she said after letting go.

"Don't know." He took possession of her mouth, delving deep, possessing her.

Because, like her, Nate worked out hard almost every day, he had a fine body. *Very fine,* Taylor thought as she skimmed her hands over his chest, down to rock-solid abs. His skin rippled under her fingers, his reaction boosting her confidence. He liked her touching him, which suited her just fine, since it was one of her new favorite things to do.

It was hard not to pause whenever she touched one of the scars inflicted by his father, but she knew Nate. He didn't want her sympathy or pity. She didn't feel either emotion for the man, but she did for the boy who'd been horribly abused.

"Pants off," she said when her hands reached the waistband of his jeans. She wanted him gloriously naked.

He sat up, straddling her. "Tiger, tiger," he said, his lips curving into the wickedest grin she'd ever seen. "That bossy mouth of yours is going to get you in serious trouble."

"I've always liked trouble."

"That's a damn good thing." He grabbed the hem of her jersey. "Cause you're in deep trouble, Ms. Collins."

"You do remember that I can take you down, right?" Special Agent Nate Gentry was as serious as they came, but she was learning that Bed Nate had a playful side, and she loved it.

"I do. But you know what?"

She shook her head.

"By the time I'm finished with you, your knees are going to be as weak as a newborn kitten's. You're not going to be able to walk, much less best me."

Every nerve ending, every bone in her body, and every pulse point screamed an enthusiastic *Yes, please!* She tugged on his jeans. "Off."

"Not yet. This goes first." He pulled her up so he could remove her baseball jersey. "Beautiful," he said, sliding his hands along her sides.

She hadn't bothered putting on a bra when she'd changed, nor had she expected them to end up in bed. When he lowered his face and placed whisper-soft kisses across her breasts, she sighed as her eyes slid closed. He swirled his tongue around a nipple and then blew on it.

"Feels so good." She felt his mouth curve into a smile against her skin.

"Yeah?" He sat up, staring down at her. "We'll get back to that, but first, you still have on too many clothes." As he inched her jeans down, his gaze followed the slow reveal of her panties and then her legs.

When he lifted his eyes to hers, she sucked in a breath at the hunger she saw in them. No man had ever looked at her the way he did, as if she were his deepest fantasy come true. He was definitely hers.

Once her pants were gone, he straddled her again, holding most of his weight on his legs. The arrow of black hair disappearing into his jeans caught her eye. She traced her finger down it until she reached his waistband. With her thumb and index finger, she slipped the button out of its hole. He'd gone as still as stone. A sleek panther just before he pounces on his prey was the image that came to mind.

She wasn't sure how eyes already black could turn darker, but his had, fathomless pools she could happily drown in. And the way he watched her—drinking her in with an intensity that set her body on fire—had her almost begging him to move. To do something. Anything. If he kept looking at her the way he was, she would soon burn to a crisp.

"Keep going," he commanded, his voice harsh.

She kept her gaze on his as she slowly pulled down the zipper. A muscle ticked in his jaw, the only indication that he wasn't unaffected by what was happening between them. He had on a pair of black briefs, and she put her hand on him, cupping his erection. It pulsed against her palm at the same time he hissed. She squeezed her fingers around him, dragging them up his length. His throat flexed as he swallowed hard.

"Off," she said, letting go of him and tugging on his jeans.

He hopped off the bed. After pulling two condoms out of his pocket and dropping them on the nightstand, he pushed his pants and briefs down. Her eyes feasted on his body. He wasn't overly muscled, more on the lean side, actually. As far as she was concerned, he was perfect. Broad shoulders, narrow hips, long legs, and oh God, his hair. She thought that was her favorite thing about him, or maybe it was his face. The high cheekbones, straight nose, full lips, black eyes, and the scruff on his cheeks were enough to send her libido into a screaming frenzy.

"If you don't stop looking at me like that, I won't last five minutes."

She licked her lips, hiding a smile when he made a noise deep in his throat. Something grew inside her, a sense that she had power over this man. She'd never felt that with her only two boyfriends, and she liked it.

"Then we'll just go for a round two." She turned onto her side, resting her head on her hand, and looked up at him. "Unless you're not man enough for me."

His lips curved into that wicked smile she was learning to love. "Are you challenging me, tiger?"

"Hmm, maybe." That was the thing about them. They were highly competitive when they got physical. When they worked out, neither gave way, both determined to best the other. The sexual tension between them always hit its zenith during those hours on the mat. She loved that, and wanted the same thing in the bedroom. A test of wills with him was a huge turn-on.

He stretched out next to her and put his hands on the sides of her head, pulling her mouth to his. After kissing her senseless, he lifted his face. "Challenge accepted. In fact, before the night is over, you'll be begging for mercy."

"You know I never beg." Before he could respond, she slid down his body. "I think you're the one who'll be begging."

"Taylor," he rasped when he realized where she was headed. He buried his hands in her hair. "You don't have to do that."

"I want to, so hush."

He didn't give her more than a few minutes before he said, "Enough."

No sooner than the word was out of his mouth, she found herself flipped onto her back, his body covering hers. "Well, hello," she said. He stared down at her as if she were a puzzle he couldn't figure out. "That was like tasting the sea. Warm and salty." She swiped her tongue over her lips, greedy for more of him. She palmed his jaw. "What are you thinking right now?"

Irritation glimmered in his eyes. "Fuck if I know how I resisted you as long as I did."

"And that makes you mad?"

"Yeah, it does."

CHAPTER EIGHTEEN

Nate covered Taylor's mouth with his before she could ask any more questions. He was venturing into foreign territory with this woman, and it scared the living hell out of him. He never saw the same woman twice, or never had before Taylor. What was he supposed to do with this need to be with her? She took his breath away, and he didn't know what to do with that either.

She arched her body when he kissed his way down to her belly and then lower. Bewitched by everything about her, he stopped thinking. He loved the sounds she made, her sighs and moans and gasps. Yet, as he'd learned the first time they'd made love, she climaxed quietly, nothing more than an exhale of breath, and a shudder that traveled through her body like the wave of an ocean.

"You're so sexy when you come," he said, crawling up her body. He grabbed a condom, ripping it open. She gave him a dreamy smile, her blue eyes soft and not quite focused. "But let's see if I can make you scream." *His name.* That was the part he liked best.

Losing himself in the rhythm of the oldest dance in the world, he held her hips with his hands as they rocked together. His muscles strained as he fought to keep the wildness inside him leashed. If he let go, taking her the way he wanted—hard, fast, and deep—she'd think she was in bed with an animal.

"I'm not fragile, Nate." She slid the pad of her foot down his leg. "You're not going to break me."

He knew that better than anyone, considering they did their best to kill each other every time they met on the mat. "Tell me what you want," he said, staring down at her.

"You." She arched against him. "The man who takes no prisoners."

"I don't think you have a clue what you're asking for, Taylor." She didn't get it. He was doing his best to treat her like a lady, the way she deserved to be treated.

"The other night when we made love? I knew you were holding back, but that was okay. It was our first time together, and we were learning each other. Now I want the real Nate."

"Are you sure?" When she lifted her head, sucked his earlobe into her mouth, and then bit down, sending pleasure searing through him, raw lust hit hard. He could smell the musky scent of her arousal, and with a low moan, he sought her mouth, needing to feed the hunger growing inside him. Fisting a hand in her hair, he thrust his tongue deep, ravishing her mouth.

Letting go of her hair, he flipped them over. "Ride me, tiger." He put his hands on her hips, helping her move. Even though she'd said she wanted the real him, he wasn't sure she understood what she was asking for. He wasn't into kink, but he liked his sex hard and fast and raw. Better to let her set the pace.

"Nate," she said, her voice breathy. Her eyes slid closed, her skin flushed a pretty pink, and she sucked her bottom lip into her mouth. Nate knew he'd never seen anything more beautiful than Taylor in the throes of passion.

"Nate," she breathed again.

"You can let go. I've got you." He dug his fingers into her skin, forgetting that he had intended to be gentle with her. She moaned, the sound of it eliciting a growl low in his throat. He lifted his hips, thrusting deep inside her, his climax close.

Rolling them back over, unable to hold back, he let out a little of the leash he'd been holding on his urges. His hair, which she'd freed earlier, hung around his shoulders, and she buried a hand in it, pulling hard. And then a shudder traveled through her as she shattered in his arms.

He looked into her blue eyes, dark with desire, got lost in them as the intensity building low inside him grew until he could no longer contain it. *Taylor,* he thought as he buried himself to the hilt, his muscles shaking from the force of his orgasm. He'd never felt anything like this with any other woman.

Taylor, he thought again as he buried his face against her neck. To say her name aloud would reveal too much. If he did, she would hear the wonder of what just happened in his voice. He had no idea what to do with the storm of emotions roiling through him, especially the possessive feeling he was suddenly hit with where she was concerned.

He rolled off her. "You okay?" She hadn't said a word, making him curious as to what she was thinking. Had it been as good for her? And why was he even thinking that? He'd never been concerned about his bed partners' *after-sex* feelings before. They satisfied him, he satisfied them, and then he went home. This new thing, worrying that she was happy with him, was unsettling.

"That was amazing," she said, turning toward him.

"Yeah, it was." And like his first night with her, he had no desire to leave her bed. Also worrisome.

She made circles on his chest with her finger. "Please don't feel weird about this, Nate."

That was exactly what he was feeling. *Weird.* "I don't. Come here." He helped rearrange her so that he spooned her, her back against his chest. At the moment, he didn't want her staring into his eyes because he hadn't a clue what she would see in them. He wasn't ready for this thing taking root inside him, didn't know what to do with the tenderness, much less the possessiveness he was feeling toward her.

"It's late. Go to sleep," he said.

She sighed as if he'd disappointed her. "Good night."

"Night." He didn't want to disappoint her, but somehow, someday, he would. Actually, he probably was doing exactly that even now by not talking about whatever it was women liked to talk about after sex.

It was a big step that he was still in her bed, but she didn't know that. Not only would he never marry, but he didn't have the first idea of how relationships functioned. It wasn't like his parents were good role models for how a marriage should work. These warm and fuzzy feelings were so foreign to him that it was a surprise he even recognized them.

Taylor's breathing evened out, and as she slept, he put his hand on her hip, wanting to sigh as her body heat seeped into his hand. But he didn't. He did, however, bury his nose in her hair, breathing her in.

For the first time, the thought of never marrying saddened him, sent an odd pain through his chest, right where his heart lived. His brothers were the happiest he'd ever seen them since they'd fallen in love. Marriage had settled them, and contentment rolled off them in waves. And when they were with their wives, love turned their eyes soft.

Nate didn't envy them. They were the only beings in the world he loved, and as their brother-mother-father—and he had been all those things to them—seeing them happy was the one thing that brought him pure joy. But that state of bliss wasn't for him. He'd never allowed himself to dream of a white picket fence, kids, a woman he looked forward to coming home to.

So how did Taylor play into his life?

All he had to do was keep their relationship on steady ground, the same as it had been for the past year. Best friends, but with benefits now added to their friendship. It was doable. Taylor never lied, and she'd said she had no desire for a husband or kids of her own, so he didn't have to worry about her getting stars in her eyes.

Satisfied that his world was as it should be, he drifted off, still inhaling Taylor's lemony scent and still with his hand on her hip.

♠♠♠

The first time in his life that he greeted the morning in a woman's bed, he woke up alone. Nate frowned as he ran his hand over the sheet, finding it cold to the touch. He glanced at the clock and groaned. The sun hadn't been up more than an hour. Because he rarely arrived home before three in the morning, he was not a morning person. Everyone's lunch hour was breakfast time for him. He closed his eyes for a few minutes, then blinked them open, and then scrubbed his hand over them.

With another groan, he rolled out of bed and collected his clothes, taking them into the bathroom with him. As he set them on the counter, he noticed a toothbrush still in its package next to the sink, along with a tube of toothpaste. A black comb was there, too. He smiled. His host was a thoughtful woman.

After a quick shower, he felt much better, the sand in his eyes gone. Except he didn't like putting on yesterday's clothes and should have thought to bring a change. Of course, he didn't know he'd be spending the night when he'd come over. Leaving off his boots for now, he went looking for his best friend, the one he'd shared some damn good benefits with.

At the end of the hallway, he leaned against the wall. She was already dressed for work in her FBI uniform of black pants and a blouse, blue today. That was the color he liked best on her. It made her eyes even bluer. Her back was to him as she stared out the kitchen window, sipping a cup of coffee. What was she thinking? He eased up behind her, his sock-clad feet quiet as he approached.

"Good morning," she said without turning.

He grinned. "Morning, tiger." She was probably the only woman in the world he couldn't sneak up on. He pressed his body against her back and put his hands on the counter, trapping her. Unable to resist, he nuzzled his nose into her hair, breathing in her scent. He loved how she smelled.

Taylor closed her eyes, doing her best not to melt against Nate, but failed. Epically. What red-blooded woman could resist that hot body wrapped around her? Apparently, not her.

She'd had a long talk with herself while staring at the window. Unless a miracle happened, he would never love her back. Oh, he liked her a lot, she was sure. He wanted her. That had been obvious last night. She'd woken up, and as she'd watched him sleeping, she'd wondered if she was wrong to just settle for an affair with him.

Affair. She hated that word. It was going to hurt so badly when he decided it was time to end their relationship. But he was worth the risk, and just maybe . . .

"You always smell so good," he said, still nuzzling her neck.

She turned in his arms, and he didn't give an inch, which put them pelvis to pelvis, chest to breasts, and because he was leaning down, mouth to mouth. And, oh God, he was shirtless, his hair wet and loose. Her dream warrior, the man of her fantasies.

I really, really could get used to having him around, her brain said, as if that would be news to her. When he kissed her, her mind decided it was time to shut up and just enjoy. She loved his lips. They were lush and soft, and, heavens, they were the most talented lips to ever touch hers. He didn't just kiss, he sucked, he nipped, he explored. She put her hands on his chest, splaying her fingers. His heart beat under her right hand, a thump-thump against her palm, pulsing faster the longer they kissed.

I can make his heart pound, she thought, and that was good enough for now. It had to be.

♠♠♠

"Poor Nate," Alex said, peering at her with mischief in his eyes. "Caught him doing the walk of shame this morning. Big brother was trying to sneak back to his condo, but I'm Super Spy. Nothing gets past me."

"Will you stop it?" Taylor said, trying not to laugh. "Besides, how do you know he didn't spend the night in his car, keeping an eye on my apartment?"

The amusement faded from his expression. "Because he had a smile on his face, one I've never seen on him before. The same kind I'd see on my face when looking in the mirror after meeting Madison." He leaned forward, scooting the desk chair closer—Nate's chair—and locked eyes with her. "You're good for him, Taylor. I know my brother, though, and because he doesn't think he deserves to be happy, he'll try to scare you off. Don't let him."

"And what if he's not what I want?"

He gave her a shrewd look. "Isn't he?"

She stirred the whipped cream into the iced mocha coffee she'd bought on the way in. How to answer his question? Honestly, she supposed. What was the point of denying it?

"Yes, but we've both agreed that . . ." She felt her cheeks heating as Alex patiently waited for her to finish. Dang, these Gentry brothers were good at interrogation.

"That we're just friends, is all." Her relationship with Nate was private, between them.

He stared at her a moment, then grinned, and then gave a deep belly laugh.

"Why's that so funny?"

Still grinning, he said, "Because you both are so full of crap." He leaned back in the chair. "Whenever you guys are in the same room together, I want to yell, 'Get a room,' and it's been that way for months. It's more than just the sexual tension between you two. You genuinely like each other. And Taylor, he won't be an easy man to love, but once he's committed, he'll be a hundred percent in."

Because that was the kind of man Nate was. She eyed Alex. "Why are we having this conversation?"

"Simple. I want my brother to be happy, and I think . . . No, I know that he would be happy with you if he'd just get his head out of his ass and see what everyone else does."

"And exactly what does everyone else see?"

He sweetly smiled. "That you two are meant for each other. Also, I want you to know that there's nothing Court and I, along with our wives, would love more than to welcome you into the family. I wanted to be sure you knew you had our blessing."

His declaration warmed her heart, but . . . "Jeez, Alex, don't go and order wedding invitations. We've only just started"—she waved a hand in the air—"you know." There was that mischievous grin again, and she braced herself for whatever was about to come out of his mouth. God, why had she even admitted that much?

"Doing the dirty?" He stood. "About time."

She buried her face in her hands but couldn't stop the laugh bubbling up. "You're impossible," she said through her fingers.

"So Madison tells me."

"What does Madison tell you?"

Taylor dropped her hands back to her desk and gave Rand a shrug. "Ignore him." Rand Stevens was tall, blond, had pretty blue-gray eyes, and was definitely eye-candy status. Why wasn't she interested in him? They'd have beautiful blue-eyed babies. Not that she ever planned to have any babies with anyone. Also, why was he carrying a vase of flowers?

"These are for you," he said, setting the vase on her desk. "Security asked me to bring them up to you."

She froze as she stared at them, dread slithering through her as her stomach threatened to rebel, the coffee she'd drunk turning to acid.

"Taylor?" Alex said, concern in his voice.

"Take them away," she said, then ran to the bathroom with her hand clamped over her mouth. Somehow, she managed to keep the contents in her stomach, but it had taken some deep breaths—her hands pressed hard against her waist and her face over the toilet bowl—before she was sure she wasn't going to be sick. She stumbled to the sink, and as she drenched her face in cold water, a memory skittered around the edges of her mind. One she didn't want to come to light. Ever. What that memory was, she didn't know, but it was there and it was ugly. That she did know.

"Taylor?" Alex softly said, pushing open the door and stepping inside.

She buried her face back into the water. "Can't you read? This is the women's room." Her words were gurgled, as if her mouth was drowning. It was. She was.

"Taylor," Alex said again, putting a hand on her shoulder. "I called Nate. He'll be here in a few minutes."

Yes, Nate. She wanted Nate.

"Can you tell me what just happened? Do you know who the flowers are from?"

No and yes. She grabbed a wad of paper towels, pressing them against her face. She was Special Agent Taylor Collins, highly skilled and trained to kill. She was a Krav Maga black belt. A woman in a man's world, holding her own. It was mortifying that she wanted to lock the door and curl into a corner with a loaded gun in her hand, ready to shoot, all because of a vase of flowers.

"I'm okay," she said. "Just had too much coffee."

"I call bullshit."

She lowered the paper towels, ready to give Alex hell, but the compassion in his eyes was her undoing. Tears rolled down her cheeks, and she didn't know why. That she was crying in front of Alex made her angry. An FBI agent didn't cry, especially a female one. It made her appear weak.

"What's the deal with the flowers?" Alex said. "Are they from a boyfriend?" He frowned. "You don't have one of those, do you?"

"I don't know. I mean, I don't have a mystery boyfriend, but I have no idea why I reacted the way I did." And she really didn't. Only that the sight of the flowers felt like a knife right through her heart. "They're from our killer." That much she did know, but not why she did.

"Shit. No wonder you're upset." He scrubbed a hand through his hair. "We need to check the vase for fingerprints."

She wasn't upset because they were from their bad guy, but she didn't correct his assumption because she couldn't explain—even to herself—why the pink tulips troubled her.

"I doubt his fingerprints are on the vase, but yeah, send them over to the lab. Also, tell Rand to talk to security. How were they delivered, and where did they come from?"

"Taylor?" Nate burst into the bathroom, practically knocking Alex over with the door.

She tossed the paper towels into the trash. "Um, you both do realize this is the ladies' room, right?"

Nate pulled the door back open. "Get lost, Alex."

"Going."

When they were alone, Nate closed the distance between them. "Why are you crying?"

CHAPTER NINETEEN

"I'm not crying."

Nate lifted her chin, peering at her red-rimmed eyes. "You were. Why?" He'd been ten minutes away from their field office when Alex had called, telling him that Taylor had freaked out over some flowers. At first, he'd thought his brother was pulling his chain. Taylor wasn't a woman who would lose it over flowers.

"What happened, Taylor?" he asked when she pulled her face away from his hand, taking a step back. Pink stained her cheeks, and knowing her, she was embarrassed. "Talk to me."

"I don't know, okay? The flowers triggered a reaction, but I don't know why." She crossed her arms over her chest. "Don't you have someplace else to be besides the ladies' room?"

Yeah, he supposed he shouldn't be in here, but he wasn't leaving until he got to the bottom of why a vase of flowers had freaked her out.

"You're upset because they came from our killer?" That much he did know, since he'd read and taken a picture of the card that came with them before they were sent to the lab to check for fingerprints.

But Rand had told him that she hadn't opened the little envelope to see who had sent them.

"No. He's trying to play mind games. He'll have to up the game to impress me."

Nate let out a sigh of exasperation. "Then what? Give me something to work with here." At seeing tears pool in her eyes, he wanted to kick his own ass. He couldn't stand seeing her cry.

"It was the flowers themselves," she said, her lips trembling.

"Okay, that's a start." Because he needed to hold her—whether she needed that or not—he leaned his butt on the counter, and then pulled her between his legs. "How did they make you feel? Angry? Scared?"

"Sad. So damn sad, Nate, but why?"

"I don't know, sweetheart. We'll figure it out. Promise." He held her while she cried, his mind busy sorting through possibilities. A vase of flowers had made her sad enough to cry—a very non-Taylor thing—but she didn't know why, which led him to the conclusion that she had suppressed a memory of something to do with flowers.

"Hey, it's going to be okay," he said after she quieted. Keeping one arm around her, he reached for a paper towel and handed it to her.

"I'm fine, really." After wiping her face, she glanced at the door. "Except that now Alex and Rand are going to fuss over me."

Yeah, she'd hate that. "I won't let them."

"Ha! And who's going to stop you?"

"I'm allowed to fuss over you." He put his finger on her lips when she opened her mouth. "And no arguing about that." The shy smile she gave him sent a strange flutter through his heart, but he quelled it. His heart wasn't allowed to flutter.

"Well, I can't hide in here all day. Let's go see if Alex found out where the flowers came from. I didn't even check to see if there was a card."

"There was." He reluctantly let go of her, and straightened, taking his phone out of his back pocket. "I took a picture before Rand sent them to the lab." After pulling the photo up, he handed her his cell.

"'Such a pretty girl,'" she read aloud. "That's it?"

"Yeah. Does that mean anything to you?"

"Other than it's creepy? No." She handed him back the phone.

He tucked a damp length of hair behind her ear. "I was on my way in to talk to you when Alex called. A psychologist who practices hypnotherapy can see you this afternoon. Dr. Gleason. He'd supposedly one of the best in his field. You still game?"

She chewed on her bottom lip, drawing his attention to her mouth. What he'd like to do was take her home with him and make love to her until the light was back in her eyes.

"Stop looking at me like that." When he raised a brow, she said, "Like you want to eat me up."

He grinned. "Can't deny that. How about this? You keep that appointment, and then we'll go back to my place, where I'll cater to your wishes all night long."

"Now, there's an offer I can't refuse." She trailed a finger down his arm. "Be warned, though. I can be very demanding."

"I sincerely hope so."

♠♠♠

The man sat at the bus stop, sandwiched between a teenaged girl wearing earbuds—her head bopping to the music she was listening to even as her thumbs furiously typed out a text—and a woman and her fussy young boy. He guessed the little brat was around three or four years old, and the man would very much like to have wrapped his hands around the boy's neck until he shut up.

The FBI building was across the street from the bus stop, the people on the bench with him serving as camouflage as he waited for his angel to appear. Would she have his flowers with her, maybe even let him see her touch her nose to them as she smelled them? Would she smile?

Although he wished he could use his camera to take a close-up photo of her when she came out, that would be too obvious. Instead, he had his phone's camera open, ready to capture a picture to add to his collection.

How long would she make him wait to see her? He glanced down the street. The bus was about four blocks away, with one stop to make before it reached his bench. Once the people giving him camouflage got on, he would be sitting here alone, making him too noticeable.

His gaze darted between the approaching bus and the FBI's front door. One block to go now. He would have to fade into the background and wait for new people to come and sit. The building's door swung open, and he jerked his head to the right, exhaling a loud breath when his angel walked out with the man he was going to kill for touching her. He just had to figure out when and how.

The man wore his usual jeans and black T-shirt, and like always, his long hair was in a ponytail. He'd been coming and going out of the fed's building lately, so he must be an FBI agent. But didn't they all wear suits and ties, like the other men who walked in and out that door? Had she possibly hired a bodyguard? Or was he her boyfriend, one who couldn't seem to let her out of his sight?

His questions were forgotten when he realized she wasn't carrying his flowers. Rage colored his vision when the man in the black shirt put his arm around her shoulder, and she leaned her head against him. He brought his camera up, but before he could snap a picture, the bus arrived, its airbrakes making their whooshing sound as it stopped, blocking his view.

By the time the new passengers had boarded and taken their seats and the bus moved on, his angel and the walking dead man had disappeared.

He slammed his phone against the bench, then, after seeing he'd cracked the screen, he did it again and again, until little pieces of glass were scattered over the wood seat.

♠♠♠

"I want him to come in with me," Taylor said after Dr. Gleason introduced himself. "He'll know what questions you need to ask me."

"I'll bring him in once you're in a hypnotic state," Dr. Gleason said. "Until then, he'll be a distraction."

Nate would have insisted on it, but it was better that it was her idea. She'd been nervous on the drive over, worried that it wouldn't work. Or that it would, and that she might learn things better left alone. Nate had briefed the doctor when he'd called, and Dr. Gleason had spent a few minutes explaining to her what would happen, his easy manner seeming to calm her.

After Dr. Gleason took her away, Nate paced the confines of the waiting room. Was this the right thing for her to do? She had no memory of her mother's murder, but according to Rosie, Taylor had witnessed it. What if she couldn't deal with remembering that night? If that happened, he would help her get through it.

"You can come in now," Dr. Gleason said.

Nate glanced at his watch. He'd expected it to take longer than fifteen minutes. He followed the doctor into the room, his gaze going straight to Taylor. She was sitting in a chair, which surprised him. He'd expected to see her reclining on a couch.

"She's in a deep state of trance," Dr. Gleason said. "I've taken her back to the night her mother was killed. Right now, she thinks she's sleeping. You'll also be able to ask her questions."

"Will she remember what we talk about?"

"If I tell her to, she will. I asked if she wanted to remember, and she said that she does." He gestured to a chair a little off to the side of Taylor. "You can sit there."

Dr. Gleason took the seat in front of Taylor. "Taylor, if I say the word *blue*, you will go to sleep again. And if I say *yellow*, you will wake up and tell me what you see. Do you understand?"

"Uh-huh. Blue sleep, yellow talk."

Nate had researched hypnosis after Taylor had agreed to it and had read that hypnosis subjects sometimes reverted to the age in question, but he was not prepared for the change in her voice. It was disconcerting.

"Yellow, Taylor. I'm waking you up so I can ask you some questions. I have a friend here, too. His name is Nate, and he's a very nice man. He's also going to ask you some questions."

"Is he one of my mommy's friends?"

"No, he's my friend. If he asks you something, you can answer."

"Okay," Taylor said in her little-girl voice.

At hearing Taylor's question about her mother's friends, Nate wondered how much she'd understood at that age about her mother's life.

"What woke you up that night, Taylor?" Dr. Gleason asked.

"Yelling. My mommy was yelling. She never does that."

"What did she say?"

"She said, 'Get out.' I think the man is hurting Mommy."

Nate moved his chair a few inches closer. "Ask her if she knows him."

"Do you know the man, Taylor?"

"No, but Mommy has lots of men friends."

"Ask for a description," Nate said.

Dr. Gleason nodded. "What does he look like?"

"He's mad."

Nate wanted to growl in frustration. "We need a description."

Dr. Gleason shook his head. "She'll get to that in her own time." He turned his attention back to Taylor. "Taylor, why was he mad?"

"He gave my mommy pink tulips. She loves pink tulips, but she doesn't want them. She threw them at him. He didn't like that."

Damn. The pink tulips *had* been a real trigger for Taylor. Nate barely resisted dragging her onto his lap and putting a stop to this.

"What did he do when he got mad?" Dr. Gleason asked.

Taylor started rocking. "He's hurting Mommy." She rocked harder. "Make him stop."

Dr. Gleason glanced at Nate before saying, "What is he doing to your mother, Taylor?"

"He's choking her." Tears streamed down her cheeks. "You're hurting my mommy," she screamed.

"Blue. Taylor, blue." Dr. Gleason sat back in his chair, his gaze on Nate once Taylor stopped rocking. "I don't see any reason to let her see her mother die, so I'm going to skip ahead."

"Agreed," Nate said, swallowing hard against the bile in his throat. Although Rosie had said that Taylor had witnessed the murder, hearing it in her little-girl voice was chilling. "I'd like to put a stop to this. If we can get a name or a description from her, that's all we need."

Dr. Gleason nodded. "Yellow, Taylor. Where are you?"

"In the bed. I'm scared."

"Can I talk to her?" Nate quietly said.

"Taylor, remember I told you my friend Nate wanted to talk to you?"

"Uh-huh. You said he was nice."

"He is. He wants to ask you some questions."

"Okay."

"Hello, Taylor. This is Nate."

"I like your voice."

"Thank you." Nate wondered if her subconscious recognized his voice. He hoped so, and that it made her feel safe. "You're in your bed. Are you by yourself?"

"He's coming," she whispered.

Nate hesitated, the urge to stop this almost overwhelming.

"Can you make him go away, Nate?"

"Sweetheart, listen to me. I won't let him hurt you, I promise. But I need you to tell me what he looks like. Can you do that?"

"Can he hear me talk?"

"No, Taylor," Dr. Gleason said. "Only Nate and I can hear you."

"Okay. He has glasses. You know, like wire ones."

"That's good, Taylor. This is Nate again. Can you see what color his eyes or hair are?"

"His hair is yellow."

Was yellow how a six-year-old would describe blond? "What about his eyes? What color are they?"

"Brown. He's sitting on the bed, Nate. I don't want him to look at me."

"Is he talking to you, sweetheart?"

"He said . . . He said that I'm such a pretty girl."

Christ. Nate took a deep breath, willing the rage away. He could be angry later, but right now wasn't the time for it. "Remember that I won't let him hurt you, Taylor." At least he could promise her that much. "What's he doing now?

"He's rubbing my neck with his fingers. He said I shouldn't cry for my mommy. That she's now an angel in heaven. He said he saved her and he'll save me." She started crying. "I want my mommy."

"Let's stop this," Nate said, unable to handle listening to her cry. "Can you make her remember without feeling like she's living through it again?"

"I'll plant the suggestion, but I can't guarantee exactly how she'll remember the event."

"Just bring her out of it."

"Rosie!" Taylor yelled.

"Do it now," Nate said, knowing what was coming. He'd learned all Taylor knew, and now Rosie had arrived with her bat in hand. The next time he saw the tiny woman, he was going to give her a crushing hug for saving Taylor.

"Blue, Taylor," Dr. Gleason said. She immediately stopped crying. "You will listen to me now. When I wake you up, you will remember everything, but you will be at peace knowing your mother is in a better place. Do you understand?"

"Yes."

"Tell me what you understand."

"That Mommy's in a better place, and I'm at peace."

"Very good. Now, I'm going to slowly count to ten. With each number, you will feel yourself growing older as you gently begin to wake up. With each number, you will feel more at peace. When I get to ten, you will open your eyes, and you will remember that you are at peace because your mother is in a better place. Do you understand, Taylor?"

"Yes."

"Very good. One. You are starting to gently awake. Two. You are beginning to feel the energy returning to your body. Three . . ."

Nate kept his gaze on Taylor as Dr. Gleason brought her out of her trance. He didn't understand how any of this worked, but he hoped that the suggestion to be at peace took hold. They hadn't gotten a name, but at least they had a partial description to work with.

"Ten," Dr. Gleason said. "Wake up, Taylor, and open your eyes."

Nate put his hand on her arm. "Are you okay?"

She blinked, her eyes focusing on him. "I remember everything, but I'm . . ." She paused, her gaze going distant, as if taking a mental inventory. After a few seconds, she nodded, giving him a small smile. "I'm fine. Really."

Nate let out a sigh of relief. He'd been afraid that she'd wake up and be sad or distressed. "I know it was hard to go back to that night, but you did good."

"I can describe him."

"Excellent. I'll make arrangements for you to sit down with the police department's sketch artist—tomorrow, if she's available."

"Yeah, the sooner the better." Taylor nodded at Dr. Gleason. "Thank you. It's always bothered me that I couldn't remember that night. Even though it was the worst night of my life, I do feel at peace now in a way I haven't before."

The doctor smiled. "I'm glad for that, Taylor. If you have any problem dealing with what you've learned, call me and we'll work through it."

"Thanks, I will."

Nate shook hands with the man. "You have my appreciation, too."

Once they were in the car, he said, "Are you really okay?"

"I think I really am."

"Are you hungry? We can stop somewhere for an early dinner." He wasn't sure, but he thought he might be more upset by her session than she was.

"You know what I really need?"

"What's that?"

She put her hand on his thigh, circling her index finger over his jeans. "You. Inside me."

Nate almost ran off the road.

CHAPTER TWENTY

Taylor hadn't taken two steps inside Nate's condo when he had her up against the wall, his body pressed hard on hers.

"Is this what you want?" he said, staring down at her.

"Yes, but I don't want to think. About anything." She brushed her thumb over his bottom lip. "Tonight, I'm at your mercy. I want it down and dirty, hot and hard."

"Mother of God, woman, you're killing me."

His mouth took hers in a crushing kiss. It was impossible to think when he was devouring her as if she were the air he needed to breathe. A kiss so demanding that there wasn't room in her mind for anything else but him and his mouth. He put his hand on her neck, splaying his fingers, holding her in place. His other hand drifted down to her hip, and he splayed his fingers there, too. All too soon, he stepped back, leaving her gasping for air.

"Take off your jacket, Taylor."

She slipped it over her shoulders, letting it fall to the floor.

His gaze went to her shoulder holster. "I never did get to see you wearing your gun on your thigh. That's on my bucket list." He unstrapped the holster, then set it on the kitchen counter. Facing her again, he said, "Blouse next."

That rough voice, full of command, sent heat spiraling through her. She reached for the top button, her gaze locked on his. His eyes followed her progress as she made her way down her top. With each button undone, his eyes grew darker, smokier.

"Drop it."

She let the blouse slide to the floor.

"Pants next."

There was something about undressing to his orders while he stayed fully clothed that she found surprisingly erotic. Surprising because she was a woman who liked to be in control, so turning that over to a man shouldn't excite her. Maybe it was only because it was Nate giving those orders. And because of the heat simmering in his eyes. Or the way his hands flexed at his sides, as if he were dying to touch her.

She toed off her shoes before stepping out of her pants. There was a moment when she wished she had on a pretty dress and sexy shoes instead of what Nate had always called her FBI uniform. But by the way he was looking at her—as if he were about to eat her alive—it didn't appear her clothes were a problem for him.

"Damn, tiger. You in those pink panties and bra is my new wet dream." His gaze roamed over her body, then he lifted his eyes to hers. "Turn around and put your hands on the wall."

"Blush," she said. "The color is blush, not pink." Every nerve ending in her body hummed with need as she obeyed. How had he brought her to this state with nothing more than a few commands and scorching looks? When her palms were flattened on the wall, she glanced over her shoulder, waiting for his next command.

He stepped up behind her and put his hands over hers, trapping her to the wall. "Blush. Pink. Doesn't matter the color. It's you in them. Do you even have an inkling of how hot you are?" he rumbled into her ear. He stroked his finger over hers. "When I tell you to come for me, you're going to obey."

She whimpered when he pressed hard against her back, the pressure of his erection and the friction of the material of his jeans rubbing over her skin, sending desire spiraling through her.

He scraped his teeth over her bare shoulder, and when she trembled, he said, "You like that?"

"Yes."

"Keep your hands on the wall." He slid his palms down her arms, raising goosebumps as his hands moved over her, finally reaching her breasts. He cupped them, one in each hand. When he slid his thumbs inside her bra, teasing her nipples, she moaned.

"Please, Nate."

"Hush. Don't think. Don't talk. Just feel."

White-hot pleasure was what she was feeling. Noises she'd never made before sounded in her ears when his fingers found their way down to her core, tangling in her curls. Already on the edge, she jerked when he stroked a finger inside her.

He stilled. "I didn't say you could come yet."

At another deep stroke, she bit down on her bottom lip.

"Beg me to let you come, Taylor," he whispered into her ear.

"You said not to talk."

He chuckled. "Can't help rebelling, can you? You have my permission to beg."

"I never beg." He was going to make her eat her words, but she didn't care.

"We'll see."

When his thumb circled her clit while his finger was stroking inside her, her knees buckled. He slipped his other arm around her waist, pulling her back against him. As soon as he realized she was on the edge again, he stilled.

"Nate," she said. She hissed out a breath when he rocked his groin, rubbing the hard length of him over her bottom.

"Here's tonight's agenda. As soon as you ask, I'm going to let you come. Then we're going to take a shower together, where I might make you come again, and then you're going to be the first woman to christen my bed."

Shocked, she glanced back at him.

"I don't bring women to my home. Just wanted you to know that."

Then where did he take them? To a hotel? She squeezed her eyes shut, pushing away the wayward thoughts his words had put in her head. He was with her right now, and that was all that mattered.

"You're thinking," he growled into her ear. "Wouldn't you rather come?"

"Yes. God, yes." She pressed her forehead to the wall. "Damn you. That was me begging."

"Good girl."

It didn't take more than a few minutes for his fingers to work their magic before she shattered so hard that she was digging her fingernails into his wall in an effort to stay upright.

"I have you," he said.

She sank into his arms, her back to his chest. "I've never done anything like that before. It was amazing."

He brought his hands to her face, cupping her cheeks. "There's more amazing to come." The moment his lips touched hers, his phone buzzed. "Damn," he said.

She sighed, knowing he would have to answer it.

"Rothmire," he said after pulling his cell out of his back pocket and glancing at it.

That wasn't good. Their boss never called after hours unless there was an urgent situation. While Nate talked to him, she gathered her clothes.

"I'll pick up Taylor, and we'll head over there," Nate said, glancing at her. "I'll call you after we talk to her."

He'd done that—pretended she wasn't with him—the last time Rothmire had called. Even though she knew that he protected those he cared about, she told herself that his guarding her reputation didn't mean she was special to him. It would be dangerous to her heart to start believing he thought of her as more than a friend and bed partner, especially because she happened to know that he had his pick of lovers.

You couldn't be best friends with a man for over a year and not know those kinds of things about him. Because seriously, he was hot, he owned a biker bar, and there were barely clad women throwing themselves at him on a nightly basis. What man could refuse that kind of smorgasbord? She forced an answering smile as she slipped on her pants, then her blouse.

"Let me," Nate said, brushing her hands away from the buttons on her shirt. He trailed a finger down the valley of her breasts to her bra, giving a little tug. "You do realize you owe me big time, right?"

"Duly noted." Because she was determined to keep secret that she loved him, and that as far as he knew, all she wanted from him was his body, she pressed her palm over the bulge in his jeans. "I'm surprised you can even walk."

He snorted. "Barely. Now stop touching me, or we'll never get out of here."

"Where are we going?"

"To the hospital. Our man attacked another prostitute tonight, but she managed to get away."

"That's not good. He's not taking any time off." But at least he hadn't killed this one. That was a win.

"Yeah, but maybe we got lucky with this one and can get a good description."

"Let's hope so."

♠♠♠

Nate glanced at Taylor. She'd gone quiet on him, spending the first ten minutes of their drive staring out the window. "We'll get him."

She shrugged. "We will."

"I know this case upsets you, and I understand why."

"It does, but that's not what I'm thinking about right now."

"And?" he said when she went quiet again.

"Before we slipped into friends with benefits, I felt like I could talk to you about anything."

"Now you can't?"

"I don't know." She shifted in her seat to face him. "I want to think I can."

His internal warning system dinged. He wasn't sure where she was going with this, but he had a feeling he wasn't going to like it. "You can still talk to me about anything," he said, mostly meaning it.

"Okay." She sucked her bottom lip into her mouth.

"Taylor, just spit it out." *And stop sucking on your lip.*

"Yeah, okay. I don't want you to think I'm trying to put a claim on you or anything like that."

Ding. Ding. Ding. Warning! "But?"

"Because I'm not. I spoke true when I told you I'm not husband hunting. It's just that, while we have this thing going on between us, I don't want to think about you in some other woman's bed. If that's a problem, then we should end it right now."

His first reaction was that by demanding an exclusive, she was putting a claim on him. Friends with benefits were free to pursue other interests. Wasn't that the way it worked? But when was the last time he'd even been interested in another woman? Months. And no way in hell was he ready to call a halt to whatever this thing between them was.

Truthfully, she already had an exclusive from him, it just hadn't been acknowledged. But if he did verbally agree, then he was entering unchartered territory. He'd rarely seen the same woman twice for no other reason than to avoid entanglements. Hang around too long, and women developed expectations. Not that he blamed them, but if they thought he'd ever put a ring on their finger, they were barking up the wrong tree. Any woman who thought he could make her happy was just wrong. He didn't have it in him.

"I see," Taylor said, then turned her attention back to the passing scenery.

No, she didn't see. An internal debate raged. *Tell her she's better off without you.* The words wouldn't come, though, because a stray thought that came out of nowhere said, *Maybe for her, you might have it in you.*

"No, you don't see," he said. "I've never done exclusive before, but I'm willing to give it a go." Wrong thing to say. He knew it as soon as the words left his mouth, and Taylor's frown confirmed it. How did they get from what had happened between them in his foyer to this?

She turned her face toward his. "Seriously, Nate? Give it a go? What kind of bullshit is that? That gives you an out card. All you have to do is come to me and say, 'I gave it a go, but then I screwed some other woman last night.' Well, that doesn't work for me."

"Is this a lovers' quarrel? I've never had one before, so just checking." Yeah, he was digging the hole deeper, but avoiding relationships was ingrained in him. Why couldn't she enjoy the ride for as long as it lasted without putting a name to it? He had no intention of seeing other women at the moment. Truthfully, he couldn't imagine being with anyone but her for a long time. So why hadn't he said all that instead of what he had?

"You're an ass."

An undeniable fact. "We're here." He shut off the engine. "We'll talk about all this when we get back to my place." Maybe he could get his act together by then.

She got out without answering.

"You really are an ass, Gentry," he muttered, then followed her into the hospital.

"Did Rothmire tell you what room?" Taylor said after stabbing her finger on the elevator button.

"Two thirty-one. The boss talked to her doctor. They're only going to keep her overnight. She got lucky." He put his hand on her arm. "Taylor—"

She pulled away. "Not now. We have a job to do."

Fine. But they were going to talk later, even if he had to handcuff her to a chair so she'd listen. The short ride in the elevator was done in silence.

They both showed their badges to the cop at the entrance to the woman's room. "Her name is Delaney Gains," he said as they entered, having gotten that information from Rothmire. Taylor nodded, and when she walked up to the bed, Nate took a position next to the wall.

He studied the blonde-haired woman in the hospital bed. She was asleep, but he didn't doubt she had blue eyes. There were bruises on her neck but no other visible injuries, unless the blanket covering her hid them.

"Delaney," Taylor said, putting her hand on the woman's arm. "I need you to wake up, hon." She brushed the woman's hair away from her face. "Delaney. Wake up, okay?"

Nate's phone buzzed, and at seeing Court's name on the screen, he stepped out of the room. "Yeah?"

"Where are you?"

"At the hospital. Our man struck again tonight, but the woman managed to get away. Taylor's interviewing her now."

"Glad to hear she escaped. I might have something. Stop by my place when you get back."

"Should be in about an hour. I'll bring Taylor with me."

"Great. See you then."

Nate eyed the door to the woman's room. If he walked back in now, he would interrupt the flow of Taylor's interview. She had a knack for remembering conversations word for word, so he decided to wait in the hallway. The cop studied him with interest when Nate leaned back on the wall. Keeping his expression blank, he closed his eyes, hoping he wasn't about to get grilled on how to become an FBI agent.

While he waited for Taylor to finish, the image of her pressed against his wall, wearing nothing but a lacy pink bra and matching bikini panties filled his mind. It was true what he'd told her. Every time he passed that spot, he would visualize her there, her quiet little sighs and moans, her fingers digging into the wall as he pleasured her. Arousal stirred just thinking about it. To get his mind off an almost-naked Taylor before he embarrassed himself, he ran through their conversation in the car.

What had brought that on? Why was she even thinking of him with other women? He'd never been a touchy-feely man, but with Taylor, anytime he was near her, he wanted to touch her. Whether it was a hand on her back when they walked, tucking hair behind her ear, or his fingers on her arm, the contact pleased him. He had no problem with exclusive, he just didn't want to say it. Putting it out there took them to relationship status.

If he were smart, he'd back away before things between them got messy—or messier—but he didn't want to. Apparently, he was a selfish bastard. She'd said she wasn't looking for anything permanent, so maybe he was making too much of this. They just needed to talk and make sure they were on the same page.

That shouldn't be too difficult.

CHAPTER TWENTY-ONE

Taylor paused at the hospital-room door. Nate was braced against the wall, his eyes closed. Her mouth went dry. He was so beautiful that looking at him was sometimes painful because he would never belong to her.

His eyes opened, his gaze landing on her. Awareness simmered through her blood as he focused on her. She could almost feel his fingers on her, his rough voice commanding her to come. Desire pulsed low in her stomach. She glanced over to see the cop watching her with appreciation in his eyes.

"Let's go," Nate said, pushing away from the wall while giving the cop a hard stare. He put his hand on her lower back as they walked toward the elevator.

She forced herself not to lean into the warmth of his palm. She was still unsettled by their conversation in the car and needed time to think. Although she hadn't intended to start a conversation about exclusivity, it had been his comment that was playing havoc with her mind. *I don't bring women to my home* hadn't been a past-tense statement.

At the elevator, he pushed the button, but his eyes stayed on her. "Taylor—"

The door opened, and she stepped inside. To give herself something to do, she took out her phone to check her text messages. There was one from each of the girls, even a snowman emoji from Annie. Taylor smiled, thinking of how much Annie loved pointing at emojis, then giggling when Rosie would make them appear in a text message.

God, she missed her girls. But they were having a blast at the beach, so she was happy for them. Also, they all apparently had crushes on the two K2 guys, since in their nightly phone conversations, it was *Saint this* and *Doc that.* According to Rosie, Annie was now adamant that Doc put her to bed every night.

"The way you're smiling, I'm guessing those are messages from the girls?" Nate said.

"Yeah. They said to tell you hi." She glanced at him. The way his eyes grew soft at hearing that did funny things to her heart. It still sometimes surprised her at how good he was with the girls. It had taken a few visits for the older ones to feel safe around him, but he'd understood that and had let them come to him when they were ready. For Annie, though, it had been love at first sight.

"Tell them I miss them," he said as they reached his car.

"I will when I talk to them tomorrow. They'll love hearing that." He opened the passenger door, but before she could get into the car, he put his hand on the roof, blocking her. Her gaze landed on his arm, on the flex of his muscles under tanned skin. What was it about his forearm that made her want to lick it?

"Listen." He glanced across the roof of the car, then focused back on her. "I'm sorry. What I said, it didn't come out right."

She wondered if he'd ever said "I'm sorry" to a woman before. She doubted it and appreciated that he was saying it now. But . . . and there was a but, a very big one. It was the bare arm she wanted to put her mouth on. She didn't want another woman to touch it. Ever. Nate Gentry didn't do relationships. He'd been up front about that, and she didn't see him changing his mind. She'd thought she could do the friends-with-benefits thing with him, but she'd been wrong. There were a lot of things she could accommodate where he was concerned, but sharing him was not one of them.

"We never should have let this thing between us get out of hand."

He frowned. "Exactly what are you saying?"

"That I want to go back to just being friends." *Tell me that doesn't work for you. Tell me you want me in your life as more than a friend. Tell me you can't bear the thought of me with another man. Tell me I'm the only woman in your life.*

His expression blanked. "Sure. Whatever you want." He removed his arm. "Get in. Court's waiting for us. Said he found something."

Willing her tears away, she slid onto the seat, watching him as he walked around the hood of the car. As much as she'd loved every intimate moment with him, it had been a mistake. She would have been better off not knowing what she was missing. But she'd known putting the brakes on was the right thing to do as soon as he'd said "sure" without hesitating. If he'd given the slightest argument, she probably would have given in, so she was glad he hadn't. Even though it was for the best, it hurt like hell.

"What did Delaney Gains have to say?" he asked as he backed out of the parking space.

They were going to be all business, then. If that was the way he wanted it, so be it. "If we're headed to Court's, I'll tell you both at the same time."

He didn't respond, and the ride back to his condo was made in silence. That hurt, too, because not only had she lost Nate as a lover, she didn't see how they could go back in time to when he was simply her best friend. She was highly trained, knew how to rein in her emotions.

When she got home tonight, she'd have a good cry, and then she'd put Nate Gentry into coworker status, where he should have stayed in the first place.

Back at the condo building where the brothers lived, she followed Nate into Court's home. When they walked in, Alex turned off the TV, tossing aside the remote.

"Court's waiting for us in his computer room. Hi, Taylor." He grinned, giving her a wink.

She smiled, something she often did when Alex was around. "Hey. How's Alex today?" Of the three brothers, she thought of Alex as being the least tortured by their childhood. From what Nate had told her, he and Court had protected their baby brother as best they could. Alex was fun to be around. She wished he could rub some of his bubbly off on his oldest brother.

"He's just peachy." His grin grew wider. "I stole that word from Madison."

Nate grunted, then headed down the hallway without giving her an invitation to follow.

"Who poked the bear?" Alex said, frowning at the retreating back of his brother.

"I did."

"Good for you. Someone needed to." He walked over and slung an arm around her. "He's a stubborn one. Don't give up on him."

"I don't have a clue what you're talking about, Alex. Where are Madison and Lauren?"

Alex lifted his gaze to the ceiling. "Pretty sure she does have a clue." He turned eyes so much like Nate's on her. "Give him a hard time, Taylor. Madison did that, and it brought me to my knees. I found, much to my surprise, that I liked that position where she was concerned." He stilled. "That didn't sound right, did it?"

She rolled her eyes. "You Gentry boys have a knack for saying things you later decide doesn't sound right."

"Uh-oh," he said, chuckling. "Want to share?"

"Nope. Where's Court?"

"He's in his James Bond room. Come with me."

He put his hand at her back, giving her a slight push. His palm on her spine didn't have the same effect as when Nate did that.

"To answer your second question, Madison and Lauren are sitting on the balcony, having a predinner glass of wine. As soon as we're done, we're heading to the bar. The girls ordered a pizza and want you to join them."

"Sure. That would be nice."

"Great." She followed him into the room, coming to a stop at seeing a wall full of weapons. "Good heavens." She turned in a circle, taking in the banks of monitors, the shelves filled with bottled water and other supplies. "Is this your doomsday room?" she asked Court.

He spun his chair around. "It's a safe room. We each have one."

"Not fair. I want one, too." She'd been in Nate's condo numerous times, but he'd never shown her his room.

"I'm sure Nate will let you borrow his anytime you want," Alex said.

She glanced at Nate, who was shooting daggers at his younger brother. He shifted his gaze to her. "Before we hear what Court has to say, fill us in on your interview with Delaney Gains."

"Sure." It was time to get down to business. She put her aching heart and all thoughts of Nate in a box and closed the lid. "One big difference between Delaney and the others is that she has bruises all over her body, not just her neck. The other women only have strangle marks. You'll understand why in a minute. So, our unsub first approached her a week ago. He asked what she charged, and when she told him, he offered her triple that if she'd stay the night with him. She took him to the Corner Motel, her usual place to book a room."

"I've seen that place," Alex said. "It's pretty nasty."

Court nodded. "And, unfortunately, not the kind of place that will have security cameras."

"The girls would avoid any motel with cameras," she said. "Anyway, when they got to the room, he told her to keep her clothes on. All he wanted was to talk. At first, she thought he was a cop and it was a sting. He finally convinced her that he wasn't the police, so she decided getting paid triple and not having to"—she made air quotes—"'fuck' to earn it was a nice change."

"What did he want to talk about?" Court asked.

"Saving her." That got their attention. "He told her that what she was doing was a sin and that he could take her away from her miserable life. At some point, she fell asleep while he was talking. When she woke up, he was gone. Two nights later, he showed up on her corner again, offering her the same deal. She decided he was a harmless kook, and since she liked the extra money for doing nothing, she took him back to the motel. The same thing happened. She said, 'He talked the same shit,' and she fell asleep again. He was gone when she woke up."

"He's definitely our man," Alex said.

Nate hadn't said a word since she'd started recapping her conversation with Delaney. Her eyes kept straying to him even though she didn't want them to. He was perched on the edge of Court's desk, his expression still unreadable. She'd give anything to know what he was thinking.

Nate didn't know what to do with the ache in his chest that had taken up residence when Taylor had told him she wanted to go back to just being friends. He'd never felt anything like this before because of a woman. Friends *only* was for the best, so why did he want to throw her over his shoulder, take her to his bedroom, and make love to her until she admitted they were more than friends?

What was wrong with him? He didn't make love. He fucked. *Admit it, dude. It's not like that with her. She means more to you than wham, bam, thank you, ma'am.* So what if she did? It didn't change anything. He'd still never marry, so he had nothing to offer.

"This afternoon, he showed up with a shopping bag in his hand."

Nate tuned back in to what Taylor was saying.

"He made the same offer, along with telling her that he'd brought her a present. When they got to the room, he took a white dress out of the bag, saying, 'Marry me, Delaney, and I'll take you away from this life. You're going to be a beautiful angel.' Delaney didn't like the way his eyes glowed. 'His eyes were wild, like some of those crazy preachers I watch on TV,' she said. So she told him that she wasn't putting on the dress, and then she tried to leave. He grabbed her, and they fought. She was smart enough to knee him where it would hurt the most. When he doubled over in pain, she was able to get away. She ran to the office, and the night clerk called the police."

"Maybe that answers why she has bruises and the others didn't," Nate said. "If they agreed to put on the dress before he killed them without fighting him."

Taylor turned to him, but instead of meeting his eyes, her gaze was on his left shoulder. "Or he could have put the dresses on the others after he killed them."

What? She couldn't even look at him now? He wanted to turn the clock back to when they were best friends without this awkwardness between them, while at the same time, he wanted to drag her onto his lap and not stop kissing her until those blue eyes saw nothing but him.

Damn her. He was off his game because of her. And if Alex didn't stop smirking, as if he knew a woman had brought his big brother to his knees, Nate was going to assign Alex dishwashing duties at Aces & Eights for the next month. Because that was how he felt—cut off at the knees by a woman half his weight with twice his brains who was his equal on the mat. A woman he wanted to handcuff to his bed and never let go.

Suddenly angry with her for making his chest hurt, he said, "You should have told me all this at the hospital so I could call Rothmire, have the scene preserved."

Icy blue eyes finally met his. "I called him as soon as Delaney told me about the hotel. He already knew where she'd been found, the cops preserved the room, and our crime scene techs are there now."

And he felt like an idiot. Of course she was on top of things. She always was. "Good. Anything else?"

"Yes. He said, 'My angels are making me angry today,' and then he tried to choke her."

"What does that mean?"

"I don't know, Nate. When I find him, I'll be sure and ask."

Alex tapped Court on the shoulder. "You feeling the chill in here, too?"

Nate scowled. His baby brother had a habit of poking his nose into things that weren't any of his business.

"Stop glaring at me," Alex said. "That was just a general observation."

"Shut up, Alex." He wondered if Court had any duct tape in his doomsday supplies that he could use to slap over his baby brother's mouth.

Court laughed. "You're asking the impossible from him." He glanced at Taylor. "Did he tell her his name?"

"Oh, right. Forgot to mention that. He told her she could call him Gabriel. She doesn't believe that was his real name, though."

"You think his reference is to the angel Gabriel?" Court said.

She shrugged. "Could be. Any of you know what his role as an angel was?"

"Let's look him up." Court swiveled his chair around and in seconds had a page on the archangel Gabriel up on the monitor.

Nate leaned over Court's shoulder, reading the screen. "'Archangel of resurrection, mercy, revelation, and death.'" He blew out a breath. "I hate these nut jobs."

When he straightened, he accidently brushed against Taylor's arm, his skin rippling where they touched. She jerked away as if he'd burned her. He put his back to the wall, crossed his arms over his chest, and scowled. She was making him crazy.

Which was why it took longer than it should have to remember the angel she'd found near her car. "Hell." At his outburst, all eyes turned to him, but his focused on Taylor. "What'd you do with that plastic angel?"

"You don't think . . ." She trailed off, her face losing its color.

"After hearing what Delaney said, I think it's entirely possible he left that for you."

"I put it in the lost-and-found box."

"Is it still there?"

"I have no idea."

He pulled his phone out and called Rand. "Are you headed this way?" At getting an affirmative, Nate instructed him to stop by the office at Taylor's apartment building and check the lost-and-found box for a small plastic angel.

Court eyed him for a moment, and then said, "While we're waiting to hear back from him, I might have something. Not sure. A few years ago, someone from the police department of Glade, a town near the Everglades, entered an unsolved murder in a Florida cold-case database, although the case isn't so much unsolved as the suspect was never arrested."

He lifted a few sheets of paper. "You can read the report, but I'll give you a quick summary. Thirty-one years ago, Gretchen Tompkins and her eleven-year-old son, Wayne, lived in Glade. Back then, the town had two cops, Bert Archer and Doug Emmitt. Gretchen was a prostitute who caught the eye of Doug Emmitt. He asked her to marry him. The wedding never happened because she was strangled on her wedding day."

"What makes you think this might be related?" Nate asked.

"Ah, good question. Because she was wearing a white dress and had a gold band on her finger even though the wedding hadn't taken place yet."

Nate glanced at Taylor. "Are you feeling the buzz?" It was a question they asked each other when instinct said they were on to something.

"Oh, yeah."

Well, at least she was still talking to him, even if she didn't want him touching her. And that thought put the scowl right back on his face.

She grabbed the pages Court was holding. "Who was their suspect? Doug Emmitt?"

Court nodded. "The one and only. He disappeared the same day, never to be seen again. Her son witnessed the murder. Said it was Emmitt."

"So this ex-cop is going around all these years later killing prostitutes?" Alex said.

Taylor grabbed on to Alex's arm. "Or the son. How old would he be now?" She scanned the report. "Forty-two. That fits with what Pauline's told us."

Nate narrowed his eyes at the hand she had on Alex, wanting to yank it away. "We need to find out the whole story. Why did he kill her? What happened to the boy?"

"Bert Archer's retired now, living in the same house that he did when he was a cop," Court said.

"That makes it easy." Nate nodded at Alex. "Tomorrow, take a ride over to Glade and interview him. Take Josh with you."

Alex nodded. "I'll call him when we finish and let him know."

When Nate's phone buzzed, he answered, saying, "Was it there?"

"No," Rand said. "I tracked down the apartment's manager, and he didn't see a plastic angel in the box or who might have taken it."

"Okay, head this way. We're leaving for the bar soon, but the girls are having a pizza party." It was Rand's night to keep watch over Taylor.

"Be there in ten."

"The angel's not there," Nate said when he hung up.

"Maybe someone did drop it and reclaimed it," Taylor said.

"Possible." He didn't believe in coincidences, though.

Alex stretched, then stood. “If we’re done here, I’ll head on over to Aces and Eights. Taylor’s going to hang with the girls tonight. They’re going to eat pizza, drink wine, and talk about us.” He winked at Taylor.

“I’ll head over with you,” Court said.

“I’ll be there soon.” After his brothers left, Nate tried to think of something to say that would fix things between him and Taylor. He had nothing.

Taylor held up the report Court had given her. “I meant to ask Court if I could keep this.”

“Sure. He’ll have extra copies. Since you don’t have your car here, Rand will be waiting downstairs when you’re ready to go home. He’s got the watch tonight.”

“Okay.” She edged toward the door. “Guess I’ll see you tomorrow.”

Nate put his hand on her shoulder, stopping her. “We need to talk. If not tonight, then have lunch with me tomorrow.”

“I don’t think that’s a good idea. Text me when I’m supposed to meet with the sketch artist.”

“Dammit, Taylor, I said I was sorry.”

“Apology accepted. Good night.”

He wanted to tackle her, keep her from leaving before he had his say, but he let her go. She’d turned into an ice queen, and he hated the frost coming off her. Why couldn’t she understand that he hadn’t meant what he’d said the way it had sounded? He kicked Court’s chair back under the desk.

He clenched his jaw. *This isn’t over, tiger.*

CHAPTER TWENTY-TWO

The minute Taylor settled into a lounge chair, joining Lauren and Madison on the balcony, a black cat jumped onto her lap. "Well, hello. Who are you?"

"That's Hemingway," Madison said. "He spends his day mostly sleeping in our bookstore window, then comes home with us at the end of the day."

"He alternates nights with us." Lauren reached over to rub the cat behind his ears. "Tonight's my night to have him."

Madison filled a glass with wine and handed it to Taylor. "It's so weird. He actually knows his routine. If it's his night with me, he follows me off the elevator when we reach the eighth floor. When it's Lauren's turn to have him, he waits for the door to open on the ninth floor."

"You're a very smart kitty," Taylor said, rubbing him behind the ears the way Lauren had, getting a loud purr from the cat. She'd love to have a cat, but couldn't bear to leave an animal alone as much as she'd have to. Hemingway made three circles, then curled up on her lap.

After the pizza arrived, they chatted about mundane things while they ate and drank wine. Getting approval from his owners, Taylor shared a little of her cheese with Hemingway. When their glasses were empty, Madison filled them all up again.

Taylor was the most relaxed she'd been in days, and she hoped she'd occasionally be invited over for more nights with Madison and Lauren. A nice breeze blew off the ocean, and as she listened to the sound of the waves hitting shore on the beach, her thoughts returned to Nate.

"At what point in a relationship does a woman have the right to ask for an exclusive?" Taylor said. Two pairs of wide eyes focused on her, causing her to giggle. She never giggled, but obviously three glasses of wine put a lie to that. "Just asking for a friend."

"Uh-huh," Madison said, then seemed to find that funny, laughing so hard that wine sloshed onto her hand.

Lauren took her glass away from her. "This friend, is she in love with him?"

"No!" Okay, more like she wished she wasn't. She made a mental note to limit herself to two glasses of wine in the future, since it appeared that she was willing to spill state secrets when she was buzzy.

"But I want her to be in love with him," Madison whined.

Taylor crossed her arms over her chest. "Well, she's not."

"I think she protests too much." Madison tugged on Lauren's sleeve. "Right?"

"And I think you're cut off." Lauren grinned at Taylor over Madison's slumping head. "Wine puts her to sleep. She'll be snoring in about two minutes."

"Don't snore," Madison mumbled, then her body slid down, her head landing in Lauren's lap.

"And she's out for the count." Lauren brushed the hair out of Madison's face. "To answer your question, I don't think there's anything wrong with your friend broaching the subject with the man she's seeing. If a certain Gentry brother happened to be the man in question, I'm pretty sure he's not dating anyone but your friend."

"Um, my friend did broach the subject of being exclusive with him while they were together . . . and I'm not saying it was one of the Gentry brothers. Anyway, he said, 'I'll give it a go.'" She really needed to shut her mouth, and she *really* shouldn't be telling this to the wife of one of Nate's brothers. But she'd never had girlfriends, women she could talk to who would understand. The wine had definitely loosened her tongue.

"He didn't!"

"Oh, yeah, he did. Well, that's what my friend said." It was silly to cling to the friend scenario when they both knew she was the friend, but it was easier to talk about as long as she was pretending it wasn't her.

"And how did you . . . I mean, your friend respond?"

"She got pissy."

Lauren snorted a laugh. "Good for her."

"Maybe. But I think she overreacted, and now she doesn't know how to . . ." It was time to shut up. She glanced at her watch. "It's getting late, and I've got an early day tomorrow."

"This was fun," Lauren said. "We should have a girls' night once a week."

"I'd like that." She handed Hemingway, who'd stayed in her lap, over to Lauren. "I won't ask you not to repeat our conversation to Court, but—"

"Girls' night conversations aren't for sharing. That's the rule."

"Thank you. I'll let myself out. Good night."

Lauren waved. "Night."

♠♠♠

Early the next morning, Taylor headed straight to the gym, with Rand following behind her. After a restless night, she needed a hard workout to clear her mind. In the locker room, she took the leather bag containing her gun and phone from her purse, then put her purse and the clothes she'd put on after a shower in a locker.

"What are you attacking today?" Rand asked.

"The treadmill."

"I'll be in the weight room. Let me know when you're ready to go," Rand said.

"I'm going to do an hour run." For some reason, she could do her best thinking when running, and she had a lot to think about. "You've been up all night. I'm safe here, and the building's right across the street. Why don't you head home and get some sleep?"

He gave her an eye roll, then headed for the weight room. Gah, she hated having to be babysat. Sighing in frustration, she wrapped a towel around her neck, then stepped onto the treadmill. She set the leather bag in the tray and then switched on the machine, setting it for a warm-up. Five minutes later, she turned the speed up.

The biggest thing on her mind was Nate, and that wasn't good. She needed to be concentrating on their case, not her love life or lack thereof. Someone stepped onto the treadmill next to her, but she didn't look over. Didn't want to encourage a conversation.

What was she going to do about Nate? Yes, she'd overreacted to his stupid comment. Between the case and being stalked, missing her girls, and her head filled with all things Nate, she was operating on a short fuse.

Thirty minutes into her run, she made a decision. She couldn't stand the way things were between them, and she was as much to blame for that as Nate. The best thing to do was to turn the clock back to before she'd slept with him, to when they were best friends. It would be hard to forget how amazing it was to be with him, but she could do it.

"You seem in deep thought, Ms. Collins."

She glanced over at the man on the treadmill next to hers. "Oh, hello, Mr. Tillman. Just trying to convince my legs that they can make it another twenty minutes." Not wanting to encourage him, she faced forward.

"How about just Wade? Mr. Tillman sounds like you're talking to my father."

"Sure," she said, not looking at him.

He was silent for about two minutes, and then said, "May I call you Taylor?"

Had she told him her first name? She thought back to when he'd introduced himself last week, remembering that she had. "If you wish," she said, letting her voice go cold. *Take the hint, Mr. Tillman.* It seemed he got the message, as he stayed silent after that.

At the end of another ten minutes, she slowed the treadmill for a cool down. Her legs were on fire. Muscles screaming in protest after a good workout always gave her satisfaction. She stepped off the treadmill, scrubbed her face with the towel, and then grabbed her leather bag.

"May I buy you a cup of coffee, Taylor?"

Crap. The man was quickly moving into pest status. He wasn't bad-looking, and fifteen or so years on her wasn't a deal breaker, but she had zero interest in encouraging him. She was still licking her Nate wounds.

"Um—" Her cell phone vibrated, signaling she had a text. "Excuse me a minute," she said, grateful for the interruption. She angled the leather bag so he couldn't see her gun and slipped her phone out. Nate's name came up on the screen.

Is he bothering u

She glanced up to see Nate leaning against the wall, a scowl on his face as he stared at Wade Tillman.

A little

Never taking his eyes off her, he strode toward her like a man on a mission. "Hey, babe," he said on reaching her.

Babe?

He put his arms around her shoulders, tucking her against his side. "Ready to go?"

Something like displeasure flashed in Mr. Tillman's eyes, then it was gone. What was that all about? She should probably introduce him to Nate, but she didn't want to start up a conversation with the man. He was beginning to rub her wrong. Besides, he wasn't a friend, and she didn't want to encourage him to think he was.

"I need to change, *babe*." She startled when Nate dropped his hand down and pinched her butt, getting a soft chuckle from him.

"Enjoy your day, Taylor," Mr. Tillman said.

She nodded, then nudged Nate to go.

"He seems to have taken an interest in you. Who is he?" Nate said when they were out of earshot.

"His name is Wade Tillman. That's all I know. I need to tell Rand I'm leaving."

He dropped his arm from her shoulder. "I already sent him home."

"Oh, okay. I need a quick shower."

"No problem. I'm here to take you to the police department. The sketch artist is meeting us there in about forty minutes."

"I'll make it fast." She handed him the leather bag. "Hold on to my gun for me."

"Can I use it to shoot your Mr. Tillman?"

"Play nice."

He lifted an eyebrow. "Me? I don't know how to do nice."

"True." She headed for the showers. So far, she was doing okay with pretending the last few days had never happened. It was hard, though, because just looking at him in his bad-boy clothes made her want to climb right up him. And he always smelled so yummy.

Yep, it was going to be hard to stop loving him, but she could do it. She hoped.

♠♠♠

Nate sat off to the side, listening to Taylor—her voice only a little shaky—describe her mother's killer. He hated that she had to go through this, but she was holding up better than expected.

The woman was confusing him, though. She'd been as chatty as a magpie on the way to the police station, an about-face from the cold shoulder she'd given him ever since he'd made that stupid comment. He didn't know what to make of it, and he didn't like it. She should be miserable, because he sure as hell was.

"His lips were a little thinner than that," Taylor said.

Janie Moore, the police department's sketch artist, nodded. "Better?" she said after a moment.

"Yes, that's him." Taylor took the clipboard with the drawing on it from Janie, holding it up for Nate to see. "There's something about his face that's nagging me."

He reached for the drawing. "Let me see that." The picture was of a blond, brown-eyed man wearing wire-rimmed glasses, maybe in his early twenties. But the lips, the jaw line, and the eyebrows—he was sure he'd seen this man not two hours ago.

"Can you do a second one?" he said, handing the sketch back to Janie. "Same face, but age him about fifteen years with brown hair, hazel eyes, and no glasses."

"Sure." She clipped the page to the board, next to a fresh sheet of paper.

Taylor tilted her head, her brows furrowed as she studied the drawing. "Oh, my God. He could be Wade Tillman's son, or maybe his younger brother."

"That's possible, but I think Wade Tillman and the young man in that drawing are one and the same."

Her cheeks paled. "You're saying my mother's killer has been under my nose all this time? But their eyes are a different color."

"Contacts." He resisted the urge to move his chair next to Taylor's so he could touch her.

"And he dyed his hair brown. I should have seen the resemblance."

"Why?" he said. "He's older, his hair and eye color are wrong, and he doesn't wear glasses now. And he's going by a different name."

She chewed on her bottom lip. "Wade Tillman is Wayne Tompkins, and the man who killed my mother had the gall to ask me out for coffee? I'm going to shoot him in the balls."

Janie chuckled.

"We're not positive yet, but I'm feeling the buzz." The bastard had asked her out?

"Yeah, me, too."

"Here's your second sketch." Janie held up the page for them to see.

"That's him all right," Taylor said. She stood and began to pace. "Okay, we need to go to the gym and get an address for him. I want that son of a bitch today."

Janie gave him a folder to put the sketches in, and after thanking her, Nate walked alongside Taylor as they headed for his car.

"I just can't comprehend that he's been under my nose all this time. I feel like he's taunting me. What the hell is his game?"

Nate gave in to temptation and put his hand on her back. "I have a theory about that, but let's hold off on speculating until Alex and Josh get back from their interview. After we hear what they learned, we'll be able to get a better handle on this guy. In the meantime, let's go to the gym and get an address for him."

There wasn't a doubt in his mind that Wayne Tompkins, a.k.a. Wade Tillman, had fixated on Taylor. The question was, did he see her as a substitute for her mother, a woman he'd fallen in love with and wanted to marry? Did he want Taylor for himself, or was he planning on killing her, too? The thought of the man being anywhere near her made him crazy. If he'd known this morning that Wade Tillman was their unsub, the bastard would be dead right now for no other reason than he'd dared to talk to her.

♠♠♠

"The address the gym had on file for him was an empty lot," Nate said. "Can't say I'm surprised." They were in the field office's conference room—him, Taylor, Rothmire, Court, Alex, and Josh. He glanced at Taylor, sitting in the chair next to him. She was too quiet, had gone into silent mode ever since they'd pulled up to the lot overgrown with weeds.

He'd tried to talk to her after leaving the police station, but she'd ignored him. He had wanted to comfort her, and it was killing him that she wouldn't let him. Wasn't that for the best, though? They'd tried friends with benefits—he hated those words—but that hadn't gone so well. He accepted the blame for that, since he apparently sucked at saying the right words that pleased a woman. But for her, he would have tried harder. That right there was a mind fuck. He'd never wanted to *try* before Taylor.

"Is Tillman at the gym every day?" Rothmire asked.

Taylor shook her head. "I've only seen him there a few times. The manager said he joined four weeks ago, around when the first victim was found."

At least she was finally talking. He knew she blamed herself for not recognizing a killer, or at least sensing something was off about the man when he was right in front of her, but why should she have?

"What about the flowers he sent Taylor?" Rothmire asked.

"Dead end," Nate said. "Paid in cash by a kid." Unfortunately, Tillman was smart enough to pay a teenage boy they'd never find to go into the florist shop. He glanced to his left where Alex and Josh sat. "You talked to the retired cop, Archer something?"

"Bert Archer." Alex leaned forward, resting his arms on the table. "He retired five years ago. Said his last act before leaving the job was to enter Gretchen Tompkins's murder into the cold-case data bank."

"He thought we were looking for Doug Emmitt, and was disappointed to learn we aren't," Josh said. "Apparently, he never thought highly of his fellow cop."

Alex nodded. "Yeah. Seems there's some bad blood there. He said Emmitt was a man you didn't want to turn your back on. The story goes that Emmitt was caught in the back of his patrol car with Gretchen, a known prostitute, while he was supposed to be on duty. He was given a week off without pay by the mayor. Turned out he kept seeing her, and when it came out, he said she'd given up the life and they were getting married."

"They moved in together a few months before the wedding was scheduled," Josh said, picking up the story. "One night her son called 9-1-1, reporting that Doug Emmitt was trying to kill Gretchen. Archer was on duty and took the call. When he got there, Emmitt was nowhere to be found."

Alex sat back in his chair. "Gretchen denied that Emmitt had tried to hurt her, but there were bruises on her neck, arms, and face. She said she'd fallen. Archer asked the boy what happened, but he claimed he'd been asleep and hadn't seen anything."

"Sounds like either his mother or Emmitt convinced him not to talk," Nate said.

Alex nodded. "That's what Archer thinks. Things were quiet after that until the day of the wedding. Another call from the boy came in. Archer took that call, too. When he got there, Gretchen Tompkins was dead—strangled." He glanced at Taylor. "She was wearing a white dress and had a gold band on her finger."

"And this was before the wedding took place?" Taylor asked.

"It was." Josh took a picture from a folder, handing it to Rothmire. "Archer made a copy of the report and crime scene photos. Said some day he was going to see Emmitt behind bars."

As the photo made the rounds, Alex said, "According to her son, Emmitt accused Gretchen of flirting with one of his friends. Yelled at her that once a whore, always a whore."

Nate caught Court's recoil. As a boy, Court had been hiding behind the couch the day their father had yelled those same words at their mother. It was the day she had left them, and if Court was right, she'd been pregnant. Nate needed to stop putting off finding answers.

It looked like this case would wrap up in a day or two, and then he'd make that trip back to Dunnellon and find out once and for all if their mother was there. If they had a brother or sister out there somewhere, it was time to find out.

"Wayne told Archer that he tried to pull Emmitt away, but Emmitt threw him across the room," Alex said. "Wayne hit the wall, stunning him. He watched Emmitt strangle her and then put the ring on her finger. 'Only good whore is a dead whore,' Emmitt said, then walked out the door, never to be seen again."

Taylor let out a breath. "It's really sad that her son had to watch her murder."

She would know how sad that was better than anyone sitting around the table. "You okay?" Nate asked.

"I'm at peace."

She smiled at him, and his stomach clenched, wanting that smile in his life forever. The thought was so startling that he didn't know what to do with it. Run? Accept that she might be the one woman in the world he could love? What about his fear of being an abuser like his father? That hadn't gone away.

He should probably put as much distance between him and Taylor as possible. A deep ache settled in his chest at the thought of not having her in his life. This was all stuff he needed to think about when he wasn't in the middle of a murder investigation. He tuned back in to what Alex was saying.

"Archer said the boy was crying, begging his mother to wake up. He said it was the saddest thing he'd ever seen, but what he told Wayne . . ." He glanced around the table. "This is important. In an effort to comfort Wayne, he told the boy that his mother was now an angel in heaven."

"And thus the seed was planted," Nate said. "What happened to him? Did he have family to take him in?"

Josh shook his head. "No, he went into foster care, and Archer lost track of him."

"I've found Wayne Tompkins's birth certificate and his foster care records. He didn't last long in any of the homes he was put in," Court said, his fingers flying over his laptop keys. "At the age of seventeen, he walked away from his last foster home. A year later, he enrolled in Miami Dade Junior College, but dropped out after six months. Looks like he worked odd jobs for a while, and then he was arrested for domestic violence on a girlfriend. Got six months for that. After he was released, his trail goes cold."

Rothmire scratched his chin. "Is there anything that connects Wade Tillman to Wayne Tompkins that we can use as evidence?"

"Looking for that now," Court said. A minute later, he raised his eyes from the screen. "It always amazes me how stupid some people can be. Wade Tillman has a Facebook page. His profile picture is an angel." He turned his laptop around so everyone could see. "His last post, dated yesterday, was that he'd found his angel."

Taylor's cheeks drained of color. "He means me," she murmured.

Nate didn't care that they were in a room full of fellow agents and their boss, all of them watching. He put his hand on her chair, swiveling it to face him. "We knew that—you knew that—already, tiger." He used her power name on purpose. Tigers killed. They didn't get killed. "It's just hearing it said aloud that's freaking us all out." He wrapped his hands around her cold ones. "I would die before I let anything happen to you." And that was the God's honest truth.

She blinked, as if coming out of a fog. Her eyes settled on him. "Would you really?"

"Damn straight I would." The room and people around them disappeared. All he saw was her, the woman he loved. And yeah, that realization was like a boulder falling on his head. One that knocked him flat on his ass.

Rothmire cleared his throat. "I expect an invitation to the wedding, but before that can happen, we have a killer to catch."

Nate managed not to smile at the sudden pale-pink blush in Taylor's cheeks at their boss's announcement. He should probably be embarrassed, too, but the ache that had been residing in his chest since he'd gone stupid, saying stupid things to her, had vanished. He didn't know if she'd ever forgive him, but he had news for her. He was hers, plain and simple. If she needed him to grovel, he'd do that. Well, he'd do it while making her scream his name against the foyer wall so she could add a few more scratch marks to it.

He met Rothmire's amused eyes. "Right. Ah, so, Court, you got an address on him?"

"You don't have to give Facebook an address to set up a page, but they do require a mobile number or an email addy that I can trace. I'll have something in a sec."

"While you're waiting, suit up," Rothmire said. "I have a judge standing by, ready to sign a warrant."

Nate stood. "You heard the man. Let's get this done."

CHAPTER TWENTY-THREE

The address was a small ranch-style house in North Miami. Their backup team evacuated the residences on both sides of their target house and had secured the premises.

"No one will blame you if you sit this one out," Nate said quietly at her side.

Taylor bit back her first retort. He wasn't saying she wasn't capable of being a part of this operation. "I'm good." She'd had to fight to be in on the arrest, arguing that after what their perp had put her through, she had a right to be here. Nate had seemed to understand that, and after getting a nod from Rothmire, he'd agreed. And considering the whole team was here, she didn't doubt they were all keeping an eye on her.

"Then let's do this."

Court and Alex were stationed at the back to make sure Tompkins didn't try to run. She, Nate, and Rand approached the door. They split up, Rand on one side, her and Nate on the other.

Nate fisted his hand and banged on the door. "FBI. Open up!" When there was no response, he banged again, repeating the words.

There wasn't any noise coming from inside, no TV or radio blaring, no car parked in the carport. She sensed the house was empty.

"There's a sliding glass door in the back that I can jimmy open," Alex said, his voice coming over their headsets.

"Do it," Nate answered. "Station yourself at the corner of the house, Rand, so you can warn us if a car pulls in. Taylor, come with me."

She followed Nate to the back. Alex had the door open by the time they walked up. Guns drawn, she, Alex, and Court entered behind Nate, splitting up to search the house. Taylor and Nate ended up in the kitchen.

"Does he ever cook in here?" She glanced around. The electric stove was spotless, as were the counters and sink.

"Doesn't appear so," Nate said, peering inside a cabinet.

She opened the refrigerator, eyeing the contents, or more like the lack of contents. Other than a dozen bottles of water, a plastic bottle of milk, ketchup, a bottle of hot sauce, and a tub of butter, it was empty.

The freezer was loaded, though. She doubted he could squeeze another frozen dinner into it. So he lived on microwaved food. Moving to the small pantry, she frowned. The only things on the shelves were video cassettes. Who used those anymore? She tilted her head, reading the titles.

"Nate, you need to come see these."

Seconds later, he stepped behind her. "What?"

She moved aside so he could see into the pantry. "*Taxi Driver, The Killer Inside Me, The Machinist*, to name a few, and one with the handwritten title of *Snuff Film*," she said. They were in the middle of a search. She shouldn't be intentionally brushing her arm over his.

His gaze landed on where their arms touched, and then he lifted his eyes to hers. An entire butterfly farm came awake in her stomach, fluttering their wings in response to the heat in his eyes. But she reminded herself that she'd put them back in friends-only status, although the butterflies apparently hadn't gotten that memo. She'd have a stern talk with them once he was no longer invading her senses.

He turned his attention to the shelves. "The snuff film's probably a fake. Most of them are, but we'll have to check it out, make sure."

"Yeah, if it's real, it will open up a whole new investigation."

"Nate, you need to come see this," Court said from the hallway.

More murder tapes? When she tried to follow Nate into one of the bedrooms, Court put a hand on her arm.

"Maybe you should wait here," he said.

There was something in his voice that gave her pause, but she shook him off. "Not happening." She was here to do her job, not be coddled. When she walked into the room, the air left her lungs.

"The hell?" She knew the bastard was stalking her, but to see pictures of her at different ages wallpapering one wall—along with ones of her walking the girls to school—caused a burning rage like she'd never felt before to roar through her bloodstream.

"My girls," she whispered. "I'm going to kill him."

A growl sounded low in Nate's throat. "If I don't get to him first."

She wanted to yank all the photos off the wall, but until they caught Wayne Tompkins, they would have to stay. "This is so creepy, Nate. He's been stalking me since my mother was killed."

Her stomach churned at seeing herself through the years, at recess on the playground, getting off the school bus, playing in her yard at home, and on and on. There was even one of her at her high school graduation in cap and gown. Rosie had taken her away to keep her safe, but it had been an illusion. He could have stolen her away at any time. Why hadn't he?

Seeing her girls on that wall brought the realization that she could commit cold-blooded murder and sleep like a baby afterward.

Nate stepped up to the wall. "Why is there a gap? It looks like there was a four- or five-year span where he wasn't watching you."

"You're right. After the graduation picture, there aren't any until I was assigned to the Miami field office. My scholarship was at the University of Maryland, so maybe that was too far away for him to keep tabs on me?"

Nate glanced at her. "That would explain it."

"Guys," Court said, standing in front of an open desk drawer.

That was all he said, but it was the sharp tone of his voice that got their attention. She, Nate, and Alex crowded around him, watching as he picked up one plastic angel after another—the same as the one she'd found near her car—setting them on the desk.

There were seven of them, six with names printed on them with a black marker. One in particular had her sucking in a breath. She picked it up with her gloved hand. "Raisa," she whispered, hating that tears stung her eyes and her lips trembled.

Nate stepped up behind her, putting his hands on her shoulders. "We'll get him, tiger."

Yes, she was a tiger. Strong and fearless. She stiffened her spine. "No. I'll get him." She looked over her shoulder at Nate. "He's mine." Gently placing the angel next to the others, she read off the names. "Raisa, Brenda, Alana, Stacy, Linda, Barb"—the last one found behind the grocery store and only identified this morning—"and we have to assume the one without the name is meant for me."

Nate's hands tightened on her shoulders. "Never."

There was such vengeance in his voice, and she closed her eyes at hearing it, hiding the love for him that must be shining in them. No matter what might happen between them after this was over, she would always know that she meant something to him.

"Never," Alex and Court echoed in unison.

These men—the Gentry brothers—were her team, her family. They would die protecting her, and she would do the same for them. She was truly blessed to have them at her back.

"Brenda Jernigan was the one he killed six years ago," Court said. "Also a prostitute. That's where you don't fit, Taylor. All the others were."

Alex glanced from her to the plastic angels and then back to her. "I think he's planning one of two things. Either he's going for a murder-suicide, or he sees you as his true bride, the one woman deserving of him."

"He can go to hell." Taylor swiped her gloved hand over the angels, dropping them back into the drawer, then slammed it shut.

As if he regretted voicing what they all thought, Alex gave her an I'm-sorry shrug, then walked out of the room.

"Where's Court?" Nate asked, looking around.

"He's here with me."

The words boomed out over loudspeakers, and Taylor was glad to see she wasn't the only one who startled. She recognized that gravelly voice, having heard it at the gym when Wayne Tompkins, a.k.a. Wade Tillman, had asked her out.

"What do you want?" Nate said, his gaze going straight to a landscape on the wall.

She followed his gaze, and damn them, how had they missed the hole in the middle of a sunflower? Their killer was watching them. She walked over to the portrait. "You want me. Isn't that right, Wayne? Or do you prefer Wade?" At the pounding of her heart, she reminded herself that she was a tiger. "How do we know you have him?"

"Your mother knew me as Wayne."

He was trying to mess with her head, and it was working. Had her mother sensed the evil in him? Had she feared for her life before he put his hands around her neck? Or had she not seen the danger facing her when he'd followed her home, offering her flowers? Such an innocent thing, a gift of pink tulips, her mother's favorite flowers. How could she have known she'd die that night?

She glanced at Nate and saw the fear for his brother in his eyes. "Prove that you have him. Otherwise, I have nothing to say to you."

The computer screen on the desk came to life, drawing her to the monitor. The screen was filled with Court tied to a chair, his eyes closed, and his chin slumped on his chest.

Behind her, Nate growled.

"Is he dead?" she said, her stomach roiling with fear. Through her headset, she heard Alex tell Rand to come inside, that their man was in the house somewhere.

"Not yet, but he will be if you don't follow my directions," that gravelly voice she hated said.

He had to be somewhere in the house, but they'd searched all the rooms. "What do you want me to do?"

"Simple. A trade. Him for you."

Nate clenched his fists. If Tompkins put one nick on Court, Nate was going to kill him with his bare hands. And no way was he letting her exchange herself for Court. Even if he did, and Court lived, Court would never forgive him if that man got his hands on Taylor. Putting his back to the camera in the portrait, and hoping there were no others than that one and the one on the monitor, he mouthed, "Fuck no."

He knew she saw him, because she was looking right at him, but she only gave him a sad smile before she turned her attention back to the monitor when Tompkins started to speak.

"There's a closet at the end of the hall," Tompkins said. "Go in there and close the door behind you. If anyone tries to come with you, I will kill him." On the monitor, Tompkins pushed a knife under Court's throat. "If you come down alone, I'll let him go with nothing more than the concussion he got when he fell. But first . . ."

"First what?" Taylor said, when Tompkins paused.

"First you have to decide who you want to live the most." He pushed the knife harder against Court's neck. "Him or the one who tried to take you away from me."

"I don't know who you mean," Taylor said, even as she glanced at Nate, both of them knowing Tompkins meant him.

Nate moved next to Taylor. "Am I to assume you mean me? Because I hope to hell you do. I'll come to you unarmed." And then he'd kill the bastard.

Tompkins laughed. "Tempting, Special Agent Gentry, but I'd rather watch her shoot you. That will be more enjoyable than doing it myself." He reached up, his hand covering the camera lens, then the camera moved. "I have a little more motivation for you, Taylor. Two lives for one. You kill your lover, and these two get to live."

He removed his hand, revealing a woman tied and gagged in a chair on the other side of him. He stroked her face. "Isn't she a lovely thing? Such pretty blonde hair and blue eyes, don't you think? Not as pretty as your mother, but she'll do."

Beside him, Taylor gasped. "Easy, tiger," Nate whispered.

"So what will it be, Taylor? His life . . ." Tompkins's gaze flicked to Nate. "Or theirs? Take that gun out that I know you have on under your jacket and shoot him. No tricks. I don't quite trust you, so do it in front of the camera."

Alex appeared in the doorway but out of sight of the camera. He held up an empty bottle of ketchup in one hand and a baggie filled with what Nate assumed was ketchup. It could work. He just had to make Taylor understand.

"I'm waiting, Taylor. You have one minute to decide before I make this pretty girl an angel." He pointed the knife at a still-unconscious Court. "Then he'll be next."

While Tompkins was talking, Nate whispered to Taylor. "Say you'll do it." When she gave a slight shake of her head, he said, "Smoke and mirrors."

She darted a glance at him and then toward the doorway. Alex held up the baggie again. Standing behind him, Rand mouthed the word *blood.*

"Thirty seconds," Tompkins said when she hesitated.

"Please don't make me do this," Taylor said. "I'll come there. He won't follow me."

"Twenty seconds, and don't doubt me, Taylor."

Nate put his hands on the desk, leaning his face toward the monitor. "She'll do it, and if she doesn't, I'll shoot myself."

"And I'll still kill them both. She has to do it. She belongs to me, always has. Killing you is her punishment for spreading her legs for you."

Where the hell was the man? He'd said Court had fallen, so he had to be below them. Florida houses didn't usually have basements, so it hadn't occurred to them to look for one. Movement to the right of Tompkins caught Nate's attention. Court's arm was moving, and Nate realized he was attempting to loosen the rope tied around his wrist.

"She's out of time, Agent Gentry. If she doesn't shoot you now, these two will die."

As much as he wanted to storm down there and rip the man's head off, he had to stay calm if they were going to save Court and the woman. Nate slipped off his jacket as he backed toward the doorway. With one hand, he pulled on the Velcro securing his vest, while putting his other hand behind him, palm up. When the bag of ketchup landed in his hand, he dropped the vest to the floor.

"He's my brother, Taylor," he said for the benefit of Tompkins. "You know I'd die for him. Do it."

CHAPTER TWENTY-FOUR

Taylor stared into the monitor, right into Tompkins's eyes. "I'll always hate you for making me do this."

Smoke and mirrors. It had to work. She removed her gun from its holster, lifted it, met Nate's steady gaze for a moment—seeing nothing but trust in them—then focused on the sliver of space he'd created between his right arm and his side. She pulled the trigger.

He jerked as he slapped his hand to his chest. Red spread across his chest, splatters of red dotted his neck, and her knees almost gave out when he grunted, crumbling to the floor.

It's only ketchup. Just ketchup. With her gun still in her hand, she walked out of the room as Rand rushed in. She glanced back to see him kneeling next to Nate.

"Christ, he's dead," Rand said.

Even though she knew he wasn't, hearing him say that about Nate made her want to vomit. In the hallway, she stopped in front of Alex. "Cameras out here?" she whispered.

"No."

"Give me your knife," she said, knowing the Gentry brothers always had a knife on them. She removed the clip from her gun, emptied it of the bullets, and dropped them in his hand after he gave her his knife.

"What are you doing?"

"The first thing he's going to do is make me give him my weapon. Damn if I'm giving him a loaded one."

"He'll have Court's."

"Yeah, I know, but why give him two loaded guns?"

"Good point. Nate always said you were the smartest out of all of us." He gave her a hard hug. "Put that knife right between his eyes, tiger."

She laughed at his calling her "tiger." "That's the plan." She put her gun back into its holster, then slipped the knife into the waistband of her pants at her back.

"There must be another way," Alex said as she turned away.

"There isn't." She paused at the door to the closet, looking back at Alex. "If it goes south, tell Nate I lov—"

"No. You'll tell him yourself when this is over."

That was what she loved about the Gentry brothers. Their faith in her. "You're right. I'll tell him myself."

That they weren't standing in front of the closet door, blocking her from going in alone, spoke volumes. It meant that they didn't see her as a woman needing protection, but as a fellow agent, capable of doing her job. Of course, they didn't like it, but any one of them would be doing the same thing if Tompkins had demanded it.

She took several deep breaths to calm her nerves, then stepped inside the closet. After finding a light switch and turning it on, she closed the door, but kept her back against it. The floor in front of her dropped down. If she'd been standing on it, she would have fallen in like Court had.

"You're smarter than your agent friend here," Tompkins said when she reached the bottom of the ladder.

"Not really." He had Court's gun pressed against the woman's head and looked so smug that Taylor was dancing to his tune. It didn't appear that he'd thought to check Court for other weapons, like the knife and second gun she knew he had hidden in his boots. She glanced at Court to see that he was still unconscious. But wait, had his pinky just twitched? She jerked her gaze back to Tompkins, but out of the corner of her eye, she saw Court tap his finger twice against the arm of the chair. Thank God he was all right. She didn't doubt he was royally pissed that Tompkins had managed to catch him, but who would have expected the floor to fall out from under them?

"Who's this?" she asked, looking at the woman.

"Ah, Taylor, dear, meet sweet Nichole."

She moved to the woman in a white dress, kneeling in front of her and meeting eyes brimming with tears of fear. "It's going to be okay, Nichole." She prayed she was right. Her stomach churned at seeing the gold wedding band on Nichole's finger. He planned to kill Nichole no matter what Taylor did.

Nichole tried to respond, but with the gag, it was a mumble of unintelligible words. In an effort to keep Tompkins's attention on her and off Court, Taylor stood, surveying her surroundings. She frowned at seeing a large corkboard covered with pictures, and was that . . . After a quick glance at Tompkins, who was avidly watching her, she walked over to the board, and yes, those were strands of human hair.

"I see you like souvenirs," she said, grateful her voice was steady. Because she sure didn't feel calm on the inside. "You're missing someone." There were only five strands.

"Your mother's."

She squeezed her eyes shut, thankful her back was to him and he couldn't see her reaction.

"I regret not having hers, but I hadn't planned on making her an angel. Everything was confusing that night."

"Yet you thought to take pictures of her." Sick bastard. There was a photo of her mother after she'd died tacked to the board that she'd caught a glimpse of, but until she reined in her emotions, she kept her eyes on the strands of hair. "Why not pictures of the others?"

"Oh, they didn't mean anything to me, not like your mother. I was simply their savior, sending them to a better life. The pieces of hair were all I wanted to remember them by."

They didn't mean anything to him. If she had bullets in her gun, she'd shoot him right now.

"Take the gun I know you have under your jacket, set it on the floor nice and easy like, and slide it to me," he said as if reading her mind.

"I'm trained to never give up my weapon, but I'll do it if you'll let her go." She faced him. "You said you'd let them both go if I came down. Well, here I am."

He laughed. "You're too trusting, Taylor, dearest. Say good-bye to sweet Nichole."

When he put his finger on the trigger of Court's gun, Taylor held up her hands. "Okay, I'm doing it."

"Real slow. You try anything and she dies."

What could she say to get him to use her weapon instead of Court's? She eased her gun out of its holster, set it on the floor, and pushed it toward him with her foot. Letting the fear inside her that she wouldn't be able to save Court and Nichole show on her face, she said, "Please don't use my gun to hurt anyone. I couldn't bear it."

As she'd hoped, delight at seeing her afraid danced in his eyes, and his mouth curved into a sly smile. She glanced at the camera mounted on a stand to see it was still recording. Did he realize that her fellow agents would be watching? It appeared that he'd forgotten about the camera. She hoped so.

He pointed Court's gun at her. "Don't move unless you're ready to die."

While he stretched a leg, put his foot on her weapon, and pulled it to him, she risked looking at Court. He was rubbing his arm back and forth on the chair arm, his muscles straining to loosen the rope. Already, his wrist looked raw from rope burns. What alarmed her, though, was the steady trickle of blood dripping down the back of his neck. He must have hit his head when he fell.

This had to end before someone was killed. As she'd prayed, her reverse psychology worked. Tompkins tucked Court's gun under his leg, palming hers.

"Will you cry if I kill them with your gun, Taylor?"

"Yes." But hell if she was going to let that happen. It was now or never. She whipped the knife from her back but had a damn moment of hesitation. She wanted to send the knife right through his black heart, but even though he didn't know her gun was useless, she did.

If she killed him, it would probably be deemed a justifiable kill, but in her heart, she would always know it was murder. Her hesitation gave him time to pull the trigger of her gun. When nothing happened, he went for Court's weapon. Taylor threw the knife, hitting him in his arm where she'd intended. Tompkins screamed, Court's gun clattering to the floor.

At the same time, Court tilted his chair, sending Tompkins, along with himself, to the floor. Chaos ensued as three big men climbed down the ladder.

Nate was the first down, torn between going to his brother or Taylor. Alex pushed past him, heading for Court, so Nate went to Taylor, while Rand moved to the woman trying to scream behind her gag.

"Damn noisy in here," Nate said, coming to a stop next to Taylor.

She let out an adrenaline-filled laugh. "I love it when a plan comes together."

"You were amazing, tiger." He'd watched the monitor with his heart in his throat as she'd had to face a serial killer alone. Alex had practically had to tackle him to keep him from rushing in to save her.

"Dude, trust your woman to handle this," Alex had said.

He did, God knew he did, but seeing her down there by herself with a deranged man had nearly given him a heart attack.

She smiled at him. "Thanks. I was worried it would all somehow go south on me."

When she walked away from him, he wanted to grab her back and keep her in the safety of his arms. Instead, he crammed his fingers into the pockets of his jeans. Whatever it was she needed to do, it wasn't his right to stop her. No matter how much he wanted to. She stared down at Tompkins.

"You want to hear something?" Without waiting for an answer, she said, "I'm sorry you had to watch your mother die. I know how hard that must have been for you, but you had choices. The same as me. I find it sad that you chose to be a pathetic excuse for a man."

Nate wanted to yell, "You tell him, tiger!"

The man looked back at her with the eyes of a petulant child who had just had his favorite toy taken away. "You tricked me."

Idiot. Still staying out of what was going on between Taylor and the man who'd killed her mother, Nate watched as she picked up her gun. Pulling out the magazine, she held it out for Tompkins to see. "Empty. Did you really think I'd give you a loaded gun, asshole?"

Alex and Rand had freed Court and Nichole and were helping them up the ladder. With his brother and the woman out of harm's way, Nate kept his attention on Taylor. Pride swelled in his heart for her, and damn if it also didn't feel something like love there, too.

Rand climbed back down the ladder. "The EMTs are here. Can they come down, or should we let him suffer a little longer?"

Nate glanced at Taylor. "Up to you."

She looked from Rand to him to Tompkins. "Yeah, let them in."

"You heard the lady," he said. "Is Court okay?"

Rand nodded. "Yeah, a few stitches and he's good to go. Alex is going to the hospital with him."

That was a relief. Seeing his brother with his chin on his chest, almost looking dead, had sent Nate back to when Alex had almost died after being shot. He was getting too old for this shit.

There would be numerous conversations with Tompkins after he was released from the hospital and returned to their custody. He wanted answers, and for sure so did Taylor. But it had been a long day and night, and he knew Taylor was exhausted. All he wanted to do now was get her out of there and take care of her.

"Stay with him until the hospital releases him, and you can book him," Nate said to Rand. "I doubt it will take long to sew him up and stick a bandage on him. Tell Rothmire no one talks to him until Taylor's present. We'll come in after lunch."

She shot him a grateful smile that he understood, both her need for answers and that she was in dire need of sleep. He put his hand on her back, giving her a push toward the ladder.

"Bitch!"

Out of the corner of his eye, he saw Tompkins pull the knife out of his arm, then rear up. Nate's first reaction was to step in front of Taylor to protect her, but she shoved him aside. Damn, his tiger was fucking fearless. He grinned at her as he moved behind her. Maybe some men would have to do the macho thing and take care of her, but she'd hate that. Yeah, that was how well he knew her.

As Tompkins came at her, the knife raised high, she twisted her body, kicking back. The heel of her shoe caught him in the chin. He grunted as he recoiled, but he didn't fall. He started for her again, aiming the knife for her chest. She dropped and rolled, taking him down at his knees. He fell, face down, and she straddled his back, grabbed his hair, and slammed his face into the floor. Blood poured out of his nose.

She put her mouth next to his ear. "You still want to play with me, turd face?"

Nate snickered.

"Well, he is," she said, looking up at him.

"I'm going to have to teach you some bad words to use in situations like this," he said. "'Turd face' doesn't quite get it." He held out some plastic ties. "I assume you'd like to do the honors?"

"Absolutely." She took them from him.

"You broke my nose," Tompkins said.

Nate bent down and stared in his face. "You're lucky she didn't put that knife between your eyes. You have the right to remain silent, so shut up."

When he stood, he held out his hand. "Let's blow this joint, tiger."

She put her hand in his. "Best idea I've heard all day. Since his prints are now on the handle, make sure the knife is bagged as evidence he tried to kill me."

"I'll take care of it," Rand said.

As Nate walked to the ladder with her, he said, "For the rest of the night, I'm in charge."

The smile she sent him went straight to his heart, and strangely, he was good with that.

CHAPTER TWENTY-FIVE

Nate took Taylor to her apartment. She'd fallen asleep within minutes of putting on her seatbelt. He was used to late hours, but three in the morning was way past her bedtime. She'd been magnificent tonight, but that hadn't surprised him. She trained as hard as any of them and was as lethal. He figured his brain was warped for thinking that was pretty damn hot.

They had some talking to do, but not tonight. She didn't wake up when they arrived at her place. He grabbed her purse and eased out of the car. As he walked to her door, he took her keys out. After dropping the purse and keys on her kitchen counter, he returned to the car and scooped her into his arms. She mumbled something unintelligible, then snuggled her face into his neck.

On reentering the apartment, he kicked the door closed. In her bedroom, he eased her onto the mattress, holding her up in a sitting position as he dropped to his knees in front of her.

"Wake up, Taylor."

She blinked her eyes, then kept them open. "What's happening?"

"A few things, the first of which is to get you out of these clothes."

"Just like a man, trying to get a woman naked."

She smiled, but he saw the exhaustion on her face. He guessed that her fatigue was as much mental as physical, considering that she'd faced her mother's killer.

"Yep. That's the only thing we ever think about. But tonight, we're just getting you out of them so you can have a shower. Unless you'd rather crawl under the covers right now. Even then, you need to undress."

"I definitely want to bathe. I feel grimy."

"Can't have that. Jacket first." He slid the jacket down her arms, then folded it, and set it on the floor next to him. "Now the holster." That and her gun, he set on the end table. When she fumbled with the buttons on her blouse, he brushed her hands away. "I'm taking care of you tonight."

For the next few minutes, he removed the rest of her clothes, doing his best not to become aroused. No such luck, though. With each piece he took away, he grew more aroused. It was impossible not to whenever he got anywhere near her. But tonight wasn't about him. His dick disagreed.

Down, boy. No Taylor for you tonight. And now he was talking to his dick, something he'd never done before. It was disturbing. When she was down to her bra and panties, he scooped her up, smiling when she gave a little yelp.

"I'm not helpless, you know."

Since he didn't know how to explain—much less understand—his need to take care of her, he didn't answer, just kept going. In the bathroom, he set her on her feet, then reached into the shower and turned on the water. She blushed when he unsnapped her bra, letting it fall to the floor.

"Seriously, tiger? I've seen you naked, so why are you blushing?" His gaze fell to her breasts, then reluctantly lifted his eyes to hers. "You're so beautiful. There's no reason for you to be embarrassed." Although the woman who could take him down on the mats was adorable with pink cheeks.

"It's just that we're back to friends only, and you shouldn't be seeing"—she waved a hand down her body—"um, me like this now."

He swallowed a growl at her *friends only*. "We're going to talk about that, but not tonight. Panties off."

"Close your eyes."

He snorted at the absurdness of that order, instead shedding his clothes, all but his boxer briefs. If he took those off, he'd end up inside her before their shower was over. Since her panties were still on, he took care of that task, stripping them off her.

"In you go." He patted her ass, resisting the urge to let his hand linger there. As he followed her into the shower, it occurred to him that this was the first time he'd ever bathed with a woman. Bathing together was too much like romance, so he'd avoided this particular intimacy.

She glanced over her shoulder. "Oh, you're coming in, too?"

"How else can I take care of you?"

Her eyes lowered to his briefs. "But you still have your underwear on."

"Consider them a chastity belt." At her puzzled look, he winked. "I'm trying to be a good boy here, Taylor." Which was next to impossible with her naked in front of him. "Stick your head under the water."

"I don't think it's normal for friends to give friends a bath," she said, then stuck her head under the shower.

There wasn't a normal thing about either of them—not their childhoods or who they were as adults—so he let her comment pass. He poured shampoo into his palm. "Close your eyes."

"You really are bossy."

He chuckled. "Both my brothers' wives say the same thing about their husbands. Must be a Gentry trait."

"The key word there is *husband.* You're not one, so you're not the boss of me." She moaned as he massaged her scalp. "God, that feels good."

No, he wasn't one and he never would be, but the thought put a weird tug in his chest that he didn't understand. His brothers were outrageously happy in their marriages. Had either one ever worried they'd be like their father? It wasn't something they'd ever talked about, but now he wondered if that had been an obstacle they'd had to overcome.

"Lean your head back so I can rinse the shampoo out." Maybe he'd ask them if that had ever been a concern. First, though, he had to finish what he'd started, find out what had happened to their mother. Then he might or might not sit down with his brothers and dredge up their past and whether they had any reservations about getting married.

He eyed the bottles on the shelf. "Conditioner?"

"Yes, please."

When he uncapped the conditioner, the aroma he always associated with her wafted up. Curious, he read the label. Lemon verbena. He brought the bottle to his nose and sniffed. "I like this scent," he said.

"Thanks."

So far, he'd done well ignoring that she was naked, but once he was finished with her hair, it was time to move on to her body, and that was going to be impossible to ignore.

"What are you thinking?" he asked, hoping if they talked, he would be able to rein in his desire. She'd been unusually quiet, and he was starting to worry.

"I miss my girls."

Interestingly, so did he. More than he ever would have expected. He poured a generous amount of body wash into his palm, then rubbed his hands together. *Listen up, dude. When you touch her, remember that tonight's all about her. No play time's on the agenda.*

"We'll call them in the morning, tell them to come home." He gritted his teeth as he soaped her body, but when she turned and looked up at him with those blue eyes filled with desire, he came within a hair's breadth of losing control.

"I don't understand you," Taylor said. Not since her mother had anyone bathed her, and it was hard to keep her walls up when he was being so considerate and gentle with her. She wanted to sink her tired body into him, but he was keeping a foot's distance between them.

"What don't you understand?"

"Why you're here. I thought we agreed that we didn't have a relationship."

"I didn't agree to anything of the sort." He stepped in front of her and made a quick job of washing himself. After he rinsed off, he turned and faced her. "I told you we have to talk, but not tonight."

Their shower done, he grabbed the towel and dried her off, then himself. A few minutes later, she was tucked up against him in bed.

"I forgot to feed Henry Too."

"Already did. Go to sleep."

He caressed the sensitive spot under her ear with his thumb, making her want to purr. *What a weird night* was her last thought before drifting off.

♠♠♠

"He won't talk to anyone but you," Rothmire told her as she stood with him and Nate, watching Tompkins through the one-way mirror. The man stared straight into the glass, letting them know he was aware they were there.

Again, she was struck by how next-door-neighborly he appeared. Killers should look deranged. Even better if they had a big *X* on their foreheads. But Wayne Tompkins was a nice-enough-looking guy, although there was nothing outstanding about him. He wasn't a man you'd remember an hour after passing him on the street.

"Well, let's get this over with," she said.

Nate frowned as he studied the man. "Want me to come in with you?"

"No, he'll just refuse to talk until you leave." Nate grunted his displeasure, but remained where he was as she headed for the interrogation room. With her back to him, she smiled. He'd been so gentle and caring as he'd taken care of her last night. And when she'd thought there was no way she'd be able to sleep with everything that was on her mind, she'd slept like a baby in his arms.

This wasn't a time to be thinking about Nate, though. She needed her wits about her when she sat across from Wayne Tompkins. Pausing for a moment, she cleared her mind, then walked into the room.

"I hear you've been asking for me." She pulled out the chair, sat, and then looked him in the eyes.

"Hello, Taylor. I trust you slept well since we last met?"

"Like a baby." She rested her arms on the table and leaned forward. "Not the answer you wanted to hear, is it, Wayne?" He was trying to toy with her, but they were going to play this game by her rules.

His lips thinned for a second, then he lifted his arms as far as the chains wrapped around his wrists and then his waist would allow. "If you take these off, I'll answer any question you ask."

"How about I don't, but you answer my questions anyway?"

"I don't think so."

"So be it." She stood. "Someone will come shortly to escort you back to your cell."

"Wait."

She sat back down, but didn't say anything.

"That was a mean trick you played, giving me a gun without any bullets."

"I thought it was rather clever, myself. Did you really want to kill me? I ask because I remember you leaning over my bed and telling me I was such a pretty girl." He was creeping her out with the way he stared at her mouth as she talked. "So I have to wonder if your original plan was to kidnap me, take me someplace where you thought no one would find us."

"You belonged to me, pretty little girl. If your mother had married me like I wanted, we would have been a family. I even bought her a beautiful white dress for our wedding, but she refused to put it on. Then I saw you, so pretty in your fear, and I knew you were mine. If that bitch hadn't come in with her baseball bat . . ."

Interesting. His voice had risen until he was almost shouting before he clamped his mouth shut. *He wants to think he's in charge and didn't like losing control.*

She leaned closer to him, keeping just out of touching range. "I was never yours, Wayne. Whether you'd taken me back then or found a way to do it today, I would have fought you with every bone in my body." Okay, now she was losing her cool, and she could almost hear Nate whispering in her ear, "Easy, tiger." She pressed her back to her chair. *I never knew how much I owed you for saving me, Rosie.*

Tompkins's smile was pure evil, and the cunning in his eyes reminded her of the way Hannibal Lecter had looked at Clarice in *The Silence of the Lambs*. She suppressed a shudder.

"I would have liked you fighting me, Taylor, as a little girl or the woman you are now."

If he knew how close she was to pulling the gun out of her shoulder holster and shooting him, he'd be the one shuddering. It was time to throw him off balance.

"How did you feel when you watched Doug Emmitt strangle your mother, Wayne? Do you relive that moment each time you put your hands around a woman's throat? Do you—"

"Shut up!" He banged the chains on the table. "You don't talk about her."

"Okay, then let's talk about the women you killed."

He closed his eyes, and when he opened them moments later, all expression was gone from his face. "You have no proof I killed anyone. I'd rather talk about you. How did you feel when you saw your pictures on my wall?"

There was no reason to lie to him. "I was angry. And a little sad for the boy who had to watch his mother die, and what you became because of that. But you're wrong, Wayne. We have plenty of proof that you killed those women. Confess or don't, doesn't matter. You're going away for the rest of your life."

"You're lying. I never left any evidence or DNA behind."

"Not even when you fucked them?"

Rage filled his eyes, and red creeped up his neck. "Don't say that word. I never did that to them. I saved them. Made them angels."

Gotcha! Not that they needed his confession. They had shown Delaney photos of a group of men, and she'd picked him out. They had his wall with all the pictures and his hair souvenirs. Along with the murder charges, they'd add kidnapping and assaulting a federal officer, in addition to Delaney and Nichole.

"You tricked me. I want a lawyer," he said, apparently realizing he'd just confessed.

"You were read your rights when you were brought into this room. Remember the part about anything you say can be used against you? But sure, we'll get you a court-appointed attorney. Have a nice day, Mr. Tompkins."

When she walked out of the room, Nate was waiting. He gave her a high five. "Well done, tiger."

"Thanks." She was just glad it was over.

It hadn't been easy keeping her cool in front of the man who'd killed her mother and those other poor women. What she wasn't expecting to feel was empty. Finally seeing Tompkins behind bars wouldn't bring her mother back, and he was such a pathetic excuse for a man that she couldn't even bring herself to hate him.

It wasn't lost on her that as children, they'd both been witnesses to their mothers' murders. If not for Rosie, there was no telling how she would have turned out. She almost felt sorry for him, for the boy who hadn't had a Rosie in his life when he'd needed one the most.

And then there was the man walking next to her with his hand on her back. She loved when he did that, but she wished he wouldn't. When he touched her, it made her want to nestle into him, made her want more from him than he was willing to give. And that, more than anything, was the reason for the emptiness residing inside her.

"Now that I don't need a bodyguard, would you drop me off at my apartment so I can get my car?"

"I can, but maybe you don't need it. We're off for the rest of the day and tomorrow."

She glanced up at him. "We are? Why?"

They came to his car, and he faced her. "Because I asked and Rothmire agreed." He looked down at the pavement, then lifted his eyes to hers. "I thought maybe we could have dinner and have that talk we've been putting off, and then you'd come with me to Dunnellon in the morning."

There was a vulnerability in his eyes that made her want to say yes, but she hesitated. What did he want for them? If it was just back to friends with benefits, she couldn't do it. And honestly, even if he was willing to use the word *relationship* with her, at some point, he would end it, leaving her heartbroken. Or more heartbroken than she already was.

"I think your visit tomorrow is something you need to do on your own. It's your discovery to make. And I'm going to pass on tonight. The girls will be home tomorrow, and I need to stock up Rosie's refrigerator and plan a welcome meal for them."

"We need to talk, Taylor. At least have dinner with me."

Dammit, her eyes were burning. She willed her tears away. "I don't think that's a good idea." Rothmire walked out of the building. "Listen, I need to stop by the office for a few minutes. I'll catch a ride with the boss. Rand or someone can run me home."

She walked away before she could change her mind, but she hated how Nate's expression had blanked. Should she have listened to what he had to say? No, she already knew. He'd offer an exclusive relationship simply because that was what she'd asked for, but then he'd explain again why he'd never marry.

What he would offer her no longer worked for her. She wanted it all. His love and his ring on her finger.

CHAPTER TWENTY-SIX

"I warned you that if you stole one more beer, you'd regret it." Nate stood toe-to-toe with Dirty Dan. Nate was ready to hurt someone, and Dirty Dan would do just fine.

Dirty Dan smirked. "Like I never heard that from you before, but you're all bark. I don't think you have the balls to take me on." He guzzled the rest of the stolen beer, then smacked his lips as he reached across the bar and refilled the mug.

Rage filled Nate's brain. He saw nothing but the asshole he was going to beat to a pulp.

That's right. Beat the shit out of him, boy, his father's voice said in his head.

Nate's heart stopped, or at least it felt like it did. He wasn't his fucking father. He stumbled back, and as he became aware of his surroundings again, he saw his brothers watching him, concern on their faces. Like a drunken man, he lurched away, heading for the office.

"Knew you didn't have the balls," Dirty Dan called after him.

Dirty Dan was wrong. He had the balls, he just chose not to use them for violence. Dirty Dan should consider himself lucky he wasn't about to be dead.

"Get the hell out and never come back. Aces and Eights is closed to you forever," he heard Court say to Dirty Dan.

"Keep an eye on things," Alex said to their bartender.

Damn pesky brothers. They were following him. He was tempted to lock them out of the office, but they'd just stand on the other side and bang on the door until he let them in.

He went straight to the bar, poured a shot of whiskey—which he hated, so it was the only liquor he allowed himself when needing a stiff drink—into a glass. Downing it, he grimaced. Christ, that was awful. But it gave him the burn all the way down to his stomach—which he craved—without making him want more. He set the glass on the mini-bar counter, then faced his brothers.

"Go away."

"Not a good sign when you're drinking whiskey, so we're not going away," Court said. He plopped down on the black leather sofa. "Talk to us."

Alex planted his ass on the other end of the couch. "You came close to losing it, bro. And it wasn't because of Dirty Dan. The two of you have always played a game of him stealing beer and you catching him. Hell, you have as much fun over that as him. What's really bothering you?"

"Do either of you not understand what 'go away' means?"

Court and Alex exchanged a glance, then Court said, "We know what it means, but when this is the first time our big brother needs us? Not gonna happen."

"What he said," Alex said.

"I don't need you, either of you. So I mean it. Go away."

Alex lifted his feet, putting them on the coffee table and crossing his ankles. "Now I'm definitely not going away." He glanced at Court. "How about you?"

"Nope, not until he tells us what's going on in his head." Court put his booted feet on the coffee table, too. Both his brothers looked as if they weren't about to budge.

"I think he's in love," Alex said.

Court frowned at Alex. "And that's a problem because?"

"Because he's afraid, maybe?"

Nate would willingly die for the two idiots he claimed as brothers, but he was going to kill them if they didn't shut up.

"Of what?" Court asked.

Alex shrugged. "Until he starts talking, all we can do is guess." Alex eyed Nate. "Or we could take him down, torture him until he tells us why Dirty Dan came within an inch of dying tonight."

"There's an idea." Court looked at Nate. "Which is it going to be, bro? Talk or fight? We're up for either."

They weren't going to leave him alone, but he didn't really want them to. He wearily sank down in the desk chair. Even though he'd grown up with these two men, they'd never talked much about their father and what the bastard had put them all through. That they each hated the old man was a given, and it had never been necessary to put that sentiment in words. The less they thought about him, the happier they were.

"I'm growing moss under my feet, bro," Alex said. "Spit it out. What's bugging you?"

Nate picked up a pen and tapped it on the desk. "You ever wonder if you could turn out like the old man?"

"Why would we wonder that?" Court said.

"Twenty-five to thirty-five percent of abused children grow up to be abusers."

"Truthfully, I'm surprised it isn't a higher percentage." Alex frowned. "But what's that got to do with anything?"

"You've never worried that you could lose your temper and seriously hurt someone?"

Court's eyes lit with understanding. "You're afraid of becoming like him."

"That's a crock of shit," Alex said. "You could never be like that man."

"You don't know that. I don't know that." None of them ever referred to their sire as their father. That would give him respect he'd never earned.

"You remember when I"—Court made air quotes—"'borrowed' your favorite shirt?"

"Yeah, you tore it."

"You were pissed, but you didn't put a hand on me."

No, he'd gone for a long walk in the woods behind their property, something he'd done back then whenever he was angry.

"Remember when I shaved off your eyebrows the first time you got drunk? All you did was yell at me."

Nate glared at Alex. "I might still beat you up for that one. And it was the only time I've ever been drunk."

"And why is that?" Court dropped his feet to the floor. "Because the old man got drunk every day, and you didn't want to be like him. And another thing. You don't do relationships because you've always been afraid you'd lose it at some point and hurt a woman. Am I wrong?"

Nate shook his head.

"Well, consider this. If it's Taylor you want, go for it. If you ever did try to hurt her, she'd give as good as she got. She can fight with the best of us."

"And if you ever did hurt her, we'd help her bury you in the backyard," Alex said.

Court nodded in agreement. "Truth."

"What about her girls? They sure as hell can't fight back against someone like me."

"Christ, man." Alex stood. "If Court and I couldn't get you to beat on us, brats that we were, you think you'd really lose it with them so badly you'd want to hurt them?" He walked to the door, then paused. "If you don't see that you're a good man, then you are really stupid." He walked out, slamming the door behind him.

Nate frowned. "What's his problem?"

"You've always been his hero, and he wants to see you happy. It frustrates him that you think you could be anything like the old man. You don't have it in you to be like that," Court said.

"I almost killed that man once, would have if you hadn't pulled me off him. I'd say that's proof that I do have it in me." That day and the rage burning inside him was marked on his brain like a giant *X*, a warning of what he could turn into.

"He deserved to die for shredding Alex's back like that and for an endless list of other reasons. If I'd been a few years older and stronger, I'd have killed him myself. That one act doesn't define you, Nate, so don't let it stop you from going after what you want." Court pushed up. "Let yourself be happy, brother. Get out of here and go talk to Taylor. If you haven't admitted it to yourself, you're in love with her. Alex and I'll close up tonight." He glanced over his shoulder as he walked out. "And for what it's worth, you're my hero, too."

Alone, Nate tried to blink away the burning in his eyes. As his brothers' words settled into his mind, he still didn't feel like a hero, but for the first time, he believed that he had as much right to be as happy as the next person.

Would he ever hurt Taylor in a fit of anger? No fucking way. Alex had it right. He'd put a gun to his temple first. He pressed his head against the back of the chair and closed his eyes. Hell, if he even dared to raise his hand to Taylor, she'd put him on his ass.

What about her girls? Could he ever lose his temper enough to hurt them? He thought about it, and the answer was an adamant no. There was nothing they could do to make him want to hurt them.

If he did get angry over something, all he had to do was walk away until he calmed down, something his father had never done. But was it really that easy, walking away? He considered it. Yeah, it really was. Just put one foot in front of the other and leave. Go for a long motorcycle ride—which always calmed him—or go to the gym and kill a punching bag.

A weight that had lived like a heavy rock in his chest for as long as he could remember vanished with the understanding that he could control his actions. So simple, and so stupid that he'd never grasped that before now. Screw the statistics. He didn't have to be like his father unless he chose to be.

If you haven't admitted it to yourself, you're in love with her, Court had said. *Love.* Not a word he'd ever allowed himself to hope for, long ago accepting he'd spend his life alone. But watching his brothers fall for their wives, he'd tried not to envy them. As surprising as it was, he was in love.

And the big question? Had he lost his chance with Taylor?

♠♠♠

Taylor stirred chocolate chips into the batter for the pancakes, the girls' favorite breakfast. The K2 guys had taken turns driving through the night, and Rosie had called to say that they would be home in thirty minutes.

The girls loved chocolate-chip pancakes, piled high with whipped cream. It was a rare indulgence for them, but Taylor planned to spoil them a little this morning. She'd missed them so much and was probably more excited about seeing them than they were to see her.

Her phone pinged, signaling a text. She picked it up and swiped the screen, her heart giving a little stutter at seeing Nate's name.

Leaving for Dunnellon. Give girls a hug for me.

She stared at the message, trying not to read anything into Nate texting her.

Hope you find your answers, she finally typed.

Me too

She thought they were done, but as she lowered the phone to the counter, another text showed up.

Can I stop by tonight?

No. Yes. She didn't know.

Call when u get back

That would give her time to decide if she was ready to see him.

K

When she'd walked away to catch a ride with their boss yesterday, she'd wanted Nate to stop her, to show her that he'd fight for her. But he'd let her go without a word. She'd cried herself to sleep last night, alone in her bed. It was the last time she'd shed tears over him, though. If not for Rosie and the girls, she'd ask for a transfer. To the other side of the country, preferably. But she could never leave them, so she'd just have to suck it up and do her best to get over him.

Besides, what did she need a man for? She had a great job she loved, her little family, and a perfectly serviceable vibrator. Oh, and Henry Too. Mustn't forget him. From nothing, she'd managed to create a pretty nice life for herself, and every time that part of her heart belonging to Nate hurt, she'd remind herself that she had no reason to complain.

At the sound of a vehicle in Rosie's driveway, Taylor rushed outside. The K2 guys already had the side door to the van open and were helping her girls out. As soon as they saw her, all but Annie, who was in Ryan's arms, ran to her.

Taylor dropped her knees to the ground and held out her arms. They tumbled into her, laughing and hugging her. "Goodness, look at your tans. Did you have fun at the beach?" She already knew the answer, as every evening when she talked to them, she'd heard how much fun they were having, especially burying Ryan and Jamie in the sand.

"Yes!" Sarrie and June exclaimed as one.

Bri wiggled out of Taylor's hold. "We want to go on a beach vacation every year. Saint and Doc said we could come to Pensacola and see them. They said that's where the prettiest beaches in the whole world are. Can we?"

"We'll see. Right now, I'm just so happy you're home. I missed all of you so much."

Elle squeezed her arms around Taylor's neck. "We missed you, too. You shoulda come with us."

Not to be left out, Robin said, "I missed you the most."

"Did not," Bri said. "We all missed her the same."

"Tay!" Annie yelled.

Taylor laughed when Ryan stuck his finger in his ear and shook his head.

"Girl's got a set of lungs," he said.

He put Annie down, and she wobble-walked to Taylor. "Tay!" she screamed again, falling into Taylor's lap.

"Hello, baby girl." Taylor wrapped her arms around Annie. "It's about time you came home. Missed you."

Rosie and the K2 men unloaded the suitcases and took them into the house. When the guys returned, Taylor kissed the top of Annie's head, then stood, holding her little girl, and walked over to the guys.

"I don't know how to thank you. Because of you, I didn't have to worry about him coming after the girls."

"Anytime you need us to watch over them, we're just a phone call away," Jamie said.

Ryan smiled at Annie. "They're a delight." He poked Annie in the stomach, making her giggle. "Especially this one. If you weren't so attached to her, I'd steal her right out of your arms."

"Tell Taylor you said we could come to Pensacola," Bri said.

"That's right. Your next vacation, you should come up with the girls. Our wives and kids would love that."

"I'll seriously consider it. You have time for breakfast? I'm making chocolate-chip pancakes."

"Yay! Chocolate-chip pancakes," Robin said, jumping up and down.

Jamie shook his head. "Tempting, but we need to get on the road."

They squatted, said their good-byes to the girls, and got hugs from each of them, with promises that they'd get Taylor to bring them to the beach in Pensacola. When they got in the van, waving as they pulled out of the driveway, Annie burst into tears.

"No go," she cried.

"Ah, sweetie, you'll see them again. Let's go feed you."

She walked into the house with her little family. She tried not to wish that Nate were here to welcome them home with her.

CHAPTER TWENTY-SEVEN

Once again, Nate sat in his car outside of the run-down house in Dunnellon. This was it, the day he'd get his answers. As he walked up to the door, he couldn't decide if he hoped his mother was in that house or not.

Before he could knock, the door opened, and Nate recognized Harmon Baker. The years hadn't been kind to him. Dressed in stained overalls, a good twenty pounds underweight, and with a gray beard that looked like it needed a wash, the man Nate remembered being kind to them narrowed his eyes.

"I wondered how long it'd take ya to come with yer questions," he said in greeting as he came out onto the porch. "Expected ya years ago. Which Gentry brother are ya? Never could get ya boys straight in my head."

So Harmon remembered them. "I'm Nate, the oldest one." He held out his hand to the old man.

"The one got beat on the most," Harmon said, shaking Nate's hand. "Yer pa weren't a good man."

Nate couldn't argue with that. He eyed the door that had been left open a crack, wondering if his mother was in there, watching. "Do you have a few minutes?"

"Ain't got nothin' but time these days. Ya finally decide to look for yer mama?"

"Yeah. Is she here?"

Harmon scrunched bushy gray eyebrows together. "Why would ya think that?"

Apparently, he wasn't going to be invited inside. "Because I saw her leave with you that day."

"So ya assumed? Ya know what they say 'bout assumin', boy?"

Nate fought a grin that the old man was calling him a boy. "I do. If she's not here, then do you know where she is?"

"Nope. I been waitin' years to tell one of you boys what I know. Ya shoulda cared about her long before now."

"I'm sorry I didn't come sooner, but I'm here now. What do you know?" He wished Taylor were with him. He had a bad feeling about what he was going to hear.

Harmon shuffled over to the porch rail—which, if the man had weighed any more than he did, would have given way when he leaned against it. "Ya sure ya wanna hear this, boy?"

Nate nodded. "I saw her get in your truck. I always thought she ran away with you, leaving us in his hands."

The old man grunted. "Then ya were a fool, boy," he said. "I took yer mama to the bus station. That's all I did. Yer daddy woulda beat my ass if'n he ever knowed that, so I left town. I din't want to git involved, but when she told me why she had to leave, couldn't say no to her."

When Harmon stared into the distance, seemingly lost in time, Nate said, "Why did she have to leave?" He already had a sinking feeling that it was because of what Court had overheard. Their mother had been pregnant.

"Why?" the old man said, focusing rheumy eyes back on Nate. "It was 'cause of the baby. Yer daddy tried to beat it out of her belly. I was there that day. Heard her screams as he whupped up on her. I couldn't cotton to that, so I helped her leave. Everything happened real fast. Your daddy took off in his truck, and soon as he was gone, she begged me to help git her away. So I did. Took her to the bus station. Last time I saw her."

The air left Nate's lungs, and he struggled to breathe. All these years he'd believed their mother had left them for the man staring back at him with disappointment. Eff him to hell. How had he let himself think that about a woman who, until she'd walked down that dusty dirt road, had never given him or his brothers a reason to doubt her?

"Do you know where she went?" he asked.

"Nope. Din't want to know in case yer papa came callin'. She sent me a picture after the baby came. Still have it. Saved it fer when you came callin'. I'll go git it."

As Nate waited on the porch, he tried to wrap his mind around the fact that he had a brother or sister. What he did know was that he'd find his mother and somehow try to make things right with her.

Harmon Baker returned, holding out an envelope. Nate took it, and the first thing he noticed was the stamp and that it had been mailed from Gainesville. A starting point in his search. Unfortunately, there wasn't a return address.

"You kept in touch with her?"

"Nope, but I kept my post-office box even after I moved so she could let me know if she needed help. Ya know, like money for the baby. But she never asked."

That didn't surprise him. Their mother had been too proud to ask for help, that much he remembered about her. He slipped his fingers inside, hesitated when he touched the contents, then pulled out a

Polaroid photo. How long he stared at the picture, he couldn't say. He guessed the baby to be about six months old when it was taken. She had the same black hair and black eyes as he and his brothers. He smiled at seeing the little pink bow in her hair. Standing on that rickety porch with an old man who was disappointed in him, he fell in love with the little girl in the decades-old photo.

Where was she now? Who was she? They'd searched for Wanda Gentry, but their mother's trail had grown cold the minute she'd walked away. What name had she taken? What was his sister's name? With all his questions, there was one thing he did know. His brothers would want to find their mother and sister as much as he did.

"Can I keep this?" he asked. If the answer was no, he was keeping it anyway.

"That's why I saved it. To give to one of you boys when ya decided to come callin'," Harmon said.

"Thank you." He pulled out his wallet, flipping it open to the bills in it. It was obvious the man had nothing to his name, and Nate meant to thank him as best he knew how.

"Don't want yer money," Harmon said, scowling at Nate. "Just go find yer mama and sister." He walked into his house, closing the door behind him.

Harmon Baker had helped their mother escape the cruelest man Nate knew, and had apparently done it out of the kindness of his heart. That he didn't have a pot to piss in was obvious. Nate jogged down the wobbly stairs, picked up a decent-sized rock, and then returned to the porch. He emptied his wallet of the four hundred dollars he had in it, put the bills on the floor in front of the door, then set the rock on top of them.

He returned to his car, and after sitting for a few minutes, considering his next move, he called Court.

"I'll be at your place for a late lunch. Get subs or something. Tell Alex I want him there when I get back. In the meantime, see what you can find on a Wanda Gentry in Gainesville." He hung up before his brother could ask any questions.

♠♠♠

"We have a sister," Alex said for the third time, staring at the yellowed photo of the baby girl. He set it on the table between him and Court. "We have to find her and our mother."

Court looked up from his monitor. "Nothing's coming up on her from the day she left us."

"Then she either stayed off the grid, or she somehow got a new identity." Nate pushed his half-finished sub aside. "Our mother wasn't an educated woman, nor did she have any friends to turn to. She likely changed her name but didn't know how to go about getting a fake I.D."

"You think she found jobs where they paid her under the table?" Alex said.

"Yeah. Motel maid, maybe a waitress at the kind of place that didn't ask questions, housekeeper for a private individual, something like that."

Court frowned. "If she didn't have I.D., then she couldn't apply for any kind of welfare, and with a baby, it would be hard to hold down a job."

For so long, thinking that she'd abandoned them for a man, Nate hadn't cared about what might have happened to his mother. Now the idea of her starving and trying to care for a child sat heavy in his chest.

"Keep looking," he said, standing. "You two need to head over to Aces and Eights soon."

"You're not coming?" Alex said.

"Nope. I've . . ." He paused, not used to baring his soul, but it was time to let his brothers into his life. "I've got a woman to win, if it's not too late."

Alex sprang up, wrapped his arms around him, and hugged him hard. "Finally."

"I'm going to shoot you if you don't let go of me, bro." Nate rolled his eyes over Alex's shoulder at Court's smirk. "I mean it, Alex. Let go." Opening up to his brothers was one thing, but this touchy-feely crap wasn't going to cut it.

"Love you, man," Alex said.

He patted his baby brother's back. "Ditto. Now get the hell off me."

Court laughed. "Ah, you're gonna hurt his feelings."

"I'm going to hurt a lot more than that the next time he goes all girly on me."

Alex stepped back. And eff him. He knew that look in Alex's eyes.

"Girly, huh?" Alex said, staring down at Nate after putting him on his back. "Want to call me that again?"

"Probably not." And because his baby brother was his favorite idiot, Nate found himself laughing. He held out his hand. "Help me up." As soon as Alex's hand was in reach, Nate grabbed him by the wrist and scissored his legs around Alex's with the intention of bringing Alex down to the floor with him.

"Knew you were going to do that," Alex said, somehow twisting his body away.

"I'm getting too old for this." Nate laughed again as he struggled up. Someday soon, he was going to have to accept that he'd never best Alex. The boy was that good. "Go on. Get out of here. Both of you."

After they left, he showered, shaved, and then spent a stupid twenty minutes trying to decide what to wear to romance a woman.

♠♠♠

Taylor dropped flakes of food into Henry Too's tank. She'd spent a wonderful day with her girls, but the fun had been dulled because a certain frustrating man stayed on her mind. All day, she'd gone back and forth, one minute deciding she'd agree to see him when he called, and the next changing her mind.

"Life is so easy for you, Henry Too. All you have to do is swim around and wait for food to fall out of the sky." He darted from flake to flake, gulping them up.

All afternoon, she'd expected her phone to buzz, but it had remained silent. At the very least, he owed it to her to let her know if he'd learned anything about his mother. Maybe he wasn't going to call after all. She should be relieved. Wasn't that what she wanted?

No, it wasn't.

Accepting that her phone wasn't going to ring, she jumped in the shower. After toweling dry, she put on her comfiest yoga pants and an oversized FBI T-shirt. She poured a glass of wine and took it and her Kindle to the sofa. It was a sad state of affairs that the only romance in her life was found in a book.

She'd made it to chapter two when her doorbell rang. "You expecting company, Henry Too?" It was probably her neighbor, locked out again. It had happened so many times that she'd given Taylor a key to keep for when she needed it. On the way to the door, she scooped Mrs. Preston's key out of the bowl. But when she looked through the peephole, it was not her elderly neighbor on the other side of the door.

"Crap," she muttered. Of course, Nate would show up after she'd put on her ugliest nightclothes. Well, it was his fault for not calling first. She cracked open her door.

"Hey. Thought you were going to call before you came over." It would make her happy if her heart didn't decide that bouncing in her chest was the appropriate response at seeing him. And even worse was how her mouth watered at the sight of him wearing a button-down white shirt rolled up at the sleeves and black dress pants.

Don't you dare drool, Taylor!

"I was afraid you'd tell me not to come over."

There was a vulnerability there that she'd never seen before in the man standing in front of her with his hands behind his back. Her stupid heart continued acting up by going soft at the uncertainty in his eyes. Nate Gentry was never unsure of himself, but he was now.

"Can I come in?"

"Um . . ." She stepped back. "Yeah, okay. Give me a few minutes to change." *And to get my heart to stop pounding.* As he walked past her, still keeping his hands hidden behind his back, she caught his spicy scent and had to fight the urge to sniff him.

"You look fine. Kind of cute, really."

She scoffed as she glanced down at herself. "Kind of cute?" Gah, she'd dripped wine down her T-shirt. "Pretty sure I have a homeless fashion thingy going on here."

"I'd take you home with me." He took his hands from behind his back. In one was a bouquet of wildflowers in a mason jar, and in the other an iced mocha coffee piled high with whipped cream.

"For me?" Okay, that was a stupid question.

He grinned. "No, they're for Henry Too."

"What's going on, Nate?" His smile faded, and she wished she could take the question back. But not really, since she was totally confused. A man bringing a woman flowers and her favorite beverage seemed a lot like he was courting her. Courting and friends with benefits were two completely different things. Weren't they?

"I guess I'll drink this myself," he said instead of answering her question.

"No way." She grabbed the coffee from him, and while she was at it, she might as well take the flowers. It wasn't like a man brought her a bouquet every day. Actually, it was only the third time, four if she counted Wayne Tompkins, and she definitely wasn't. Twice from Nate, and one of her two boyfriends had given her flowers once on her birthday.

"I'll just go put some water in this." The mason jar was really cute. "Then I'll go put some decent clothes on."

"No, don't. I should have called."

She hated how unsure of himself he seemed tonight. That was so not Nate, and she didn't like it. "Okay. How did it go this morning?" After filling the jar with water, she took it and her iced coffee to the living room, setting the flowers on the coffee table where she could see them. Curling up on the sofa, her legs tucked under her, she waved her hand for Nate to take a seat.

He shook a Tic Tac into his palm, then popped it into his mouth as he sat at the opposite end, angling his body to face her. "It was what Court said. She was pregnant. But all Harmon Baker did was take her to the bus station."

As he told her what he'd learned, tears filled her eyes. All these years, he'd believed the worst of his mother, and she saw the guilt of that on his face.

"You couldn't have known," she said when he finished. "Considering you saw her get in that truck with him, along with the fact that until recently, you guys didn't share with each other what you knew."

He shook his head. "It's like Alex said. We should have known she wouldn't abandon us without a good reason."

"How do all of you feel about having a sister?" That had to have come as a shock.

"I don't think it's really sunk in yet for any of us. We're trying to find them."

Of course they were.

"We don't even know what names they might be using." His gaze shifted to the fish tank, then returned to her. His throat flexed as he swallowed hard. "But that's not what I want to talk about tonight."

"Oh?" She sipped her iced coffee as she tried to ignore the hope that had been building in her chest ever since she'd opened the door. There was no reason for it. All he was going to do was try to convince her to take up where they'd left off.

"I'll say this straight out, Taylor. I'm in love with you."

Aaaand she choked, dribbling coffee all over herself. "Crap." She set the cup on the table, then brushed at her T-shirt, doing nothing but smearing the stain. *Real cool, Taylor. The man tells you he loves you, and you spit coffee at him.*

He blew out a breath. "Not exactly the reaction I was hoping for."

She had no response to that. Had she even heard him right? She had thought that if he were ever to say those words to her—and sometimes late at night, she'd let herself dream of that happening—she'd always imagined the moment would be straight out of a romance novel.

The setting would be somewhere romantic, she'd be wearing a sexy dress, and they'd stare into each other's eyes as he said the three little words she longed to hear. It had never occurred to her to imagine a scene from a romantic comedy if this day ever came. Well, he had brought her flowers, so that was pretty romantic.

"Seriously, can I go change my clothes?" His eyes blanked, so she hastened to add, "I refuse to tell you that I love you with wine and coffee stains on my shirt."

A slow smile lifted his lips. "How about I help you change?"

"That'll work." Weirdest avowals of love in the world. It suddenly struck her funny, and she burst into laughter. Or maybe it was the way her heart was doing a jig in her chest that had sent her straight into silly.

She grabbed his hand and pulled him into her bedroom with her.

CHAPTER TWENTY-EIGHT

Nate could breathe again. He'd never thought he would tell a woman he loved her, and when he finally had, her first word had been *crap* as coffee had dripped down her chin. About the time he'd decided to leave—to retreat and regroup—she'd started laughing and had insanely said that she couldn't say the words back in a stained T-shirt.

So instead of temporarily walking out—temporarily, because there was no way he was going to give up on her now that she owned his heart—he found himself laughing with her as she led him to her bedroom.

"Oh, my flowers. I need them."

When she tried to return to the living room, he tugged on her hand. "Go on. I'll get them." He liked that she wanted them with her. At the florist shop, he'd considered roses again, but he'd done those already. And then he'd spied the wildflowers in a mason jar, and they'd seemed to be something she'd like. Halfway to her house, he'd had second thoughts, questioning his decision not to go with something fancier.

The jar of flowers in hand, he headed for Taylor's bedroom. Seriously? Wildflowers? He'd really screwed this night up. What he should have done was plan a special night. Except he had no experience in planning romantic evenings. He should have asked his sisters-in-law for advice, but he'd been too anxious to see Taylor to even think of doing that.

He snorted. Who was this man wishing he'd asked for romance advice? But when he walked into the bedroom and saw Taylor, wearing nothing but tiny blue panties, standing at the end of her bed, a shy smile on her face, whatever he'd been thinking was lost.

"Tur . . ." He cleared his throat. "Turn around." She slowly pivoted. Yep, it was a thong. His eyes landed on her creamy-white ass cheeks. God help him. He might never be able to think again.

She peeked at him over her shoulder. "I was going to put a shirt or something on, but I figured you'd just take it right back off."

"You figured right. Don't move." He set her flowers on the nightstand, then prowled toward her, his gaze focused on her back. When he reached her, he lifted her hair and put his mouth to her neck. She was warm, with that hint of lemons he'd come to love.

"You smell good. You taste good," he said, moving his lips against her skin. She shivered, and he nipped at her neck and was rewarded with another shiver. He loved that he could make her do that. Truthfully, there was nothing he didn't love about her. Except maybe that she still hadn't said she loved him. He would torture it out of her if he had to, but it would be a torture she'd enjoy.

When she wiggled against him, he put his hands on her hips, holding her still. As turned on as he was already, he'd lose it before he had his clothes off if she kept doing that. What he wanted tonight—wanted for them—was something so special that they'd still be talking about it years from now.

He wrapped one arm around her chest, holding her tight against him. "I'm going to make you come," he whispered into her ear. She moaned as he danced his fingers down her stomach, occasionally pausing, waiting for her to push her belly against his hand, wanting him to keep on going.

There was something sexy about the thin barrier of his shirt and pants between them. He was dying to be inside her, but not yet. He trailed his tongue from her neck to across her shoulder. Out of the corner of his eye, he noticed the mirror over her dresser.

"Walk," he said, pushing her with his body to that mirror where he could see her face when he made her come. Standing in front of it, her eyes found his in the reflection. Taylor, when not in the thrones of passion, had blue eyes that made him think of the sky on a cloudless day, but Taylor turned on? Hot damn. Those eyes were as dark blue as storm clouds just before they turned black.

Right then, there was nothing he wanted more than to chase that storm, even if it destroyed him. He watched her in the mirror as his fingers found her sex. She watched him back. She let out a low moan when he dipped his hand under the band of her panties and slipped a finger inside her. And wasn't that the hottest thing he'd ever heard?

He toyed with her, played her with his fingers. At the moment he recognized she was going to come, he stilled.

"Tell me you love me."

"I might tell you that later," she said as she put her hands over his, trying to force him to continue pleasuring her.

She could out-technique him on the mat, but she wasn't strong enough to make his fingers move when he didn't want them to. "That doesn't work for me, tiger. Tell me now." And there, that was what he loved about her, that challenge in her eyes. His equal. She wasn't going to say a word until she was good and ready. Well, he'd see about that.

"If you want to come, say it." He played with her some more, stopping again when he saw that she was on the edge. "Say it, Taylor."

Now he was the one pleading. And interestingly enough, he didn't care. She could fight him all she wanted if she'd just say the words he wanted to hear. The ones he needed to hear.

She smirked. "I don't feel like saying them yet."

"Little brat." He hoped this was like it would always be between them. Neither giving an inch.

"You have too many clothes on," she said, trying to turn around.

"They'll come off when you say what I want to hear." He tightened his arm around her breasts, holding her in place. As he let his fingers move again, he pressed against her, letting her feel how much he wanted her. "Say it." In the mirror, he watched her bite down on her bottom lip, challenge lighting a fire in her eyes.

"Make me."

"Now you've gone and done it." He fought a grin and failed. Yeah, the woman was going to always keep him on his toes. He spun her around, then pulled her panties down as he dropped to his knees. She was going to say the damn words.

He peppered kisses on her inner thighs, smiling against her leg when she bucked. He hadn't even reached the best part of her yet. With each kiss on her skin, he inched closer to his prize. She buried her fingers in his hair, then tried to guide him to her core. He wasn't having it. This was going to happen on his terms.

"Nate, please."

"You know what you have to do." He teased all around her sensitive flesh with his lips and tongue.

"You're a bastard." She pulled the band out of his hair, letting it drop to the floor.

He chuckled. "But I'm your bastard." He flicked his tongue over her sex, and she fisted her hand around his hair, pulling hard.

"Please," she begged.

"Say it." He stroked his tongue over her. "Say it, Taylor."

"Dammit, Nate, I love you."

As much as he'd wanted to hear the words from her mouth, he hadn't been prepared for the pure rush of pleasure that surged though him. It was a good thing he was already on his knees, because he would have ended up on them.

Maybe any other man would have taken offense at how she'd said them, but it had been perfect for them. She was for sure going to make his life interesting, but he wouldn't have it any other way. Giving her what she wanted, it only took seconds before she cried out. He loved hearing his name on her lips.

When she put her hands on his shoulders for support, he stood, scooped her up, and carried her to the bed. She watched him undress, her gaze lowering with each piece of clothing he removed. By the time he stood in front of her in nothing but his briefs, he feared he was going to embarrass himself.

"Turn around," she said, echoing his earlier command to him.

He obeyed, then glanced over his shoulder. "Do I pass inspection?"

She quirked a grin. "Can't answer that yet. You're well on the way, but I have to touch the merchandise first."

It occurred to him that sex had been on autopilot before her. Get in, get what he needed, and then get out as fast as possible. He made sure the women got their pleasure, too, but even that had been on automatic. Step A, step B, step C in a learned routine of what women liked.

But with Taylor, everything was different. There was fun—something he'd never experienced where sex was concerned—and there was . . . He wasn't even sure he could explain it if he tried. There was just more. Of everything.

"Touch away," he said, coming to the bed after discarding his briefs. He climbed over her, bracing himself on his hands and knees. "Make sure the merchandise meets your approval."

"Mmm." She put her hands on his hips, then trailed them over his ass. "So far so good."

He kissed her then, starting with one corner of her mouth, teasing her with soft nips until she wrapped her arms around his neck, opened her mouth and thrust her tongue against his. As was the way with them, their kisses became a duel, a battle for supremacy. He pressed his body against hers, his shaft finding its way to the *v* of her sex, seeking entrance. Gasping, he pulled away and grabbed the condom he'd put on the nightstand when he'd removed his pants.

"Hurry," she said, as if the few seconds it took to roll it on was too long.

When he covered her body with his, she put her hands on his waist, sliding along his ribs, and then down his back, exploring every inch of him. He guided himself inside her, groaning as he slid home. Leaning over her, he braced himself on his elbows and stared down at her. Her lips were moist and swollen from their kisses, her eyes were that deep blue that made them shimmer like pools of water.

He withdrew, then slid back in, slow strokes as he watched her face, loving the way she looked back at him, as if there was nothing in her world but him.

"I love you," he said, and her soft smile filled his empty heart and soul.

Taylor would never get tired of hearing him say that. "I love you, too." He laughed, except it wasn't really a laugh. More like a rusty sound of happiness. "That's five," she whispered.

"Five what?" He thrust deep into her.

"Oh, that felt good." She lifted her hips, meeting his rhythm. "Five times I've made you laugh."

Another thrust. "I laugh."

"No, you don't, or at least you didn't used to." She gave her hands free rein to explore, loving the feel of his body, of the hard planes and muscles and the firm roundness of his butt.

He buried himself to the hilt, and she moaned a raspy "yes." She wrapped her legs around his thighs, urging him to go faster, harder.

"Talk dirty to me, Nate."

"Sweet Jesus," he growled. He lifted onto his elbows and stared down at her with glittery eyes. "I'm going to whisper dirty things in your ear, do more dirty things to you with my mouth, and when I'm done with you, you're going to be ruined for any other man but me."

She already was. He smiled then, a very wicked smile that had her toes curling. Oh, God, she knew that look. She'd freed the beast, and the beast was hungry. He put his devious mouth to work on her breasts as he moved inside her slow and deep.

"Oh, God," she cried when he whispered into her ear what he was going to do to her. He was relentless, bringing her to the edge, then pausing, refusing to give her more until she begged.

"Please, Nate. I need . . ."

"What do you need?" He licked a nipple, then kissed her hard. "Tell me," he said, lifting his mouth from hers.

"I need you to let me come." She lifted her hips to meet this thrust. "Please," she added, loving the way his eyes smiled at her plea.

"Only because you said please."

The cords in his neck strained, and as he picked up his pace, she let go, exploding in waves of ecstasy. Her eyes tried to close, but she willed them to stay open, to watch him as he gave in to the pleasure rolling through him. His eyes never left hers, a muscle in his jaw ticked, his lips were pressed firmly together, and his beautiful hair formed a curtain around the sides of his face. She reached up and combed her fingers through the silky strands.

"Taylor," he said as his body visibly shuddered. He lowered his body, burying his face against her neck. "Taylor," he said again.

She'd heard him say her name a thousand times, but it was different tonight. There was love in the sound of it. Overwhelmed with happiness, she squeezed her eyes shut before the tears leaked out.

When his heavy breaths eased, he rolled away. "Be right back."

Even knowing he'd return in a minute, the bed felt empty without him. She pressed her nose into the pillow she now considered his, breathing in his scent lingering on the case. If he was going to spend nights in her bed, she needed to buy something bigger than the double mattress she had now.

Where would they go from here? she wondered.

"Come here," he said when he slid back into the bed. He pulled her against him, her back to his chest. "I'm not done with you tonight, tiger, but let's talk a little."

His warm breath blew against her ear, sending shivers through her. "Okay. What's on your mind?"

"A lot. First, how are the girls?"

Warmth filled her heart that he'd asked about them. She laced her fingers with the hand he had resting on her stomach. "Great. All tanned and happy. They can't stop talking about the beach, sandcastles, and the K2 guys."

"Annie better not be replacing me as her boyfriend. I'll go with you in the morning to see them, make sure I haven't been forgotten."

Taylor smiled. "I think she still considers you her boyfriend, along with Ryan and Jamie. She asked for you about a dozen times today." She peeked over her shoulder to see his reaction to that.

His eyes narrowed. "Unacceptable. I'm her one and only." He nipped at her earlobe. "Just like I'm your one and only." He chuckled. "I never thought I'd say that to a woman."

She turned to face him. "Does that scare you?"

"It should." He put his hand on her hip, pressing his fingers into her skin. "But strangely, not at all. Truthfully, it excites me."

"Me, too." She only hoped tonight was real and she wasn't dreaming. If she woke up to an empty bed, it would break her heart. "I love you, Nate Gentry."

"Move in with me."

She blinked. Well, she hadn't been expecting that.

"At least think about it," he said when she didn't respond. "I'm not talking marriage. It's too soon for that, although I'm hoping we get there someday. But living together makes a lot of sense. We've gone and fallen in love. I plan to spend every night with you, either here or at my condo. My place is bigger, and—no offense—nicer. And also, no offense, but my bed is better. When I'm at Aces and Eights, you'll be close to Madison and Lauren, and they already hang out. They'd love to include you. If you don't want that, you can sit on the balcony, listen to the ocean, and read your romance books."

She'd never told him what she liked to read, but it only proved that he was an observant man.

"And think of the money you'll save that you can use on your girls." He glanced away, then his eyes returned to her, and she saw longing in them. "Can they be our girls?"

Could a heart really burst from happiness? Because she thought hers was about to do just that. "I think they already are our girls." The smile on his face was beautiful to see. "Is there anything else you want to talk about? Because I want you again."

"So you're going to ignore my question?"

"Oh, that. Is Henry Too invited?"

"He's the only reason I'm asking. I'm only including you because I doubt you'll give him to me."

She punched him in the stomach, her fist connecting with stone-hard muscles. "Very true. Henry Too and I are a team. Yes, I'll move in with you." This playful side of him was new, and she loved it.

"When?"

She laughed. "Impatient, are you? How does tomorrow sound?"

"Fucking great."

Deciding she wanted to be the boss of their next bout, she tackled him.

Much later, as she floated in a state of almost asleep, he whispered in her ear, "I do too laugh."

And she'd make sure he kept on laughing. She fell asleep with a smile on her face.

CHAPTER TWENTY-NINE

"It's time for you boys to turn over Aces and Eights. With all that's gone down with each of you, your faces are becoming too well known. You'll still own the bar on paper, but no one will know that."

When Rothmire had mentioned a few weeks ago that he wanted to talk to them about something, Nate had assumed a new case was on the burner. He glanced at his brothers, seeing the same shock on their faces that he was sure was on his.

Yet, as he let the idea sink in, he found that he had no desire to protest. A month ago, he would have fought tooth and nail against letting go of Aces & Eights. But that was before Taylor. And as his eyes shifted between his brothers', he knew they were thinking the same thing. It would mean nights at home with their wives, or in his case, his girlfriend.

Taylor had been living with him for two weeks now, and he'd never been happier. There wasn't an inch of his condo that hadn't been christened by the two of them. And now they were starting over tonight on their balcony after he got home from the bar—usually around three in the effing morning. That was her favorite place to make love, thus it was his. If she wanted to make love on the moon, he'd find a way to make that happen.

Yeah, he was ready to have a normal life, and he was pretty sure his brothers felt the same. But what did Rothmire have in mind for them? And who would take over Aces & Eights? The bar was a bitch queen, demanding and volatile. She would require special hands to keep her happy. He and his brothers had always thought of the bar as the queen of diamonds, but turned out they were wrong. There was a queen of diamonds in the Gentry family. Their sister. All they had to do was find her and their mother.

"I think Rand and Josh could step in and do a good job," Rothmire said. "Maybe not at the level you boys reached, but the only other choice is for you to sell out or shut the bar down, and I'd rather not do that. It's proven too useful for carrying out covert operations."

So that was why the boss had been keeping Rand out of sight lately. And Josh was so new that very few outside of their field office knew he existed. They would both be able to slip into undercover roles without difficulty.

As for Aces & Eights, Nate didn't want to see it shut down either. He and his brothers had put too much blood, sweat, and tears into the place to see it become nothing more than an FBI legend before it was forgotten about completely.

He raised a brow at his brothers, getting nods from both. "How are we going to make that happen?" he asked their boss.

Rothmire smiled—a canny one, in Nate's opinion—and said, "You boys are going to have a public falling out, and then just as publicly say the bar is up for sale because you can no longer work together. Your supposed buyers will be Rand and Josh."

"How fun," Alex said.

Nate rolled his eyes. Of course Alex would find that fun. He was probably already planning how to put him and Court on their asses—in public—and crow about it.

"You so much as touch me, baby brother, and I'll delete you from existence," said Nate's computer-nerd middle brother. Court apparently guessed as Nate did that they'd better keep their eyes on Alex during the little charade Rothmire had in mind.

Nate gave them both an evil grin. "Either of you come at me, and I'll tell your wives about that time you two streaked through the Florida State campus, wearing nothing but matching pink bras and pink thongs." They'd done it on a dare, and his only regret was that he didn't have a picture.

Rothmire snorted, then coughed, then choked. "Need water," he gasped as he left the room.

"You play dirty, bro," Alex said.

Nate smirked. "Always have, but you know that, *bro*." He settled back in his chair. Yeah, the boss probably did need a drink of water, but he'd also left them alone to talk. "So, you two good with turning over the bar?"

"I am," Court said. "Being gone every night but Sundays is putting a strain on my marriage."

That got Nate's attention. "Problems?"

"Nah, not like that. It's really me more than Lauren. I hate leaving her alone every night. I know she doesn't like it, but she never complains. She accepts that it's my job. It's just that lately, I've been thinking that I'd like to have a somewhat-normal life. As much as the FBI will allow it."

"Madison's amazing," Alex said. "She never makes me feel guilty for my late hours. But I'm echoing Court. A somewhat-normal life without the crazy hours we put in sounds agreeable to me."

It did to Nate, also. It would mean he could join Taylor and the girls for dinner whenever she spent an evening at Rosie's. And although the idea of finding a house big enough for all of them had been brewing in his mind, he hadn't mentioned that to Taylor. With the bar, his hours were too disruptive for a family, especially since Taylor often welcomed him home by jumping into his arms the minute he walked in the door, usually without a stitch on.

"Look at the way he's smiling. He's thinking dirty thoughts about his girlfriend," Alex said.

Court smirked. "Pretty sure he is. Actually, I've been seeing that smile on his face a lot since she moved in."

"Stuff it," Nate cheerfully said, then couldn't help grinning. When had he ever thought he'd be *cheerful* about anything?

"Who are you and what have you done with our sourpuss-faced brother?" Alex put his elbows on the table and leaned forward. "In all seriousness, I've thought for a long time . . . no, more like I've been afraid that you'd never figure out how to be happy, and I hurt for you." He lowered his eyes to the surface of the table. "I didn't like it."

"What he said," Court said. "You raised us. You were our mother and our father. If not for you, I hate to think where we'd be now. If anyone deserves to be happy, it's you, Nate."

"We're going to be crying in a minute if you two don't shut up." Although it was a lame attempt to lighten the mood, he was deeply touched by his brothers' concern. As for raising them? What choice had he had as the oldest brother? Sure, there'd been times when he'd both hated and resented the responsibility, but the two clowns he called brothers had brought him great joy. Still did, and he was damn proud of them.

He pushed away from the table, scowling at the gleam in Alex's eyes. "No, I'm not doing a group hug."

Alex snorted. "I can make you."

"True, but remember what you said yourself. I play dirty." He smirked. "You really want your wife to know you like wearing pink panties?" He left his brothers laughing as he went to find Rothmire. Just what plans did the man have in mind for them once they turned over Aces & Eights?

CHAPTER THIRTY

"So you get to sleep with the boss," Madison said, her amused eyes on Taylor.

Taylor grinned. "Oh, yeah." As the newly promoted special agent in charge of the Miami field office, Nate was now her boss. "And let me tell you, my boss is a very talented man." She winked. God, was he ever! The man's mouth—not to mention other parts of his body—was so, so very talented.

Lauren laughed. "And so is his new intelligence analyst."

"Saying the same about his special agent in charge of investigations," Madison said, a dreamy smile on her face.

His brothers had been happy with their new assignments, Court as an intelligence analyst and Alex supervising their operations. Taylor thought it was a brilliant move on Nate's part, but then she might be a bit prejudiced where her man was concerned.

With Rothmire's transfer to a troubled field office in the Midwest happening in three weeks, Nate had been offered his job. They'd talked late into the night about it. At first, he hadn't been thrilled and had seriously considered refusing, but she couldn't imagine a better replacement for Rothmire. The thought of the bureau bringing in an unknown for the job if Nate didn't take it was what had finally won him over.

"What if they send someone like your first boss?" she'd asked. From all she'd heard, that man had practically run the Miami office into the ground, had even been the reason one of his agents was killed.

That one question had decided it for him, and now Taylor sat in the office of Aces & Eights, waiting to watch the Gentry brothers' "falling out" on the monitor. For the past several days, they had left her, Madison, and Lauren in stitches as they acted out different scenarios of how that could go down. Whatever they had finally decided to do they'd kept a secret, so Taylor sat with her new girlfriends, each of them practically bouncing with anticipation.

She'd never had close female friends before, and she treasured their friendship. If a tiny part of her heart envied that they could call their guys *husband*, she did her best to ignore it. She and Nate had agreed that they needed time together before considering marriage, and even if she was ready for that next step, he wasn't. That was understandable, really.

Although he claimed he was over his worry of being an abuser, she believed that was still a fear in his mind. Not in hers, though. The man would walk into the ocean and keep going until he drowned before he would touch her or the girls in anger. So time was what he needed and what she would give him.

As for the girls, they adored him and he them. And Rosie? She'd loved him at first sight, and all she'd said when they'd told her they were living together was "About time." Neither one of them suspected that Taylor knew about the money Nate slipped Rosie on a regular basis. How could she not love a man who did things like that? Since they had too much fun thinking they were pulling something over on her, she let them have their little game.

"It's starting," Lauren said.

Taylor snapped her eyes to the screen, her gaze following Nate as he stomped toward his brothers.

♠♠♠

Nate strode up to Alex and Court. "Which one of you assholes put that dent in my Harley?" he snarled, his voice raised. They'd spent the last week arguing about anything and everything with each other in front of their customers, building up to this moment.

At their silence, he poked Alex in the chest. "Was it you?"

Alex knocked his arm away. "Get your hand off me. I'm damn tired of you blaming me for every little thing that goes wrong."

"He's just pissed because he's not getting any," Court said.

Nate wondered what Taylor's reaction to that was, considering they couldn't keep their hands off each other. She was probably laughing hysterically. None of their customers knew that his brothers were married or that he had a live-in girlfriend, since they fiercely protected their private lives.

He turned on Court. "You think not? That sweet little thing you've had your eye on? Guess whose bed she woke up in this morning."

"You son of a bitch." Court came at him with a fist.

Nate spun, using his legs to knock Court's feet out from under him. They'd been tumbling on the floor for a few minutes when beer splashed on their faces. He looked up to see Alex standing over them, holding an empty pitcher. He and Court both went for Alex, ending up in a three-way brawl.

At tasting blood from the cut on his lip, Nate decided to end this charade. They'd done enough to make the final scene believable. Not to mention the bikers in the bar tonight were about to join in the fun.

He pushed up from the floor, dragging Alex—rather, Alex letting him pull him up—with him. "Go. I don't care where. Just get out of my face."

"I'll go all right, but don't ever expect to see me back here covering your ass again," Alex spat. "I got much better things to do."

Nate watched him walk out. Baby brother should have been an actor. "Did you put that dent in my Harley?" Nate yelled just before he walked out the door. His only response to that from Alex was a middle finger lifted in the air.

"Anyone tell you that you're a total dick before?" Court said, looking up at Nate with his back flat on the floor. He rolled over, brought his knees under him, then stood. He glared at Nate. "If not, let me be the first. I put the damn dent in your bike. If you'd given me half a chance to tell you that before you hurt our baby brother, I wouldn't be saying this . . . Go screw yourself. I quit. Q-U-I-T." He took a few steps away, then came back, putting his face too close to Nate's. "I used to think blood was thicker than water, but you proved me wrong. See you in hell, brother."

Nate stood in the middle of the floor of Aces & Eights—his hands fisted at his sides, his breaths fast and heavy—feeling strangely sad. They'd planned everything that had just happened, yet it felt real. Final.

As soon as he could realistically announce new owners, he would never come back to Aces & Eights. His brothers would never return. Alex and Court would have already left with their wives, but Taylor would still be watching. Although he'd wanted her to go when the other ladies did, she'd refused.

"Even though tonight will be for show, it's going to hit you that this part of your life is really over. I'll be there for you," she'd said before they left for the bar.

How had she known? He turned in a circle, eyeing the bikers, all standing silent as they looked back at him. "As of this moment, Aces and Eights is for sale." When no one moved, he waved a hand in the air. "Go do whatever it was you were doing and stop looking at me."

As soon as they wandered off, he looked up at the camera. "Love you," he mouthed.

Although he rarely drank during business hours, he was making an exception tonight. As he headed for the bar, a body barreled into him.

"Say it ain't so, Ace. You boys gotta make up. You can't be selling out."

Nate peered down at the little man who had his nose dug into the *v* of Nate's ribcage. "Dammit, Spider, you're blubbering all over my shirt." He pried Spider's arms from around his back, frowning at the tears rolling down Spider's face.

He sighed. "Stop crying, and I'll buy you a beer." That seemed to do the trick, and he followed Spider to the bar. Strangely, he was going to miss the little man. He'd have to make sure that Rand and Josh kept an eye out for him.

Truthfully, as much as he was looking forward to more normal hours, he was going to miss this place, even the biker clubs that gave them so much trouble. But Rothmire was right, it was time to move on.

♠♠♠

"Spider cried like a baby," Nate said. Even though it was three in the morning, they were all sitting on Nate's balcony. His brothers and their wives had been waiting for him and Taylor to come home after closing Aces & Eights for the night.

Alex laughed. "I knew he would. He loves us, especially me."

That was true, Alex was Spider's favorite Gentry brother. "I'll spread the word next week that I found buyers."

Taylor, sitting next to him, squeezed his hand. "It's going to be hard for you guys, letting it go."

Yeah, it was. He was afraid he wasn't going to enjoy his new job nearly as much as working undercover. "We'll survive. Any progress on finding our mother and sister?" he asked Court.

"I'm running a program now, looking for any records of a woman named Wanda who gave birth to a daughter the year our sister would have been born. Even if our mother changed her last name, I'm hoping she kept Wanda. If not, then it's going to be harder to find them."

"But we will," Alex said. "In the meantime, I need my beautiful wife to tuck me into bed. I'm wiped out from beating you two up tonight."

Nate scoffed. "Like hell you did. I whipped your ass."

"Did not."

"Did too. And shut it, Alex, if you don't want your new boss to put you on desk duty."

Alex looked at Court. "Can we still beat him up when we're off duty? 'Cause if we can't, that's not gonna work for me."

"Come on, Ninja Man," Madison said, pulling Alex up with her. "Let's get you to bed before you get fired."

"Nah, he wouldn't fire me. He loves me too much." He bent and kissed Nate on the cheek.

"Dude, stop kissing me. Stop hugging me." Swallowing a grin, Nate scrubbed at his face where Alex had kissed him.

"Make me," Alex said, laughing as he walked out, his arm around Madison's shoulder.

Court rolled his eyes. "Baby brother ain't right in the head. We're out of here, too. At least tomorrow's Sunday, and we don't have to do anything but sleep all day." He waggled his eyebrows at Lauren. "Well, maybe not sleep the entire day away, but we are spending it in bed."

"TMI," Nate muttered.

Alone with Taylor finally, he stretched out his legs, patting his thigh. "Come here, tiger." After she was curled up on his lap with her head resting on his shoulder, he wrapped his arms around her.

"Tired?"

"Strangely, no. Why? You got something in mind?" She licked his neck.

"I have a few ideas. The question is, do you want me to show you here or in our bed?"

"Why don't we start here and see where we end up?"

"I like how you think." He tilted his head and looked into those beautiful blue eyes, already turning dark with desire.

"I love you, Taylor."

She straddled him. "Why don't you show me how much?"

"I can do that." He tugged on her T-shirt. "But I can do it even better if you're naked."

"Ah, you need inspiration for this love business?"

"Yes, but you're all the inspiration I need. That I'll ever need."

And no truer words had ever been said by him.

EPILOGUE

She'd found them! Kinsey Landon held her mother's letter in her hand. She'd read it a hundred times or more in the past year, ever since learning she had brothers. Three of them, to be exact. "Alex, Court, and Nate," she murmured, testing their names on her tongue for what was probably the hundredth time. It was strange that she knew about them, but they didn't have a clue of her existence.

The surprise was that they were the owners of a biker bar. That didn't sound like men she'd want to know. But they were her brothers. Since finding them, she'd researched bikers, learning there were two kinds. The men and women—doctors, lawyers, businesspeople—who rode mostly on the weekends were one kind.

Then there were the clubs, what the bikers referred to as the one-percenters. They were the outlaws of the motorcycle world, men who called their wives and girlfriends their "old ladies." She snorted. Seriously? The Hell's Angels came to mind, along with what little she'd heard of them—nothing good. It appeared her brothers belonged to the latter group, the one-percenters. Not the kind of men she could see herself liking.

Did she want to let them know of her existence? The part of her that had never known she had brothers said no. She'd done just fine without them for her twenty-two years on this earth. Yet, she had brothers. She wasn't alone, or wouldn't be if they wanted her in their lives. That was the biggie. Well, the second biggie. The first, did she want them in hers? What if they were members of the Hell's Angels or the Outlaws? If so, she didn't want any part of that.

She read her mother's letter again, even though she had it memorized.

> *My darling Kinsey,*
> *If you are reading this, then I am no longer with you. Please don't cry too much, sweetheart. I've been blessed to have you in my life, and having you has kept me sane.*
>
> *You see, I had three sons who were taken from me, and my heart has cried each day from missing them. Without you in my life, I don't know how I would have gone on.*

Before she finished reading the pages she held, her gaze strayed from her mother's words, landing on the birdbath outside her window when she caught the flutter of wings. The parrot was back. Like so many parrots one could glimpse around Miami, this one had once been someone's pet that had either been let loose or had escaped. She knew that because he talked to her.

She grabbed the baggie of birdseed she kept just for him and slipped outside, careful not to make too much noise. He was skittish.

"Hello, Oscar," she quietly said as she lowered herself to the ground, far enough away as to not send him flying away.

"Hello, Oscar," he parroted in a high-pitched woman's voice, tilting his head, one beady eye on the bag of birdseed.

He'd said that shortly after he'd appeared at the birdbath, which Kinsey took to mean that was his name and he was a male. She tossed birdseed onto the stone slates, a little closer than the last time. She was slowly getting him used to her.

"Hello, Oscar," he chirped as he fluttered his wings, landing on the opposite side of the birdseed. "Oscar's a naughty boy." He eyed her again, before hopping forward until he could dip his beak to scoop up the food.

As he pecked at the seeds, she said, "I don't know what to do, Oscar. See, I found out I have brothers. Brothers, Oscar. Imagine that. I want to meet them, but what if I don't like them?"

Oscar paused, looked at her as if considering her problem, then said, "Hello, brothers."

Kinsey laughed. "So it's that easy, huh?"

There was one part of her mother's letter that she'd read the most and had memorized: *I had to believe that I had instilled in my sons honor and a love of learning so they would grow to be fine young men. I know in my heart they grew into men I would be proud of.*

She needed to find out if that was true before she burned her mother's letter and forgot she had brothers. Kinsey pulled her phone out of her jeans pocket and called Aiden, asking him to meet her for breakfast.

♠♠♠

"I need you to go with me to a biker bar," she said the next morning.

"Huh?"

Kinsey lowered her menu, peering over the top at her best friend. "I said, I need you to go with—"

"I heard what you said." His eyebrows scrunched together. "I'm just trying to figure out why you said it."

"It's a long story."

Aiden leaned back against the booth, spreading his arms along the top. "I'm listening."

"Read this." She handed him her mother's letter.

"I found them," she said when he finished. "They own a biker bar, Aces and Eights. So what are you doing Saturday night?"

"Going to a biker bar?"

ACKNOWLEDGMENTS

Where to start? I've written enough acknowledgements that you'd think it would get easier. It doesn't. With each book, there are more readers, friends, authors, and so on to thank. And with each book, I find myself more grateful for the support and encouragement given me. I keep expecting to wake up and discover that this wonderful journey I'm on is all a dream. I sure hope it's not.

First, I have an amazing family. Thank you, Jim, for your unwavering support and belief in me. Also, I really appreciate that you eat burnt dinners without complaint when I'm on deadline. Even better are all the dinners you cook for me. You will always be my hero. Love you!

Since my first book was published in 2013, I've become friends with so many readers throughout the world, and I'm so in awe of that. I love our online chats about everything under the sun, but especially about books. I wish I could thank each one of you in person for loving my books. And to those who take the time to post reviews, thank you so very much! That means the world to an author.

I dedicated this book to my Sandra's Book Salon group on Facebook, but I want to say here, y'all rock big time! I love every one of you. If you'd like to join us, just click here: https://www.facebook.com/groups/1827166257533001/.

Jenny Holiday, remember back when we were just starting out? Yeah, the good old days. I'm not sure I'd be where I am today without you. Jenny and I have been friends and critique partners from the very beginning, when seeing our books in print was only a dream. And then that dream came true for both of us. If you haven't read a Jenny Holiday book, do it now! Her stories are fabulous.

The team at Montlake Romance are simply the best! They make everything as easy on their authors as possible, and I've learned so much since my first book came out with Montlake. Maria, Jessica, Melody, and everyone else on the team, I wish there were better words than *thank you*, but thank you!

Courtney Miller-Callihan, you are the best agent an author could hope for. Thank you for believing in me, for supporting me, for being there for me. May our journey together continue for many years!

ABOUT THE AUTHOR

Photo © 2015 Cat Ford-Coates

Bestselling, award-winning author Sandra Owens lives in the beautiful Blue Ridge Mountains of North Carolina. Her family and friends often question her sanity but have ceased being surprised by what she might get up to next. She's jumped out of a plane, flown in an aerobatic plane while the pilot performed death-defying stunts, gotten into laser-gun fights in Air Combat, and ridden a Harley motorcycle for years. She regrets nothing.

Sandra is a Romance Writers of America Honor Roll member and a 2013 Golden Heart Finalist for her contemporary romance *Crazy for Her*. In addition to her contemporary romantic-suspense novels, she writes Regency stories.

You can connect with Sandra through her website, www.sandra-owens.com, or on Facebook at www.facebook.com/SandraOwensAuthor.